D1098982

Julian Critchley has been a Tory MP for twenty-six years in two incarnations. He has sat at the feet of Mr Harold Macmillan, Lord Home, Mr Edward Heath, and trod on the toes of Mrs Margaret Thatcher. He escaped office, and has not been knighted for long and silent service (Mrs Thatcher, when the honour was tentatively suggested, cried 'Never!'). He has taken up writing instead, mainly but not exclusively about politics. He has written regularly for every good newspaper, and several bad ones. His three non-fiction books, *Westminster Blues*, *Heseltine: The Unauthorised Biography* and *Palace of Varieties* have all been bestsellers. In 1991 he turned to fiction with *Hung Parliament*, which was an immediate success in (almost) all quarters.

Floating Voter

An Entertainment

Julian Critchley

HEADLINE

Copyright © 1992 Julian Critchley

The right of Julian Critchley to be identified as the Author of
the Work has been asserted by him in accordance with the
Copyright, Designs and Patents Act 1988.

First published in 1992 by Hutchinson
a division of the Random Century Group Ltd

First published in paperback in 1993
by HEADLINE BOOK PUBLISHING PLC

10 9 8 7 6 5 4 3 2 1

All rights reserved. No part of this publication may be
reproduced, stored in a retrieval system, or transmitted,
in any form or by any means without the prior written
permission of the publisher, nor be otherwise circulated
in any form of binding or cover other than that in which
it is published and without a similar condition being
imposed on the subsequent purchaser.

All characters in this publication are fictitious
and any resemblance to real persons, living or dead,
is purely coincidental.

ISBN 0 7472 3987 8

Typeset by
Letterpart Limited, Reigate, Surrey

Printed and bound in Great Britain by
HarperCollins Manufacturing, Glasgow

HEADLINE BOOK PUBLISHING PLC
Headline House
79 Great Titchfield Street
London W1P 7FN

Principal Dramatis Personae

ARCHER, Lord (Jeffrey Howard); politician and author; *s* of William Archer and Lola Archer, *née* Cook; *b* 15 April 1940; *Educ* by his wife since leaving Wellington School, Somerset; Brasenose, Oxford Athletics Blues, 1963–5, Gymnastics Blue, 1963, Pres OUAC 1965; ran for GB (never fast enough), Oxford 100 yards record (9.6 sec.) 1966; *m* 1966, Mary Weeden (scientist; Cheltenham Ladies' Coll; St Anne's Coll, Oxford); 2 s; *Career* Mem GLC for Havering, 1966–70; MP (C) Louth, 1969–74; Dep Chm, Cons Party, 1985–6; Trustee, RWS, 1989–; Pres Somerset AAA, 1973; Hon Pres, Glasgow Univ Dialectic Soc, 1984; FRSA, 1973. *Pubns*: Not a Penny More, Not a Penny Less, 1975 (televised, 1990); Shall We Tell the President?, 1977; Kane and Abel, 1979 (televised, 1986); A Quiver Full of Arrows, 1980; The Prodigal Daughter, 1982; First Among Equals, 1984 (televised, 1986); A Matter of Honour, 1986; Beyond Reasonable Doubt (play), 1987; A Twist in the Tale (short stories), 1988; Exclusive (play), 1990; As the Crow Flies (1991); *Address* 93 Albert Embankment, SE1

BARTON, Ronald; Father unknown; *b* 2 Dec 1961, Felday Road, Catford, SE; *Educ* Lewisham Comprehensive, London School of Journalism; *m* Sophie Tucker 1989; *Career* Bexley Bugle, Sun, True Brit; winner (1990) of the Kelvin Mackenzie Award for services to the Written Word; *Book* Tell It How It Is (with Harold Harris); *Address* c/o Raymond's Revue Bar, London W1.

CLARKE, Rt Hon Kenneth (Harry); PC 1984; QC 1980; MP (C) Rushcliffe Division of Nottinghamshire since 1970; Home Secretary, since 1992; *b* 2 July 1940; *e c* of Kenneth Clarke, Nottingham; *m* 1964, Gillian Mary Edwards; one *s* one *d*. *Educ* Nottingham High Sch; Gonville and Caius Coll, Cambridge (BA LLB). Chm, Cambridge Univ Conservative Assoc, 1961; Pres, Cambridge Union, 1963; Chm, Fedn Conservative Students, 1963. Called to Bar, Gray's Inn 1963, Hon Bencher, 1989; Mem, Midland Circuit. Research Sec, Birmingham Bow Group, 1965–66; contested Mansfield (Notts) in General Elections of 1964 and 1966. PPS to Solicitor General, 1971–72; an Asst Govt Whip, 1972–74 (Govt Whip for Europe, 1973–74); a Lord Comr, HM Treasury, 1974; Parly Sec, DoT, later Parly Under Sec of State for Transport, 1979–82; Minister of State (Minister for Health), DHSS, 1982–85; entered Cabinet as Paymaster General and Minister for Employment, 1985–87; Chancellor of Duchy of Lancaster and Minister for Trade and Industry (with additl responsibility to coordinate Govt policy on Inner Cities), 1987–88; Sec of State for Health, 1988–90. Sec of State for Education and Science, 1990–92; Mem, Parly delegn to Council of Europe and WEU, 1973–74; Sec, Cons Parly Health and Social Security Cttee, 1974; Opposition Spokesman on: Social Services, 1974–76; Industry, 1976–79. Hon LLD Nottingham, 1989. *Publications*: New Hope for the Regions, 1969; pamphlets published by Bow Group, 1964–. *Recreations*: modern jazz music, watching Association Football and cricket, bird-watching. *Address* House of Commons, SW1A 0AA

GRUNTE, Sir Ralph Redvers (Kt 1980); MP (C) Arden 1974–; *s* of Percy Haines; *b* 8 Dec 1930; *Educ* Sutton Coldfield GS; Univ of Birmingham; *m* 1960 Marjorie Grunt; no chdn; *Career* motor trader and garage owner; pres Midland Motor Traders 1970–4; dir Harry Greenway plc, tyre distrbrs, Steve Norris and Sons; Rotarian; del to the Cncl of Europe and the Western European Union 1974–80; vice-chm Party's Europe Cttee; *Address* The Copper Beeches, Warwick Road, Arden, Warwickshire (2345 54321)

GUMMER, Rt Hon John Selwyn; PC 1985; MP (C) Suffolk Coastal, since 1983 (Eye, Suffolk, 1979–83); Minister of Agriculture, Fisheries and Food, since 1989; *b* 26 Nov 1939; *s* of Canon Selwyn Gummer and Sybille (*née* Mason); *m* 1977, Penelope Jane, *yr d* of John P. Gardner; two *s* two *d*. *Educ* King's Sch, Rochester; Selwyn Coll, Cambridge (Exhibr). BA Hons History 1961; MA 1971; Chm, Cambridge Univ Conservative Assoc, 1961; Pres, Cambridge Union, 1962; Chm, Fedn of Conservative Students, 1962. Editor, Business Publications, 1962–64; Editor-in-Chief, Max Parrish &

Oldbourne Press, 1964–66; BPC Publishing: Special Asst to Chm, 1967; Publisher, Special Projects, 1967–69; Editorial Coordinator, 1969–70. Mem, ILEA Educn Cttee, 1967–70; Dir, Shandwick Publishing Co., 1966–81; Man Dir, EP Gp of Cos 1975–81; Chairman: Selwyn Shandwick Internat 1976–81, Siemssen Hunter Ltd, 1979–80 (Dir 1973–80). Contested (C) Greenwich, 1964 and 1966; MP (C) Lewisham W, 1970–Feb, 1974; PPS to Minister of Agriculture, 1972; an additional Vice-Chm Conservative Party, 1972–74; an Asst Govt Whip, 1981; a Lord Comr of HM Treasury, 1981–83; Parly Under-Sec of State for Employment, Jan–Oct 1983; Minister of State, Dept of Employment, 1983–84; Paymaster-Gen, 1984–85; Chm, Cons Party, 1983–85; Minister of State: MAFF, 1985–88; DoE 1988–89. Mem, Gen. Synod of the Church of England, 1979–. *Publications*: (jtly) When the Coloured People Come, 1966; The Permissive Society, 1971; (with L.W. Cowie) The Christian Calendar, 1974; (contrib.) To Church with Enthusiasm, 1969; (contrib.) Faith In Politics, 1987; Christianity and Conservatism, 1990. *Address* House of Commons, SW1A 0AA.

HARVEY, Charles Witherspoon; MP (C) Long Melford June 1987–; *s* of Charles and Diana Dorrington Harvey; *b* 8 Dec 1952; *Educ* Edgeborough, Charterhouse, Pembroke Coll, Oxford; *m* 1980, Miriam Joseph; 2 *d*; *Career* merchant banker; parly sec to the Min Tport 1989–. *Address* 30 Onslow Square, London SW1 (071–546 3125)

MAJOR, The Rt Hon John; MP (C) Huntingdon 1983–; PC (June 1987); *s* of Thomas Major (*d* 1963), actor (real name Abraham Thomas Ball), and his 2 *w*, Gwendolyn Minnie, *née* Coates, (*d* 1970); *b* 29 March 1943; *Educ* Rutlish; *m* 1970, Norma Christina Elizabeth, *d* of Norman Johnson (*d* 1954); 1 *s*, 1 *d*; *Career* sr exec Standard Chartered Bank plc to 1979; assoc. Inst of Bankers; MP (C) Huntingdonshire 1979–83; pps to Min. of State, Home Office 1981–3, asst govt whip 1983–4; Lord Cmr of Treasury 1984–5; parly under-sec of state DHSS 1985–6, min. of Social Security 1986–7, chief sec to the Treasury June 1987–July 1989, foreign sec July 1989–Oct 1989, Chancellor of the Exchequer Oct 1989–90, Prime Minister and First Lord of Treasury 1990. *Address* 10 Downing Street, London SW1

MORRIS, Joshua George; MP (C) Shropshire West June 1970–; *s* of George Evans-Morris and Goldeth Jones; *b* 7 Sept 1930; *Educ* Broughton Hall, Shrewsbury; Queen's Coll, Oxford; *m* 1960, Fay Greene (*d* 1982), 3 *d*, 1 *s*; *Career* journalist and author; delegate Cncl of Europe and the Western European Union 1979–83; pres, Sherlock Holmes Soc of Gt Britain. *Books* incl. The Young Margaret (1986), A Short Life of Leon Brittan (1987); A Short Life of William Cash (1989). *Address* 23 Broad Street, Ludlow, Shropshire (0584 872222)

SCRAGG, Hyacinth; *d* of Bob and Joan Scragg; *b* 9 June 1973; *Educ* Warwick Comprehensive; *Career* Beautician; Chm Arden Young Conservatives; TV reporter for TVS; 'Miss Birmingham Young Conservative' Oct 1992. *Address* Flat 2, 34 High Street, Arden, Warwicks (0987 3452)

SWAN, David Liam; *s* of Ben Swan and Ethel Walker; *b* 23 May 1954; *Educ* Longton Comprehensive, Staffs; *m* Carole Price; 2 *d*; *Career* builder and developer; winner, Golden Shovel Award, Birmingham Chamber of Commerce 1986; Mayor of Arden 1987–8. *Address* Mon Repos, Eddington, Warwicks (3462 4364)

THATCHER, The Rt Hon Baroness Margaret Hilda; PC (1970), MP (C) Finchley 1987–92; *yr d* of late Alfred Roberts, grocer, of Grantham, Lincs, and Beatrice, *née* Stephenson; *b* 13 Oct 1925; *Educ* Huntingtower Primary Sch, Grantham, Kesteven and Grantham Girls Sch, Somerville Coll, Oxford (MA, BSc; hon. fellow 1970); *m* 1951, Sir Denis Thatcher (Kt 1989), company director; 1 *s* (Mark), 1 *d* (Carol (twin), radio journalist, presenter (freelance) with LBC; *Career* former research chemist; called to the Bar Lincoln's Inn 1953 (hon bencher 1975), contested (C) Dartford 1950 and 1951; MP (C) Finchley 1959–74; Barnet, Finchley 1974–83 and 1983–7; jt parly sec Min of Pensions and Nat Ins 1961–4; memb Shadow Cabinet 1967–70 (spokesman on: Tport, Power, Treasury matters, Housing and Pensions); chief Oppn spokesman educn 1969–70; Sec of State Educn and Science (and co-chm Women's National Commn) 1970–4; chief Oppn spokesman environment 1974–5; Leader of Oppn Feb 1975–9; Prime Minister and First Lord of Treasury (first woman to hold this office) from 4 May 1979–Nov 1990; Minister for Civil Service Jan 1981–; freedom of Borough of Barnet 1980; hon freeman of Worshipful Co. of Grocers 1980; freedom of Falkland Islands 1983; Donovan Award USA 1981; FRS. *Address* c/o Dickins and Jones. London W1

WEBB-BOWEN, Sir Charles Alexander (Kt 1991); *s* of Percy Webb and Hilda Bowen; *b* 15 April 1930; *Educ* Summerfields, Eton, Hertford Coll, Oxford; *m* Sarah Dobbs; 2 *d*; *Career* Nat Serv Comm Rifle Brigade; served in Korea; Senior partner in firm of solicitors; Chm 1992 Tory Party conference. *Books*: Lust in the Dust (with Harold Harris); A Short Life of J. Enoch Powell (with John Biffen). *Rec* Bird-watching. *Address* Flaxford, Much Hadham, Herts (9876 2341)

WILIKINS, Amaranth; *d* of Charles and Enid Snape; *b* 4 Nov. 1953 at Stone, Staffs; *Educ* Obadiah Sherratt Sch for Girls, Burslem; Birmingham Univ; *m* (1) Henry Wilikins 1970 (divorced 1975) (2) John Jones 1976 (div. 1978); *Career* 'weathergirl' Harlech TV; radio/tv personality; on Conservative Central Office list of approved candidates-to-be. *Address* 15 Nelson Street, Warwick (0652 453 7865)

WORTHINGTON EVANS, Peter Jackson; MP (C) Edgbaston West 1983–; *s* of Campbell Evans and Margaret Lewis; *b* 12 Sept 1960; *Educ* Sparkbrook Sch, Univ of Keele; *m* 1984, Shirley Worthington; 1 *s*; *Career* pub rels offr, Pig Marketing Board; chm Sparkbrook YCs; memb, YCs' nat ctee; asst govt whip 1990–. *Publications*: Out and About in Edgbaston (with Jill Knight), 1985. *Address* 34 Litchfield Avenue, Edgbaston (0987 56432)

WYLDEBORE-SMITH, Maj-Gen Sir (Francis) Brian (Kt 1980); CB 1965; DSO 1943; OBE 1944; *s* of Rev W.R. Wyldebore-Smith and Mrs D. Wyldebore-Smith; *b* 10 July 1913; *m* 1944 Hon Molly Angela Cayzer, *d* of

1st Baron Rotherwick; 1 *s* 4 *d*; *Educ* Wellington Coll;
RMA Woolwich. *Career* served Middle East, Italy,
France, Germany, 1941–5; Military Adviser to CIGS
1947–9; GSO1, 7 Armoured Div 1951–3; Comd 15/19
King's Royal Hussars 1954–6; IDC 1959; BGS Combat
Development 1959–62; Chief of Staff to C-in-C, Far East
Cmmd 1962–4; GO Commnding 44th Divn (TA) and
Home Counties District 1965–8; dir Conservative Board
of Finance 1970–; Col 15/19 Hussars 1970–7. *Address*
Grantham House, Grantham, Lincs (0476 64705)

Prologue

An October mist, blown in from the Channel, hung around the rusted legs of the derelict pier. A muffled moon could be glimpsed through its broken deck, a pier long closed to those who once sought to find out what it was the butler saw. A bitter-sweet smell of excrement, orange peel and old ice-cream papers mingled with the sea and sand. In Brighton, the Prince Regent's city, people do not go to bed early, and an observer would have noticed a small group of revellers making its way along the strand to the accompaniment of snatches of song and bursts of loud laughter. The party were clearly conference goers, for plastic-covered 'photo-passes' hung from their lapels; indeed, there was something familiar about their faces. Their voices, a blend of proud and plebeian, would, when taken with the early autumnal chill, have suggested they were Tories in Brighton for their Party's annual conference.

One of them was certainly Kenneth Baker, glossy, sleek and cheerful; behind him plodded his detective, a literate and unhappy member of the Special Branch who much preferred Brighton rock to Brighton beach, especially at such a late hour. John Gummer, who was not considered to be in need of protection, was singing 'Lead Kindly Light' in a falsetto voice. Terry Dicks, not so well known, was crushing beer cans and tossing them in the direction of France. Their wives, hand in hand, stepping carefully in expensive shoes over the summer's jetsam, brought up the rear. They had met when dining at English's Oyster House, and were on their way back to the rebuilt Grand Hotel for a night-cap and bed.

It was the former Home Secretary who first noticed the deck chair, its legs awash with the incoming tide, part-hidden by the Victorian metal-work of the pier. The back of the canvas chair had been turned towards the town, and in the gloom it was not immediately apparent that someone was sitting in it. A second glance revealed a pair of pretty legs and a tousled, damp head of hair. The sea, in which were reflected the lights of the promenade, surged uneasily around the sides of the chair, covering Baker's black brogues with a film of sand. The four men ventured farther out and turned to face the chair; their wives hung back. All were silent. The bodyguard concluded that the seated woman was undoubtedly dead; Baker thought anxiously about the political consequences of the discovery; only Terry Dicks spoke.

'Sod me,' he said almost under his breath, 'it can't be? It is! It's that bloody woman!'

Ken Baker pulled himself together. A bookish man, and as such an untypical Tory, he was never at a loss for a quote, however unusual the circumstances. 'Oh, is it weed, or fish or floating hair . . . ?' he intoned, and then added for no one's benefit, 'Charles Kingsley.'

It had been a perfectly bloody conference. Sod's law. Everything that could go wrong had gone wrong. And now this. One of the wives started to cry. Midnight clocks struck the hour. It was the morning of Friday, the last full day of the Party conference.

Tuesday Morning

'All mink and no knickers,' said Amaranth Wilikins, running her wicked pink tongue over her lipstick. It was a phrase often used by her mother to describe women whose husbands had made money and moved to Edgbaston. Amaranth, thirty-nine rising forty, darkly blonde and almost beautiful, stood posed before the glass in her room at 'Mon Repos', a genteel boarding house in Gardner Street, Brighton.

It was eight o'clock on Tuesday morning, the opening day of the Tory Party conference. Her suit was by Mondi, her shoes by Harrods, her make-up by Max Factor. Twice married, a former BBC Radio 4 panellist and one-time Harlech TV 'weathergirl', Amaranth was a woman in search of a husband, an income of £100,000 a year and a seat in Parliament. Especially a seat in Parliament. Why else should she have come to Brighton on her own, and out of season?

She pinned her conference photo-pass to her lapel, dabbed 'Adieu Sagesse' behind her ears, and tripped lightly downstairs to breakfast. The elder of the two men who ran the establishment shook muesli on to her plate.

'You don't look like a typical Tory woman to me,' he said. 'I thought you all wore terrible hats.'

'I'm not,' said Amaranth, taking a spoonful of Greek yoghurt. 'I'm very untypical. I'm here to make a killing. Watch me on telly.'

Having finished her breakfast, Amaranth walked down to the front and entered the Grand Hotel. Where better to sit and be seen? Just after nine she would join the throng of the *prominenti* and walk the two hundred yards or so to the conference centre. Who knows whom she might meet? Although she could not afford to stay there, she certainly intended to give the impression that she was lodging under the same roof as the leaders of the Party. Indeed, she had dined in the Hotel the night before and had been introduced to her local MP, Sir Ralph Grunte.

'I'm sure I know your name,' he said.

Amaranth was delighted. She did not appreciate that this was his normal greeting, and assumed that her reputation had preceded her.

'You might have heard me on the radio,' she said. 'I was a panellist in "Out of Order" and "Looking Forward to the Past".'

Grunte nodded, and Amaranth told him of at least one of her ambitions: she wished to be adopted as candidate for a safe seat. A party conference is a natural stamping ground for those who have barely four days in which to make a mark. Grunte had seized his chance. They were to take lunch together today, at Langan's Bistro.

'I can be of help to you, my dear,' he assured her. Ms

Wilikins was unconvinced, but she had accepted the invitation.

Before she left the Grand Hotel for the opening of the conference, she was chatted up by a ponderous Patrick Cormack, a chastened Colin Moynihan and an eager Charles Harvey. Cormack promised to take Amaranth 'under his wing'. No fear.

Moynihan, once a junior minister, who had lost his seat at the election, had had the good fortune to buy her a drink the evening before and had suggested 'an exquisite light lunch' at Macau, the town's only Portuguese restaurant. Amaranth, who was over 5 feet 8 inches in height, had her eye on someone taller. Moynihan had been in his time a University cox and a flyweight boxing blue, and barely came up to her elbow. Anyway she was promised for lunch to Sir Ralph Grunte. 'You poor thing,' said Moynihan, promptly jogging off in the direction of Hove.

Charles Harvey, on the other hand, was tall, six foot, and he was wearing an Old Carthusian tie. At least Amaranth thought it was an OC tie, but she was not entirely sure. The pink stripe was not quite right. 'We met', he had said, 'at the Goodharts' party.' Amaranth, who had never heard of the Goodharts, said how much she had enjoyed the party. She told him that it was her intention to make her maiden speech at the conference. Harvey replied that as a junior Minister at the Department of Transport, he did not have to speak. His sole task was to listen to a speech made by his master in reply to a short debate. 'MacGregor speaks, I listen.'

Amaranth liked the look of Harvey. Cormack had smelt of Old Spice, and Moynihan of embrocation. Harvey, with his public school accent and laid-back

manner, was a different kettle of fish. Would he kindly
help her with her speech? Harvey said he would be only
too delighted, and suggested they might meet that
evening. He would leave a message for her at the desk in
the Grand Hotel foyer.

Hyacinth Scragg accepted her hotel breakfast with dis-
gust – the statutory sausage, a tepid tomato and an
institutionally fried egg.

'Sauce, dear?' said her companion. It was indeed
bloody sauce putting the Party's delegation up at such a
crummy hotel. Hyacinth, who worked as beautician in a
hairdresser's in Arden, was nineteen, big-busted ('It's
like seeing Fylingdales Early Warning system coming at
you') and handsome. She was the chairman of the Forest
of Arden Young Conservatives which she had joined
three years previously at her mother's prompting. 'Such
a nice class of young men.'

On the previous evening she had been told by her MP,
Sir Ralph Grunte, that she reminded him of 'the young
Alma Cogan', but she had no idea who Alma Cogan
was. Sipping her milky coffee from a thick cup, she
resolved to find out. The bread was sliced-white, the
butter was packed in New Zealand, and the marmalade
came in a tiny plastic box. It was not user-friendly. The
Malcolms, Kevin and Janet, who were fellow members
of the delegation, were bickering as usual.

She pinned on her photo-pass, without which no Tory
is properly dressed, and, avoiding her colleagues,
walked briskly along the front in the direction of the
conference centre. Two window-cleaners threw her a
cheerful obscenity, but she took no notice. It was her
first Party conference, and she was certain she could do

far better than them. 'Almost makes you think of voting Tory,' said one ladder-bound youth to the other. 'My dad did,' was the reply, 'but not after what they gone and done to Margaret Thatcher.'

An unseasonal sun shone brightly on Brighton, the gulls ducked and dived, and a breeze of summer tickled the gutter-borne rubbish. The elderly pushed one another along the prom in wheelchairs. There was even an open-topped double-decker bus, defying the calendar. Blue-haired widows who had lived out their prime in Hendon Central, were bound for Sainsbury's, their husbands abandoned in Golders Green. An old man in a long overcoat rummaged in a hotel's bins. As Hyacinth walked, the long line of hotels, great and small, disgorged its residents on to an increasingly crowded pavement. They came down the side streets in droves, like T.S. Eliot's clerks over London Bridge, swelling the river of the anointed. There was much hand-shaking, waving and pecking of cheeks.

Hyacinth felt excluded from it all, and rather wished she had waited for Carole Swan, or for Angela Cartwright, the delegation's leader. The prospect of four days 'politicking' at Brighton now seemed daunting. She ought to have stayed at home, or gone to stay with her boyfriend in Halesowen. But it was too late for second thoughts. Grasping her conference handbook tightly, she took her place in the queue where, she had been told last night over supper, she ran the risk of being stripped and searched by an army of discharged traffic wardens. After the bomb of 1984, nobody was taking security lightly.

Joshua Morris stood in line waiting to be searched for an

offensive weapon. As an occasional journalist his only 'offensive weapon' was his pen, or rather his word processor. Morris was in his early sixties, and Tory MP for Shropshire West. Tall, silver-haired, and a touch overweight, he had become, over the years, a somewhat cynical observer of the political scene. *Who's Who* listed his hobbies as 'collecting Staffordshire and reading military history'. He was also the chairman of the Sherlock Holmes Society of Great Britain, a body of self-appointed sleuths who dined quarterly in Baker Street. Both on duty and off, Morris wore the uniform of a Conservative MP, the double-breasted suit.

The IRA had seen to it that getting in and out of the Party conference building was like a rich man confronted with the gates of the Kingdom of Heaven, or, what was worse, like checking-in at Gatwick on an August flight to Marbella. Tories, long, short and tall, queued with the stoicism that had once made us the envy of the world. Pockets were emptied of loose change, parcels scanned as if for a malignant tumour and handbags rifled for evidence of evil intent. The ordeal, which lasted all of twenty minutes, was repeated twice a day; a high price, thought Joshua, for having to listen to Bill Cash warn of the dangers of Europe.

While he waited, Morris picked out from the throng those whose names he knew. Charles Harvey, a sleek and ambitious junior Minister: Peter Worthington Evans, an earnest Government whip who wore waistcoats, watch and chain; and Nicholas Budgen, Enoch Powell's puck-like successor in Wolverhampton. In the parallel line of the submissive, a pretty, dark girl of about twenty was emptying her handbag on the instructions of a uniformed harridan. A lipstick, a packet of tissues, a ball ticket for the Young Conservatives and a Jilly Cooper paperback were put on view.

'Any good?' asked Joshua.

'Not a patch on *Riders*,' was her reply.

A large man in a purple pin-striped suit standing behind her was complaining about the political bias shown by the BBC. A group of the young set up a chant of 'why are we waiting', and the line duly moved forward another inch. Joshua was sorry he had turned his back on sunny Brighton. He should have gone for a walk on the Downs or gone shopping in the town for antiques, or spent the morning browsing in bookshops. But it was too late; the warders in charge of the metal detector waved him through, and the press of the crowd propelled him, willy-nilly, into the conference hall itself.

The noise suddenly abated. The platform had summoned them in to give thanks to God, and to pray for wisdom. It was, thought Joshua, probably the least he should do.

'Dear Lord and Father of mankind, Forgive our foolish ways . . . '

Seven thousand Tories were on their feet. As is the custom, the annual Conservative Party conference begins with a brief religious ceremony followed by an official greeting from the local Mayor. In Brighton at nine-thirty on this Tuesday morning in October, the singing could only be described as 'tentative', not at all like the rendering of 'Land of Hope and Glory' which invariably follows upon the Leader's speech on the Friday afternoon.

The representatives of shire and suburb had arrived on

the Monday evening, and had drunk and dined exceedingly well. In consequence, the level of the Party's blood sugar was low; their expectations none too high. A benign observer of the event, sitting in among the press and nursing his hangover, would have cast his eye unenthusiastically over the massed ranks of what Sir Peregrine Worsthorne had once described in Mrs Thatcher's golden days as 'the most successful political party in the world': 'Essex Man' and 'Wessex Woman', stockjobbers, garage-owners and a scattering of country women in lavender tweeds.

Towards the front of the hall, which was coldly functional and had none of the baroque charm of Blackpool's Winter Gardens, sat a group of Young Conservatives, their tattooed arms hidden beneath designer jackets. One large young man was wearing a T-shirt bearing the legend, 'We want ink in our Pen'. He meant Monsieur Le Pen. They were likely to make trouble, having not yet come to terms with the hurried departure of Mrs Thatcher following upon the events of November 1990.

On the opening day the congregation, for that was what it had become, listened uneasily to the local Rector whose refusal to wear a clerical collar had not gone unnoticed. The Church of England was not what it once was; but neither was the Conservative Party. He spoke briefly of the responsibility the rich owe to the poor of the Third World. All too often sensible Tories at conference had to endure the views of unsound parsons and leftish Mayors, an aberration which was soon to be submerged beneath a torrent of party oratory, obsequious loyalty and special pleading.

★ ★ ★

'Through the night of doubt and sorrow, Onward goes the pilgrim band, Singing songs of expectation, Marching to the Promised Land.'

Joshua Morris had given up hope of ever reaching the promised land. A long-serving backbencher (and amateur detective who had recently helped to unmask the murderer of a woman MP whose body had been found hanging in a House of Commons lift), he sat uncomfortably at the back of the hall. His part in the murder proceedings had attracted unwelcome publicity; the tabloid press invariably referred to him as 'the Shropshire Sherlock', a nickname which had not afforded his rustic constituents much pleasure. The then Leader of the House, John MacGregor (who was today sitting on the platform with the great ones of the party, wearing a kilt to which, strictly speaking, he was not entitled) had called upon him to help with the inquiries.

Joshua, whose conceit it was to prefer the old gods to the new, took no part in the singing. He believed, with Gibbon, that the value of Christianity lay in the fact that it was a 'magistrate's religion', a necessary cement in society's fabric. But he could not take its mythology too seriously. He scrutinised the crowd, looking for a friendly face. His agent in Shropshire West had tried to persuade him to stay with his local Party members in a small, temperance hotel, but he had refused. Instead, he had put up in a hotel some miles out of town, high up on the Downs, which owed more to Laura Ashley than to Nancy Astor. Wenlock Manor was some twelve miles out of Brighton, far enough away to discourage conference-going Tories, the more important of whom preferred to stay at the rebuilt Grand Hotel, and the more humble at sea-front bed-and-breakfasts.

He was to be joined the next day by his mistress, Felicity. Their affair could be described either as 'passionately discreet' or as 'discreetly passionate', the relative anonymity of Wenlock Manor being preferred to the sodium-lit splendour of the Grand Hotel. And bored journalists, lodged there on expenses, with nothing better to write about, were dangers to be avoided.

He would entertain his local Party members to lunch on Thursday at English's, a sea-food restaurant which usually attracted the *prominenti*. It was their duty to permit themselves a swift handshake and a kindly word to those, less august than themselves, whose long evenings on the 'knocker', canvassing for the party, sustained them in the political positions to which they had become all too easily accustomed. 'Daphne, have you met Norman Lamont? Norman, this is Daphne Cadwallader, the chairman of my local Party . . . ' Such encounters were lubricants, confirming, at one and the same time, the importance of all the people concerned.

'Not for our sins alone, Thy Mercy, Lord, we sue.'

Joshua's roving eye discerned Gerald Kaufman of all people. Kermit-like, he was peering disapprovingly at the massed ranks of his political opponents, a stare that was returned, by those who caught his eye, with surprise tinged with disapproval. Kaufman was nobody's favourite Labour MP, whom Joshua Morris had once described, somewhat rashly, as a salad dressing – one part oil to five parts vinegar. In his Beverly Hills suit and hand-painted 1950s tie, Kaufman looked like a divorce lawyer in 'LA Law'; his presence at the Tory Party's autumn festival could be explained only by the need to earn a crust; he had been invited by the BBC, no doubt, to comment on the proceedings. Morris had once done as much at a Labour Party conference in Blackpool. What a pity the invitation had not been extended to someone more congenial, such as the ubiquitous Austin Mitchell.

The platform party sat smugly in extended line. Next to the Rector was the Mayor of Brighton, on his left was the Chairman of the Conference, a party worthy who had been knighted for his pains. Sir Charles Webb-Bowen was a Hertfordshire solicitor with views. It would be his task to summon speakers to the rostrum (from a list supplied by Central Office) and to introduce in appropriate terms of admiration and approval the Ministers of the Crown who would respond to a series of debates.

The Prime Minister crouched behind his spectacles, while spread out on both wings of the platform sat the members of his Cabinet. Behind and above the platform, like cherubim around the head of the risen Lord, sat the members of the Party's national executive committee, spiced with a scattering of MPs. Edwina Currie was opening her post, Sir James Spicer was picking his nose.

Joshua was suddenly overcome with a feeling of cafard; why the hell had he bothered to come? He had spent the last twenty years attending the Party conference, four days of gin and oratory. In recent years he had stayed only a day or two, until, overcome with boredom, he had returned home to watch Mrs Thatcher's Leader's speech on the telly. Thirty minutes of oratory and twelve of applause; or had it been the other way round? Would this year in Brighton promise better?

The service over, Joshua repaired to the clinically clean Gents. Sir Ralph Grunte, ('the "e" is sounded, dear boy, as in Brontë') stepped out of the next stall with pee on his brightly polished brown brogues. 'Men of my age frequently need a new washer,' was his cheerful comment, an unsolicited reference to his urinary difficulties. The MP for a seat in Warwickshire, Grunte was not one of the better-loved Tories, but he rarely went unnoticed. A Midlands motor dealer ('A fair deal with Grunt' – the 'e' had been added later, upon his election to Parliament), he was built like an elderly Land Rover. His enemies in the Party, who were numbered among the brightest and the best, suggested unkindly that his libido was turbo-assisted, and that he traded in his women after two years. In business, his practice was sharp. It was the universal view of the members of the 1922 Committee of Tory back-benchers that, given Grunte's probity in matters financial, the Governorship of the Cayman Islands would be the most suitable place for him.

Ralph Grunte was very large, bald, and wore a 1914-type subaltern's moustache. His suits were as chequered as his career. He was one of those men who, once the bloom had gone (in his case his hair), never seem to age, although a glance at Vacher's *Guide* would have revealed him to be sixty-two. He was a keen Party conference-goer. Thirty years previously a slimmer Grunte had seduced the female chairman of the Bridgwater Young Conservatives. They had lain on the damp sand under one or other of Brighton's twin piers, having spent the evening dancing to the music of Joe Loss. The girl, whose name was Marion, was now a magistrate, and a grandmother, but the escapade had sharpened the young Grunte's appetites and he had made it his business in the intervening years to keep up what he cheerfully called 'my rate of strike'.

His record, however, was not one of unbroken success. Lynda Chalker had smacked his face in the crush bar of the Grand Hotel. Edwina Currie had rejected his advances ('What sort of girl do you think I am?') while Emma Nicholson had not caught exactly what it was he had proposed. Did he want her to speak in his constituency?

Grunte was not so easily discouraged. Youth might have given way reluctantly to late middle-age, but his victims had grown old more gracefully with him, dalliance being preferred by many Tories to oratory. The more mischievous of his colleagues, bored by the proceedings and with time on their hands, watched with fascination the progress of his affairs. So too, did the Gentlemen of the Press.

Now he strode towards the hall, acknowledging the respectful salutes of Party agents. After the service, the Mayor had said his piece: 'I welcome you warmly to the city of the Prince Regent.' Sir Charles Webb-Bowen was delivering himself of a homily. He had a hearty manner and his heavy spectacles suggested an even greater myopia than is usually the case with conference chairpersons.

Last night, Amaranth Wilikins had told Grunte that she had yet to make up her mind in which of the many debates she would try to speak. Should she demand, as had the young Edwina, the return of the rod and the rope? Her instinct told her that atavistic attitudes, once so popular under John Major's predecessor, might not now be the thing. In the eighteen months since Mrs

Thatcher had taken up employment at Dickins and Jones, the mood of the Party had perceptibly changed for the better, the great bulk of the membership having transferred its loyalty smoothly from the old Leader to the new. John Major was not a hanger and flogger and the conference would take its tone from him.

Ms Wilikins might speak in favour of female emancipation, but as the majority of the representatives were women, too strident an approach would be dangerous. Her sisters under the skin would man the constituency selection committees. Perhaps the best course would be to speak in the debate on policy and public relations, a pretty appeal for less of the first and more of the second?

Grunte had promised to think it over and would give her his advice at lunch over Langan's warm salad of duck followed by white chocolate ice cream. (Amaranth never travelled without a copy of the *Good Food Guide*.)

Sir Ralph was careful not to take his place among his constituents, although his local chairman, Mrs Angela Cartwright, had kept a seat vacant for him. He had begun to suspect that, despite his many years of unstinting service to the Party in both Warwickshire and Westminster, he was not as loved as he once had been. There had been the regrettable occasion in the Chamber when he had kissed the Labour Party's spokesman for the Arts, a Mr Mark Fisher, on his bald pate, an escapade that had attracted what his wife Marjorie had called 'bloody bad publicity'. And had not a pupil of the Arden Convent school complained that he had pinched her bottom while conducting a group of girls on a tour round the Palace of Westminster? He had denied it emphatically, of course.

Grunte could not be described as being a sensitive

man, but even he had become aware of a general climate of disapproval. It was as an exercise in the restoration of goodwill that he had booked an alcove table at the Hospitality Inn's restaurant for that evening. The time had come to splash out to the tune of forty quid a head for the eight members of his party who had travelled with him from the Forest of Arden to Sussex by the Sea. Amaranth Wilikins for lunch, Angela Cartwright and Co. for dinner: Grunte hoped that the one would prove as profitable as the other.

He found a seat and settled down to listen to the opening speaker in the first of the day's debates.

The long line of leading Conservatives on the platform fixed their faces into expressions of interested concern, and prepared themselves for what could only turn out to be a surfeit of oratory. In the old days, when Margaret Thatcher was still a chemist, and John Major was John Major-Ball, most MPs and many Ministers stayed away from the Party conferences, regarding it as a necessary vulgarity, an annual opportunity for the spear-carriers and party bit-players to travel to a seaside resort out of season to spend a few days in the proximity of the great. Those MPs who succumbed to the pressures of Party democracy brought their golf clubs with them and spent long days on the sandy links of Southport and elsewhere, returning to their hotels in the evening to take part in an entertainment such as the Agents' dinner and dance.

Today, attendance for Ministers (or shadow Ministers, as the case may be) is compulsory. Even the Prime Minister, who once used to arrive on the last day by aeroplane in order to déliver his speech, sits every day on the platform listening to rebuke, complaint and exhortation. It is an innovation for which Edward Heath was responsible. Many run-of-the-mill MPs turn up, some in the hope of speaking in the debates, others, like Grunte, to feed the faces of the faithful and to press all available flesh.

No sooner had the debate begun than people began to leave the hall. What fun there was at Party conferences could most often be found outside it – in the Grand Hotel, where the *prominenti* stay and the Irish plant bombs, at the many and various meetings of the conference 'fringe' and among the bars, coffee stalls and bookshops which accompany the conference on its triangular three-year odyssey between Blackpool, Bournemouth and Brighton.

Joshua Morris began a slow progress in the hope of refreshment and of meeting old friends and enemies. He had been an MP for many years in two incarnations, for a seat in South London and now for Shropshire West. His political ambitions, once strong, had burnt themselves out and he now watched carefully the progress of others. He made for the travelling bookshop, where he found Jeffrey Archer sitting at a portable desk to one side of the bookstall. In front of him stretched a long queue of women each clutching a copy of *As the Crow Flies*. Jeffrey was doing his customary book signing. He gave each supplicant twenty seconds – 'name, please' (pause for boyish smile) and a swift signature. One by one, the women departed, clasping their treasures.

Lord Archer occupied an equivocal place within the ranks of the Conservative Party. An influential minority disapproved of him, disliking his bumptiousness, cringing before the armour of his self-confidence. Unlike the rest of Mrs Thatcher's 'court', he had survived her downfall, and John Major claimed to have taken *Crow* with him when he flew to Spain for a week's holiday. The more sophisticated Tories might have their doubts but not the hoi polloi. Jeffrey Archer's tireless energy and folksy oratory were much in demand at constituency lunches and dinners. Joshua Morris had not invited him to break bread in Clungunford, Clunbury, Clunton or Clun, but Ralph Grunte had booked him for his Warwickshire Tories' annual dinner and dance.

'Say what you like about Jeffrey, he's a damn good read,' was Grunte's view. It was shared by many.

Joshua took refuge within the bookshop. Two girls, who both turned out to be called Fiona, were still unpacking the stock. The flavour of the booth was political: memoirs by forgotten Cabinet Ministers, *Night and Day* by Nicholas Ridley, *The Hand on the Tiller* by Sir Norman Fowler and *Leading Man* by Cecil Parkinson, stood shoulder to shoulder with a company of Archers. *What Every Woman Wants* by Edwina Currie stood cheek by jowl with a thriller by Douglas Hurd. There were stacks of unreadable pamphlets produced by the Party's Young Turks, and a remaindered copy of a Michael Heseltine. Joshua asked one of the Fionas if she sold fiction. He had in mind a Brookner, a Lively or a Colegate; a Pym (Barbara, not Francis) would be a comfort; anything but Martin Amis. The girl pointed impatiently towards the Archers. Unsatisfied, Morris resumed his tour of inspection, buying a raffle ticket from a woman who claimed to have once heard him speak.

A glance at the television monitor showed that the Chancellor was on his feet, replying to the brief debate. Age had given Norman Lamont a faintly oriental look; the sound had been turned off, but it was plain from the speaker's gestures that jam, or whatever was its Japanese equivalent, if it were not on today's bill of fare, was certainly expected to be on the morrow's. The object of the whole conference exercise was the boosting of Party morale. Joshua noticed the tall, willowy figure of Charles Harvey, one of several Tories who had enjoyed the favours of the late Emma Kerr, the MP who had been murdered. He was in the company of a smartly dressed older woman to whom he seemed to defer. Kenneth Clarke drifted by under his Home Secretarial escort. The better-known Cabinet Ministers moved in a stately fashion as if speed of foot might trample accidentally a party worker bent upon homage; better to tread slowly so as to receive fittingly the admiration of many.

Suddenly a posse of television men with lights, hand-held cameras and furry sound-amplifiers like caterpillars on sticks arrived in front of Morris with Amaranth Wilikins in tow. The presenter was as black as Viv Richards but his accent was West End and not West Indies. The lights were switched on, and Amaranth stood, illuminated for all to see. She was tall, wasp-waisted with the kind of hair women's mags called 'dark blonde'. Joshua thought she would be in her early forties. A small crowd of the curious and respectful gathered round the impromptu studio.

Had Ms Wilikins political ambitions? She had. Did she hope to stand in a winnable seat at the next election? She did. Had her career as an actress come to an end? Morris had no idea she had trodden the boards. Could that be the reason her face was familiar? Politics, it appeared, now came first. Did her recent divorce now mean that she was foot-loose and fancy free? Ms Wilikins did not look too happy with the question for which she had been given no prior notice. She smiled bravely and replied to the effect that next time she would take care to marry a politician.

'Not if you have any sense, duckie,' shouted a stout Northern female bystander to much laughter. 'They're all in love with themselves.' Producer and presenter switched off their lights, and Amaranth Wilikins vanished with a toss of her mane.

Sir Ralph Grunte raised his hand dutifully at the end of Norman Lamont's reply. Votes were a mere formality, a gesture towards Party democracy. The motions which were chosen for debate all hovered marginally above the lowest common factor of Party opinion and were designed to be carried *nem con*. As the crowd edged towards the exits, and Sir Charles cried manfully for silence so that the next debate could start, Grunte stepped on the heel of his local party agent, Bill O'Farrell who, cursing silently, thrust a newspaper in Grunte's direction. It was the *Forest of Arden Recorder*.

'Have a look at the correspondence column, and tell me what we ought to do about it.'

Grunte left the hall and found a seat. He turned to the letter page, and felt his guts constrict as he began to read a letter that carried the headline, 'Grunte to be de-selected?' The letter was short and pointed, and bore the signature of a Tory local councillor who had been, in his time, the Mayor of the Borough. He had also, ten years ago or more, worked for Grunt's Garages before setting up on his own as a builder/developer.

Sir,
Ralph Grunte has represented the seat in Parliament

for nearly ten years. He has made few speeches and passed no Bills. But he is rarely, if ever, out of the papers which, if they are to be believed, have told of Grunte's drunken exploits in Parliament and have recounted his talent as a 'serial buttocks fondler'. [A what? thought Grunte angrily.] Grunte is rarely to be seen in the constituency and even more rarely in the House of Commons. Isn't it high time that his local Party found another candidate?
Yours etc., David Swan, Mayor of Arden 1987–8.

How was I to know that Grace Swan was a pupil at the Arden Convent School? Snotty-nosed little bitch. Grunte looked anxiously around him in the hope of spotting O'Farrell. De-selection had become something of a fashion in the Tory Party: an attempt had been made to de-select several Tory MPs who had campaigned for Heseltine in the leadership contest of November 1990. John Browne had been sacked in Winchester while others who had incurred the disapproval of their local parties had gone quietly. All that was needed was a fifty-signature petition, a special general meeting and a simple majority in favour of the proposition. The local party would then choose a replacement in time for the next General Election. How far had the disaffection spread? As far as Bill O'Farrell, who had worked on the pumps on the forecourt of Grunte's first garage? Surely his loyalty could be relied upon.

But could it? Grunte's treat that evening at the Hospitality Inn was well timed. Sir Ralph (he had been knighted by Margaret Thatcher in 1980 for raising money from commerce and industry to finance the activities of Conservative Central Office when in Opposition) bought a coffee and sat down at a corner table. Taking an envelope from his pocket he wrote down the names of his guests.

Angela Cartwright had been the chairman of the local Tories for the past two years. She was a bossy little woman of about fifty whose non-political husband was an accountant. She tended to wear frightful hats with feathers. She had a tiny mouth ('like a hen's arse' was Grunte's privately expressed opinion) and had, because of her aggressive plainness, so far escaped Grunte's 'paternal' – or should it be 'fraternal' – sexual attentions. She had in the past been supportive, and Grunte marked his card 15/20 for loyalty.

Bill O'Farrell, the party's agent, had achieved over the years something of the status of a retainer. He had certainly been paid one by Grunte over and above his salary, which was met by the local Tory Association. He was unmarried, wore cavalry twill trousers and a 'RAFF' tie, and was a Warwickshire drinking companion of Grunte's. Grunte put him down as 16/20.

Carole Swan was a very different matter, the mother of the bruised Grace and wife of the outraged David, once Mayor of the Borough. Grunte had been surprised to see her on duty at Brighton. She had not acknowledged his cheerful greeting that morning, but had, nevertheless, put the dinner invitation safely away in her bag. She was a big, handsome woman, a larger Grace with a noble bum, by which Grunte in happier times might well have been tempted. She spoke with a Brummy whine and had roots that were invariably darker than her ends. Her husband, although not a 'representative', was expected to join her later in the day. Grunte marked her 0/20 on his card.

The Malcolms, Kevin and Janet, were both incredibly dim. He was tall, dark and far from handsome; she was small, chirpy and was for ever brushing Kev's shoulders free of scurf. In consequence, they moved, at Party functions, within a cordon sanitaire. An ironmonger and former captain in the TA, Kevin Malcolm had become, thanks to Buggins, Chairman of the local Chamber of Commerce. Grunte had taken him earlier in the year to a lunch at the Connaught Rooms where he (Malcolm) had been introduced to Lady Porter. This had pleased him mightily as his admiration for Lady Porter was nearly as great as that for Margaret Thatcher, and, in consequence, his attitude to Grunte had warmed. Janet who had, a lifetime ago, gone dancing with the young Grunte, would, even so, do, or vote, as Kev dictated.

Grunte marked the Malcolms down at 10/20 each.

Hyacinth Scragg had caught Grunte's roving eye. A 19-year-old brunette who worked in 'Back and Sides', an Arden hairdresser's, she reminded him of the young Alma Cogan. Had he not told her so last night? Or, at least, she had done so at the Young Conservatives' Summer Dance in July. She was big and busty and wore the sort of extravagant 'gowns' favoured by La Cogan in her prime, and now only to be glimpsed on BBC1's 'Come Dancing' which Grunte proclaimed to be his favourite programme. 'It might well be naff, but, by God, it's sexy.' As the divisional YC chairman she had views on the ozone layer, the council tax and Michael Heseltine ('He's disloyal'), but she could not sustain them, and any attempt at talking politics inevitably ended in a fit of the giggles. Carole Swan had drawn her attention to the Member's assault upon her daughter in the Mother of Parliaments, but Hyacinth had been unshocked. 'Men,' was all she had said.

Grunte who had, as yet, made no move in Hyacinth's direction, adopted a joshing manner towards her, as if to a favourite niece. I'll give her 17/20, thought Grunte: the exercise was rapidly becoming a beauty competition.

Paul Franklin was a nasty bit of work. He worked at Jaguars in Coventry in a department called 'Human Resources'. He had grown a moustache in order to look like Ian Botham and he drove a 1960s Jag like Inspector Morse. He gave the impression of having little time for the Member, despite Grunte's many years spent in the motor trade. His wife, Pamela, whom fortunately he had left behind, was an acid-tongued woman who managed a fleet of launderettes. Franklin, who liked his beer, and Pam who was more witty than wise, were known in the Arden Conservative Club, where the slot machines never sleep, as 'lager and lime'. Franklin had once written a letter to Sir Ralph which the Member thought highly offensive and relations between them had since remained frigid. He marked Franklin down as 5/20.

The eighth guest was Leroy Burns, a Brummie whose parents had come from Antigua. He was a huge man in his early thirties who had been for a time a heavyweight boxer. He had been one of Frank Bruno's sparring partners. But, like most fighters, he had a placid disposition and a great good nature. The fact that he was black and a Tory gave him a value out of proportion to his contribution to the local Party, so he was frequently trotted out at functions, and encouraged to ask questions of visiting speakers. Grunte had run into him on the forecourt of one of his garages where he had come to buy a second-hand Sierra. With that instinct for survival that had kept the Member for Arden in Parliament for so long, Grunte had sold him the car at a nil rate of interest. As a result Leroy was as loyal as a hound dog and had undertaken to 'look after' Sir Ralph at election campaigns. He had made a formidable minder so far.

Grunte closed his card by awarding Leroy 20/20. He took a calculator from his wallet, added up the marks and divided them by 8. The result was an average loyalty-factor of just over 11 out of 20. There was precious little margin for survival.

If MPs do not look forward to an annual visit to Babel by the Sea, the Party's rank and file spend twelve months ticking off the days in happy anticipation. Four whole days in the company of the famous. The political correspondents both of the written and the spoken word adopt a world-weary pose, but four nights in the Grand Hotel at the expense of their bosses, together with the inevitable excitements, real or manufactured, make a welcome change. And October is the start of the political year. Alan Watkins of the *Observer* had spent August and September as a guest in Great Houses; Michael Jones of *The Sunday Times* had spent six weeks in Tuscany avoiding, whenever he could, the Gilmours, Jenkinses and Mortimers; Peter Riddell of *The Times*, Hugo Young, Julia Langdon, Simon Heffer, Sir Robin Day – they were all in Brighton on expenses, refreshed and ready for the fray.

Even Ron Barton of the *True Brit*, the paper which the Saatchi Brothers claimed had taken the heat out of the *Sun*, had moved into his brother-in-law's house in Kemp Town 'for the duration'. Party conferences were not just piss and wind; among the 7,000 pilgrims there were not a few for whom the hotel bedrooms of Brighton were the promised land, a weakness shared by some Tribunes of the People. If another bomb were to go off, just who would come through the ceiling? And in the company of whom? 'The Poison Dwarf' (Barton was 5 feet high in his Littlewood's socks) was determined to be the first to find out.

Simon Heffer, gingery and right-wing, took his vile coffee and sat next to Joshua Morris. Together they watched the passing parade. Heffer wrote for the two *Telegraph*s and had not been himself since Mrs Thatcher had been sent packing. 'Shall I see you at Jeffrey's party?' Morris said it was unlikely.

Alistair McAlpine, the merchant builder, had, when he served as the Party's treasurer during the Thatcher years, begun the tradition of a lavish party to which only *la crème* had been invited. The champagne was vintage, the pâté Fortnum's, and the air blue with the smoke of Cuban cigars: only the lobsters were pink. But Alistair had quit, and the beano had been taken over by the only Tory rich enough to take his place: Jeffrey Archer. The party was for the Wednesday night in Archer's Bridal Suite in the Grand, and tickets were like gold. Scribblers and the telly-presenters came as of right, together with the Cabinet and other Ministers, the prettiest women, and a handful of Jeffrey's cronies. Joshua Morris was not among them.

He took out of his briefcase a sheaf of invitations. There were parties paid for by the interested ranging from Lord King of BA to *The Times* newspapers. Morris laid out on a table spotted with spilt coffee, invitations from Peter Stothard, Andrew Neil, Granada Television and TV-AM.

'I'll swop you Stothard for an Archer.'

Heffer declined. He had an extra Archer however, grace of the *Telegraph*. 'I'll make you a present of it. Take care. I know some ambitious Tories who would kill for it.'

There was a loud noise. A party of Young Conservatives, led by their national chairman, Wullie Robertson, a hairy, bearded Scot with a beer belly, wearing a T-shirt with the legend, 'She was stabbed in the back', across it, made its way towards the exit and the real world outside. Maggie's praetorian guard were abandoning the chairman of the Party. Norman Fowler's speech was far too left-wing for them, so they were heading for the 'Hedgehog and Hogshead', a railway pub north of the main Brighton railway station. They had patronised it the previous night, taking to heart its motto (in Latin), 'drink yourself to hell'. The police had had to be called. Now, as they shoved their way through the audience, two wooden chairs were knocked over and there were drawn breaths of outrage.

'We shall have trouble with that little lot,' said Heffer.

At ten minutes to one the remaining 'representatives' got to their feet to applaud Fowler's speech. Nowadays, the standing ovation is given indiscriminately; only rarely is a halting speech or a lame performance marked by bottoms obstinately stuck to seats. After three minutes, the crowd made its way slowly but cheerfully towards lunch.

Hyacinth Scragg had sat quietly throughout the morning's proceedings, although she had not gone unnoticed. She had amused herself by awarding marks to the platform party for sexiness. Sadly Cecil Parkinson was no longer a member of the first eleven, although Hyacinth liked his very English good looks. He has worn well, she mused. John Major had a nice smile, Douglas Hurd carried himself well, while Michael Heseltine was dishy. Could he really be almost sixty? Like all of the young, Hyacinth believed 'sex' to end at some arbitrary, and unimaginable age, like thirty-five.

Kenneth Clarke could lose some weight to his advantage, but Richard Ryder, the Party's Chief Whip, was boyishly good looking. Norman Lamont, she thought, would look good in a gangster movie of the kind she occasionally watched on the telly, playing opposite George Raft or James Cagney. She could not see Lamont's feet, but she was sure he ought to wear spats. Angela Rumbold looked like a Derby winner, while Virginia Bottomley was quite lovely.

While Hyacinth awarded marks, others, just as predatory, were giving her the eye. Wullie Robertson had 'made a mental note'. She was a right good-looker. Charles Harvey had spotted her drinking milky Nescafé at half-time, and had told himself that he should make inquiries as to who she was. Lovely-looking girl. She stood out from the general run of Tory women like a Bird of Paradise in Trafalgar Square.

She had not gone unnoticed by Ron Barton of the *True Brit* who was, as always, in search of local colour. Sadly unaware of the interest she had caused, Hyacinth made her way back to her undistinguished hotel, and the prospect of a dullish lunch (fried fish in red breadcrumbs, tinned peas and mash) in the company of her fellow 'delegates', Angela Cartwright and the boring Malcolms. All they would talk about would be the even more boring Sir Ralph Grunte and the plot to de-select him. Grunte was ancient, but he had always been nice to her.

At lunchtime the Party workers, their appetites sharpened by contention and sea air, quit the conference hall in their thousands. The more humble queue within the centre for cold cuts and Bakewell tart, sorting themselves out into tables of four or five. Old victories are savoured; ancient defeats glossed over, and the Party's leaders held up to a not always affectionate scrutiny.

The more fortunate cluster together, striding out down the windy front past a long line of protesters, the disenchanted who, with banners in support of some unspeakable cause, line the entrance to the building, their passivity guaranteed (at the poll-tax-payers' expense) by half-a-hundred provincial policemen. The happy ones are on their way to their annual free lunch, provided, as is the custom, by their MP or prospective candidate. These occasions are marked by much conviviality, and the temporary burying of hatchets, promises of continuing support being matched, on the part of the host, by rashly given undertakings to draw a thousand raffles. Many a career has been cemented for a further twelvemonth over well-done rump steaks and bottles of Bulgarian wine.

The very fortunate indeed slip discreetly into Brighton's better restaurants. Greeted by a rubbing of practised hands, the Tory Party's celebrities take their seats before well-appointed tables where they listen to the supplications of their hosts while scrutinising the menu.

At Langan's Bistro, with its gallery full of prints, plates and drawings, a waiter stood ready to whisper into more receptive ears a list of the day's specialities. The head waiter showed Ms Wilikins to her chair; Sir Ralph, wearing his County Show tweeds, noticed with some satisfaction a general turning of heads. Alan Watkins, who was awaiting the arrival of the Chancellor himself, gave Amaranth his approving eye. She had, he mused, the build of a junior Welsh wing three-quarter.

Jeffrey Archer, who was discussing the size of his tax bill with the Features Editor of *Woman's Own*, momentarily lost his thread; who was she? A tall, fair woman with legs as long as Julia Roberts', she would be a catch for his grand party. He rose and came over to Grunte's table. 'Who's your pretty friend, Ralph?' Jeffrey had a roguish charm which he used like a bludgeon. It went down a treat with the matrons in safe seats like South-West Surrey.

Introductions effected, Archer gave Amaranth a large gold-edged card, on which he filled in her name. 'Come at nine and we'll dance the night away.'

Grunte, to whom the suggestion had not been made, and who had not been invited to Archer's bloody party in the first place, watched the novelist return to his table. 'Sold him a Rover once. Number plate ARCH 1. Never stopped complaining,' he commented, adding, 'never mind about him – I'll introduce you to the people who really count before we go.' Not to be outdone in the amatory stakes, Grunte recommended a dozen oysters.

'We are in for a long afternoon,' he said cheerfully.

That was true enough, although Amaranth Wilikins had no intention of spending it with Ralph Grunte. There would be a debate on Europe, a topic which tended to divide the Party, and it was rumoured that Norman Tebbitt, known to his friends as 'The Earl of Essex' – a reference not only to his place of origin, but to his courtier-like qualities – would be speaking. He was to oppose the motion, an act of 'disloyalty' of which many disapproved. It would add to the gaiety of nations although many, including Joshua Morris, discounted the possibility of Norm's intervention, believing that Sir Charles Webb-Bowen's myopia could be relied upon in emergencies. What was his 'K' for, after all? An angry Norman would be left turning in the wind, waving his papers in a desperate attempt to attract the conference chairman's attention. The boat might be rocked but it would not ship water.

Amaranth refused the offer of oysters, giving a little shudder. 'They are alive when they go down,' she said. 'Peter Mayle, you know the man who writes about his life in Provence, says that the best starter in the world is strips of foie gras, lightly fried in butter and dropped into a well-dressed salad.'

Sadly, it was not on the menu. Amaranth, whose figure was her fortune, chose Vichyssoise: Grunte, whose fortune, such as it was, owed more to Nissan motors, asked for a smoked trout with horseradish sauce.

'Well, my dear,' he said, pressing his knees against Amaranth's, 'so it's your intention to stand for Parliament?'

He had to consider his rate of strike. Hyacinth Scragg was certainly younger, and she had big tits (Grunte, who was a page three man, had crossed swords in the House with Clare Short, who quite definitely was not a page three woman). But Grunte was no chicken; at his age La Scragg could well be altogether too much of a good thing. Lady Grunte, who was cooking her lover's lunch in Solihull at that very moment, had warned her husband off the Young Conservatives. 'I know you can't help it, Grunt,' she had said, amicably enough for her, 'but for Christ's sake stop fouling your own nest.'

Marjorie Grunte held a majority shareholding in Grunte plc (registered in Liechtenstein), and her support, were Grunte to remain solvent, was essential. He had paid for his latest second-hand Roller out of the firm's pension fund, a fact about which only his accountant knew.

Amaranth moved her knee away, and studied the menu. 'Tell me, Ralph,' she cooed, 'do you know of any safe seats that are coming up in your part of the world?'

After lunch, she permitted herself to be steered from Langan's Bistro by a tipsy Sir Ralph, who, as good as his word, interrupted their retreat by repeated introductions to the Great and the Good. Amaranth had her hand kissed by Sir Thomas Arnold himself. Arnold was of Tom Arnold's circus, and his post as the vice-chairman of the party in charge of candidates made him a target of all those who were eager to stand for Parliament. He had a shrewd eye for the false and the fraud. Amaranth was at her loveliest. By God, she would look good on a platform. 'Good luck,' he murmured, and then suggested that he might be of further help to her. 'Worcester West,' he said, 'could very well be coming on the market.'

Amaranth wondered who it was who sat so comfortably for Worcester West. Some old sod in his late sixties ready to take up his Parliamentary pension (fifty-three per cent of the annual salary after twenty-five years of unbroken service), she supposed. She liked Worcester. Brown's was a decent restaurant and she might find a small Georgian house in the Close. She had a Worcester teapot, first period. She would ask old Grunte for the MP's name.

After Tom Arnold's encouragement, Amaranth was propelled in the direction of the chairman of the Party himself, Norman Fowler.

'This lovely lady,' Grunte boomed, bowing in Amaranth's direction, 'is the rising hope of us stern, unbending Tories.'

Fowler, who had little time for him, was mildly surprised at his erudition. He had always thought the MP for Arden read little save for the *Motor Traders' Gazette*.

'She doesn't look much like Gladstone to me,' he murmured, getting to his feet.

Amaranth, who loved his clean-cut looks, rewarded him with a blinding smile, and said she had much more time for Disraeli. 'I hope to speak in tomorrow's debate on policy and public relations,' she told him. 'Will you keep your fingers crossed for me?'

Fowler said he most certainly would do so. He might even, he mused, have a word with old Webb-Bowen's minder. Better her than Teresa Gorman.

Ushered to the door of the restaurant by minions, Amaranth, disregarding Grunte's magisterial signal to his hovering chauffeur, plunged into a waiting cab. She blew Grunte a kiss. The old fart had served his purpose. His advice as to her speech before a selection committee ('Take my tip, Ama,' he had said, 'three parts to a good speech. Ten years of ceaseless fight against socialism; in favour of flogging and hanging; and something nice about whoever it is who happens to be leading the Party. Like a charm.') was not original, but at least she had met Norman Fowler and Jeffrey Archer. She had, as her Petty Officer father would have put it, 'shown the flag'.

Her every move had been followed by jaundiced and world-weary senior politicians; she had noticed a gleam of lust in the good eye of a privy Councillor, and Peter Riddell of *The Times* had made a note of her name. The food was not at all bad, either.

Amaranth had no wish to be caught napping in the lounge of the Grand Hotel; how much better to return to 'Mon Repos' and put her feet up for an hour or so. She could then descend upon the Grand Hotel to take tea. Lying on the bed in her Marks and Spencer's slip, she read with interest of the range of conference delights available that evening for those who were otherwise unengaged. They included the Young Conservatives Ball, Tim Janman's Conservative Political Centre lecture entitled 'Some of my best friends . . .', and Andrew Neil's party on behalf of *The Sunday Times*. Perhaps she could persuade Charles Harvey to take her to Andrew Neil before they went out to dinner. Wasn't he the one who had been friendly with Pamella Bordes, or was it Donald Trelford of the *Observer*?

And there was her speech to write. Harvey was, she had read in the *Daily Mail*, 'Cabinet material'. His 'input' into her speech might well make all the difference. Amaranth fell into a gentle sleep at more or less the same time as did the bulk of Sir Teddy Taylor's conference audience.

Tuesday Afternoon

This October the weather is as balmy as it is in spring,
mused Joshua. The sea shone, the waves sparkled, and a
Royal Navy frigate steamed slowly up and down, sent by
the Ministry of Defence to deter a seaborne landing on
the part of the boyos of the Provisional IRA. Somewhat
ominously, it appeared that its guns were trained upon
the town. The streets were thronged with packets of
policemen, drawn from several county forces each with
its different helmet. They stood watching the girls go by,
small groups of foreign students or au pairs, leggy and
lithe, Indian Summer girls whose presence in Brighton
was a far bigger draw for young males than the Royal
Pavilion.

There was no sign of Pinky and his razor-wielding
gang: Joshua supposed that Graham Greene had drawn
his inspiration not so much from Hove as from Kemp
Town, where smelly pubs and mean little houses cluster
under railway arches, and supermarket mums push twins
in Siamese prams.

He was standing outside the conference centre, savouring the sunshine, watching for the return of the Party's *prominenti* from their lunch. He watched Gerald Kaufman buy a copy of the *Evening Standard*; he had probably been lunching with the BBC. The knot of demonstrators summoned up a ragged cry and waved their tattered banners, but whether it was the sight of Edwina Currie or of Virginia Bottomley was not immediately evident. Lord Whitelaw, a figure from the past, alighted from a black Rover, and, turning towards France in order to return the salutations of the mob, found himself staring into the bloodshot eyes of Class War. He turned smartly on his heel and trotted into the foyer, greeting the stewards with indiscriminate effusion. There goes dear old Willie, thought Joshua, the non-playing captain of the Wets, who was finally persuaded to advise Margaret Thatcher that famous November that 'the game was up'.

Inside the building Joshua stood in line with the multitude to endure the long wait and the thorough search, the emptying of pockets and the impudent fumblings of security. It took the usual twenty minutes, and, when he finally entered the conference hall, the motion in favour of Europe was being moved by Gerry Malone, a personable Scot who was now the MP for Winchester. The choice of Malone was, in itself, surprising; several years ago he had, in cahoots with Nicholas Ridley, stampeded the conference in favour of the early introduction of the poll tax, thereby sealing Margaret's fate.

Joshua hoped that Malone had learnt wisdom with his advancing years. His words came out in a seemingly endless flow of support and approbation. Her Majesty's

Government were to be warmly congratulated for standing up for Britain at Brussels. At this there was a muted growl of support from those in the hall who had not succumbed to a heavy lunch. Indeed, the speaker would go further; never in his experience had Britain been so ably represented in the councils of the Common Market. The audience turned over in its sleep. Had not the Prime Minister himself said, and here I quote: 'We would be at the heart of Europe.' Well, that is exactly where we were, backing Britain.

Joshua Morris, who had been standing near the door, slipped out into the foyer. Perhaps a quick cup of coffee? He took an armchair near a monstrously large television screen (the sound had been turned right down) and silently challenged Malone, the conference, and indeed the Party, to bring him back to life.

He was awakened later by the sound of laughter and, heaving himself out of his chair, he joined two Tories, John Taylor, the unsuccessful candidate for Cheltenham, and Mirj Deva, who had been elected for Brentford and Isleworth. They had lunched together. Approaching them were three people in line abreast: Nigel Lawson, his son Dominic of the *Spectator*, and his beautiful daughter, the journalist Nigella Lawson. As the six of them met, Joshua congratulated Nigel on his hand.

'What hand?' was the reply.

'Three of a kind beats two spades.'

There was a pause and then much laughter, not all of it forced. John Taylor's huge hand slapped Morris painfully between the shoulder blades. 'You're a racist, man,' he cried in mock West Indian accent. Heartened by this exchange, Joshua re-entered the conference hall just as Norman Tebbit was getting to his feet. The motion had been ably moved and seconded – according to Sir Charles. What was more to the point he was not, or so it appeared, prepared to invite Mr Tebbit to oppose it. Somnolence, which had enveloped the hall, vanished; static political electricity took its place.

Gaunt, even spectral, the figure of Norman Tebbit ('Big Norm' as he was known to the irreverent, 'Little Norm' being Lamont, and 'Nice Norm', Fowler) stood in his place, waving a sheaf of papers. Without a mechanical aid, he had difficulty making himself heard. He was protesting at the injustice of the world; the word 'referendum' could be distinguished from a flood of complaint. He was sitting among friends who promptly set up a chorus of 'hear, hear's.

Sir Charles Webb-Bowen offered his ear to the urgent promptings of a party apparatchik; the fact that it was his 'bad' ear, lent a certain comedy to the proceedings. The supplicant scampered round to the chairman's better side, and said, more loudly than he perhaps intended, the microphone picking up his words quite clearly, 'Say no to the bugger.' At this there was a roar of mingled laughter and outrage. Wullie Robertson, of the Young Conservatives, began to blow blasts on a tin trumpet, and was quickly surrounded by newspaper cameramen and reporters.

Sir Robin Day, who had been taking a nap on a sofa in the BBC room in the balcony, was hurriedly awakened. His sense of shock was swiftly communicated to the nation.

Sir Charles, whose practice as a family solicitor in Hertfordshire had not prepared him for this sort of thing, was losing control. Norman Tebbit was still on his feet, waving what appeared to be a small Union Jack, and trying manfully to make himself heard above the din. The conference chairman shouted into the microphone that he had got his little list and he was damned if he was not going to stick to it. At this there was more uproar and, encouraged by their chief, a posse of seven Scottish YCs in kilts paraded in front of the platform singing 'Rule Britannia' to the uncertain sound of Robertson's trumpet. At a word of command, the file of Scots turned towards the hall, bent forward, and at the same time presented their bare arses to the platform party. John Gummer hid his face in his hands; Dame Angela Rumbold took off her glasses.

At a further word of command the file did an about turn and repeated the gesture, this time for the benefit of 7,000 Tories. Written in lipstick, one letter to each cheek, was the slogan, 'Up Yours Delors'. At the cry of 'stewards', forty leathery men of uncertain age, who, as agents, had devoted their lives to the Party, frogmarched the YCs out of the hall to loud applause. Sir Charles, pink in the face, commanded the hall to settle down, and when it had reluctantly done so, summoned Sir Teddy Taylor MP to oppose the motion.

He was stocky, bald, and invariably gabbled in an incomprehensible West of Scotland accent. His appearance, conjured up by the magic of Central Office, had a curiously calming effect, and it was not long before those who had been so rudely awakened by Tebbit's *démarche*, to say nothing of the sight of so many Scottish rumps, were, once again safe in the arms of Morpheus.

David Swan, who had arrived that afternoon to join his wife Carole at the conference, spotted Amaranth Wilikins almost as soon as he entered the Grand Hotel. The one time Mayor of Arden, father of the bruised Grace ('Had it been Paddy Ashdown I wouldn't have minded one little bit'), had checked in at the desk and was about to carry his overnight bag up to his room when he noticed her through the glass door of an adjoining room. She was crooking her finger around a cup of Earl Grey.

Wilikins had been the name of her first husband, Henry, who had been at King's School, Birmingham with Swan in the 1960s. As two young married couples they had been close for a time when they lived near Stoke, although Carole had not got on at all well with Amaranth. She gave herself airs, was the tenor of her complaint. David had heard of the Wilikinses' divorce – there had been quite a lot about the circumstances surrounding it in the *Birmingham Mail* – and he had been told of a second, short-lived marriage. To whom, he had not the least idea. Swan took a careful second look through the door. There could be no doubt. It was clearly Amaranth. She must be pushing forty, he thought, but she's still a good looker.

He remembered the occasion when they had paid a visit to St Whatever-it-was on Magdalen bridge in Oxford. At Carole's insistence they had climbed the long metal ladder which led inside from the roof of the nave to the top of the tower: Henry went first, Amaranth second; by some accident of fate, David followed on her heels, leaving an indignant Carole to bring up the rear. The view from the tower was as nothing compared with the view Amaranth unwittingly presented. David did not know quite where to look, but it was one occasion, he subsequently recounted to his friends, when it was better to travel than to arrive.

Would Amaranth remember him? He carried his case into the lounge, determined to find out.

'Amaranth? Remember me, Dave Swan?' He thought better of mentioning Oxford. 'Married to Carole. We used to be friends. Years ago.'

Amaranth certainly did remember him. She noticed, with a feeling of disappointment, that he was not wearing the obligatory photo-pass without which no true Tory could enter the Party conference. Nevertheless he wasn't bad looking, and she could recall nothing to his disadvantage. Was he not a prosperous builder? She asked a waiter for another pot, and settled down to catching up with the story of Swan's life.

Carole was well; what was more to the point she was here at the conference, 'a queen bee' of the local Tories – Chairman of the Forest of Arden Women's Association. Grace was sixteen, at school, and wanted to become a vet. Dave was in the property business, and had had a baddish time during the recession. He built houses, shops. But he couldn't complain, really.

Amaranth's eyes wandered: the hotel foyer was almost empty, and the only other couples seemed as old as the hills.

'Do you know Ralph Grunte?' she asked. 'I've just had lunch with him.'

As Amaranth listened to what David Swan, Carole and the local Party thought of Grunte (it even appeared that Grace Swan had suffered physical assault within the portals of Parliament), her thoughts of representing Worcester West in the Commons swiftly receded. Was Arden a safe seat? It was certainly closer to London.

It appeared from what Dave was saying that Grunte's days were numbered. 'I don't mind telling you, but keep

it under your chapeau' – Amaranth shuddered slightly –
'that Carole and her crowd are having a little meeting
early this evening to work out their tactics. They have in
mind the order of the boot. Years of devoted service, but
time to make way for a younger man. You know the sort
of thing. We will then be in the market. I must say we
could do a lot worse than you. A lot worse.'

Amaranth smiled warmly; she felt the fish on the line.
If Dave were not to take part in the cabal ('I'm a
member of the Party, but that's all'), what was he doing
later on that evening? But she had to take care. Harvey
was the better catch, and there was her speech to worry
about. She needed the help Harvey had promised. With
any luck she would be on her feet in front of conference
some time early tomorrow afternoon. 'Why not a drink
in the bar at six-thirty?' she suggested.

Swan countered, 'What about a bite to eat?' That old
bugger Grunte had not included him in the invitation to
dine at some poncy joint called La Noblesse, the smart-
est part of the Hospitality Inn. Amaranth hesitated. 'Not
tonight, but we could lunch tomorrow. We'll talk about
it when we meet this evening.' She dismissed Swan with
a smile and, having fumbled in her shoulder bag for her
copy of *The Times House of Commons*, turned to
Arden.

GRUNTE, Sir Ralph Redvers (Kt 1980), MP (C)
Arden 1974–, *s* of Percy Haines; *b* 8 Dec 1930; *Educ*
Sutton Coldfield GS; Univ of Birmingham; *m* 1960,
Marjorie Grunt; no chdn; *Career* motor trader and
garage owner; Pres Midland Motor Traders
1970–74 . . .

★ ★ ★

There was much more of the same but it was not long before she found what she was looking for. 'Cons majority 10,445.' If Charles Harvey would write her speech, and David Swan sponsor her candidature, little Amaranth would be sitting pretty, very pretty indeed. She paid for her two teas and quit the hotel. There was still an hour or so left of debate.

Charles Harvey disengaged himself from his constituency chairman. He had taken her to lunch at La Noblesse where they had eaten cod in a watercress sauce and drunk between them a bottle of Chinon, Clos de l'Echo '86. He had apologised for his wife's absence. Miriam had no time whatever for Party conferences. A woman with money of her own, she was only happy with a pencil in her hand, a telephone at her elbow, and a copy of the *Financial Times* on her lap. She loved to move her money around, a process which had suffered from acceleration since the stock market collapse of the autumn of 1987. Theirs was a *marriage blanc*; Harvey was occupied for eighteen hours a day at the Ministry of Transport where he was one of two Parliamentary Secretaries with responsibility for roads.

Since his affair with the late Emma Kerr, he had behaved himself. Rudely, Miriam had advised that he tie a knot in it; she had known of their friendship but was too astute, or too calculating, to dig more deeply. In his turn, Charles suspected discreet goings-on with one or other of her team of brokers, in all probability the braying Harry with the pencil-line moustache.

Charles, who was in his late-thirties, found celibacy a trial; his fancy had been caught by Amaranth Wilikins. Once the vote on Europe had been taken (an overwhelming majority in favour of the platform's motion), he had slipped out of the hall, pausing only to watch and listen while, at the bidding of the cameras, the national chairman of the YCs blew his trumpet for the umpteenth time. The young man was sweating under the lights. He sported several tattoos: on the back of one wrist was the word 'left' in blue; on the other 'right'. So wet was his shirt that the stencilled words, now reading 'I'm an Essex Man', had no doubt transferred themselves to his chest. He stank, and Charles moved swiftly out of range.

The ante-rooms of the hall itself had turned into a miniature promenade or fairground. The Gas, Water and Electricity Companies all had stands as if it were an exhibition. Mark Lawson of the *Independent* asked him whether he thought Tebbit should have been called to speak. 'In an ideal world,' Harvey replied with what he hoped was a cynical grin. A loudspeaker called his name, asking him to collect a message. His progress towards the bureau was remarked upon by two elderly ladies who beamed appreciatively in his direction. What a nice-looking young man! Harvey smiled back, hesitated, then continued on his march. As far as he could tell they were not his constituents.

The message was from his private secretary at the Ministry. It read, simply: 'Motorway route confirmed; no public announcement until the House reassembles in the middle of the month.' The M432 had been subjected to inquiry and appeal. It was something at least that the route itself had now been agreed on. With any luck it would go straight through Grunte's Warwickshire front garden.

Charles telephoned a message through to the desk at the Grand. Would Ms Wilikins come to *The Sunday*

Times's party with him this evening? He would meet her in the bar around six o'clock.

David went upstairs to his room, pecked Carole on the cheek and told her he had run into Amaranth Wilikins. His wife gave no sign of pleasure at the news.

'I expect she's looking for another husband,' she said.

'Not a husband, a seat. Or perhaps both,' was the reply.

Carole said it was no good hoping to replace 'that awful Grunte' with that blonde tart. She changed her shoes, did her hair, dabbed her neck with Chanel and slammed the bedroom door. 'I will be late.' The sound of her steps died away. So, with any luck, shall I, thought Swan. With his hand control he killed the television News and swapped it for 'Home and Away'.

Carole hurried to the Queen's Hotel, where Angela Cartwright was staying and where the cabal plotting to de-select Grunte had agreed to meet. It did not go as well as Carole had hoped.

To start with, there were only five of them. They had decided against inviting Bill O'Farrell, the agent, or Leroy Burns, Grunte's 'minder', as the conspirators were pretty certain that those two would leak everything to the MP. And to Carole's annoyance, Hyacinth Scragg had not turned up, despite the reminder she had received over a cup of tea at the conference centre. She was a silly girl, and far too easily impressed by Grunte's elephantine attentions. She was no better than she should be. Carole would take the first opportunity to get her on her own and have a word with her in private. As the 'chair' of the YCs, she was an officer of the Association and as such had a vote in the matter.

Paul Franklin was sound, and Angela Cartwright confessed that she too had long thought it high time Grunte gave up. She wondered whether 'dear John' would do the decent thing and send Ralph to the Lords. Franklin thought not.

The Malcolms said very little although that daft Janet mumbled something to the effect that the meeting, held prior to Grunte's 'treat', was in bad taste. She said that despite his little weaknesses (here Carole thought of Grace's bruised bum), she had always found Sir Ralph to be a proper gentleman.

Angela Cartwright, as chairman of the local Party, explained the procedure for calling a Special General Meeting if Grunte was to be de-selected, and the meeting adjourned after Carole Swan said she would take soundings among members of the Party after the conference.

Then it was time to adjourn to attend Grunte's dinner. The five of them filed into a cab and were decanted outside the Hospitality Inn. Flunkeys led them into a private part of La Noblesse where they were warmly greeted by an expansive Grunte, who presented the ladies with a flower and with grave courtesy showed each to her seat. Hyacinth was already there, wearing royal blue taffeta. It was low cut, and by some welcome if unseen feat of engineering her bosom had been thrust up beneath her chin. She looked a bit like Margaret Lockwood in *The Wicked Lady*. Her hair had been freshly done, after hours spent at the Brighton branch of 'Back and Sides'. If her complexion were any guide, she had drunk several glasses of wine already, and was talking to Leroy Burns. Was she telling him about the plot to de-select Grunte? Carole stared at her reprovingly.

In fact, Hyacinth was thinking about Wullie Robertson who, to her great surprise, had said he would pick her up from the Hospitality Inn after dinner, and take her on to the Young Conservatives Ball. Apparently he was the National Chairman, which was a bit of a thrill; on the other hand, he was also a terrible scruff. And there was that dreadful beard. She had seen him on the telly – he had been on the early evening news tooting his trumpet. It was Hyacinth's first party conference, but at nineteen she had been around. If Wullie Robertson was not to her liking he would soon enough know what he could do with his bloody trumpet.

Sir Ralph Grunte had gone to some trouble over his constituency dinner party, La Noblesse being by no means cheap. There was a set dinner for nine at £40 a head and an unlimited supply of Mateus Rosé, a pink Portuguese wine curiously attractive to women. He had also arranged for a small box of hand-made chocolates to be given to each of them upon departure. 'Rome', said Grunte to himself, 'is worth a Mass.'

He placed Hyacinth upon his right hand, where he could keep a fatherly eye on her, and Angela Cartwright, his chairman, upon his left. Carole Swan found to her horror that she was sitting next to Leroy Burns. 'Hungry, Missus?' he impertinently inquired. Enoch Powell had been right all along.

Grunte knew she was rather uppity about blacks. He put Franklin on the other side of Burns, and separated the Malcolms by making a sandwich of Bill O'Farrell.

He was pleased with the menu: liver pâté, followed by scampi with avocado and a julienne of mango, Summer Pudding and *petits fours*. If that did not guarantee another five years at Westminster, nothing would. The cost would be borne by Grunte Accessories, but that was neither here nor there. Grunte ordered a large gin for himself.

Many gins later, his guests had just come to the end of the *petits fours* when Wullie Robertson turned up, forcing his way into La Noblesse, looking like the wrath of God, or the son of some Pictish chieftain, and demanding, 'Hyacinth! Where's the Scragg?'

He had changed but not bathed, and the new slogan on his T-shirt, 'Maggie rules, OK?' did not compensate for the stench of the great unwashed.

Ralph (Hyacinth had been swiftly urged to drop the 'Sir' by her genial host) called for him to be removed, by force if necessary, refusing to believe that so demotic a figure belonged to 'our great Party'. Robertson was carrying a can of Tartan Ale from which he frequently refreshed himself, and in turn denied any knowledge of the great part Sir Ralph Grunte had played for so long in the counsels of the Tory Party.

Hyacinth thought it best to leave with him at once, so as to cut short the unpleasantness. She insisted on a cab to the conference centre where the dance was being held, and when they arrived escape came in the figure of a party agent, who quickly took Hyacinth to one side, and asked whether she would like to start the dancing.

A small crowd of the young, together with a party of celebrities were waiting for the band, which consisted of five yobs and an amplifier, to take up their position on the rostrum. The agent was older than her father, but Hyacinth had been well brought up, and at least it was an escape from the national chairman; prettily she agreed to dance with him.

'Not with me, dearie,' was the response. 'With John Major.'

Hyacinth, who could not catch her breath for excitement, found herself in the arms of the Prime Minister. The band played 'Blue Moon', and to the flashes of cameramen, cheers and ribaldry, the dance began.

'Was your father really a trapeze artist?' asked Hyacinth, emboldened by Grunte's Mateus Rosé. John Major gave a Brixton twirl, and, spinning Hyacinth round, replied, 'Can't you see how quick I am on my feet?' He smiled in a way that had charmed the matrons of Europe, and led Hyacinth over to the cameras.

'Miss Scragg dances like an angel,' he told them. He then said 'God bless!' to her, and was carried off into the night.

Later that night, much later – for there are no early nights at the Party conference – Hyacinth Scragg lay happily in her hotel bed, flanked by a small teddy bear and a copy of the Gideon Bible. What bliss! She had danced with a man who had danced with a girl, who had danced with the Prince of Wales.

Six o'clock in the evening heralds the start of the Party conference's 'magic hour'. The 7,000 representatives together with the party's professionals and the MPs and Ministers of the Crown make themselves ready and, in some cases, available, for a night of pleasure. Doors slam along hotel corridors and bathrooms fill with steam. Gin, ice and tonic water dull the pain of a long day. Cabinet Ministers struggle into dinner jackets that have seen better days (so, too, do their detectives), their wives sit long before dressing tables applying powder and paint. Should they wear their blue or their blue?

There is no chance of a quiet evening slumped before the telly, or even to read a novel. There are functions to attend, after-dinner speeches to be made. They are all on parade: Norma and John, Judy and Douglas, Anne and Michael, theirs will be a royal progress under close escort, the firm handshake, the sincere greeting, the steady gaze and the simulated pleasure at the renewal of past friendships. Old acquaintance should never be forgot, not at Brighton.

The Grand Hotel comes into its own in the evening. The foyer is packed with pilgrims ready to reach out and touch the hem of any passing garment. Eager Tories with careers in mind light candles to their ambition. 'Look, there's Michael Heseltine!' The bars admit to standing room only (early birds perch on stools), and the extensive lounges with their arm chairs set in fours soon fill to capacity. The air is filled with cut-glass as handsome women in the prime of life peck at each other's cheeks and cry welcome; their heavily built, blue-suited, florid-faced husbands exchange boxers' handshakes with a contrived, Golf Club conviviality. 'Good to see you, Charles.'

Despite Mrs Thatcher's Granthamite certainties, and the rise of 'Essex Man', the Conservative and Unionist Party on parade can still muster the English professional and upper-middle classes. At the Grand, magistrates are two a penny, bankers of the sort who never lent Maxwell a farthing can be seen sipping sherry, chairmen of publicly quoted companies compare salaries, and retired officers of field rank renew old NATO friendships.

Were Harold Macmillan to return to earth and go (reluctantly, no doubt) to Brighton, he would find that little, if anything, has changed. Fewer of his kinsmen, perhaps, more yuppies and certainly more yobs, but the complement of the Grand Hotel would be much the same: lots of officers and very few 'other ranks'.

The two bar stools at either end of the crush bar were occupied by Ron Barton and Joshua Morris. Ron's little legs did not touch the floor. In his left hand he held a pocket Philips dictaphone into which he would occasionally confide; in his right, a pencil poised over a reporter's pad. He was the Roving Correspondent (politics) of the *True Brit*, an appointment that carried a salary of £75,000 a year, plus expenses. He had already interviewed Norman Tebbit about his exclusion from the afternoon's debate on Europe – ' "Diabolical liberty", says Norman, in conference outrage' – and tried unsuccessfully to have a word with Sir Charles Webb-Bowen. 'Sir Charles has his feet up,' he had been told.

That was enough politics for one edition; he would now revert to being its 'roving' correspondent. He spotted Amaranth Wilikins drinking champagne with Charles Harvey and a second man whose name he did not know. He had quite a bit on Harvey, a Kennedy Catholic who had been 'the good friend' of the late Emma Kerr. Barton was keeping the info for a rainy day and he would ring his secretary in the morning and ask her to look in the paper's library for any cuttings on Amaranth Wilikins. Looks a goer to me. He could do worse than spend his evening keeping an eye on her. Where she goes, there go I. Ron called for a Horse's Neck, carefully noting its cost (£3) in his pocket-book.

Joshua Morris sipped his vermouth and felt his strength returning in waves. He was undecided what to do with his evening. Felicity did not arrive from Herefordshire until Wednesday afternoon. He could drive out to Wenlock Manor and dine but he had already lunched on his own. It would probably be better to drop in at *The Times'* party, see who he could find to have dinner with and take pot luck in a town not noted for its restaurants. He would have to watch the amount he drank. Tories more famous than he had come nasty croppers in the past at conference time, returning tight to their hotels. Deferential coppers were a thing of the past; they had all been conscripted into the House of Commons' police.

Upstairs in the Bridal Suite, where sniffer dogs do their business once a day, Jeffrey Archer sat before his telephone. He was ringing people he did not like to tell them that they were not invited to his party on Wednesday night. He had told Mr Rory Knight Bruce of the *Evening Standard* Londoner's Diary that 'whereas people in Cabinet have told me you are fair, I have not found you so. I am ringing to say that you will not be welcome at my party in Brighton.' Mr Bruce seemed unimpressed. He had turned up uninvited last year and no doubt would try it on again. Jeffrey Archer's 'private office' had brought an Amstrad to Brighton; at the push of a button, he could summon up a blacklist of his very own. It contained many names: journalists whom he deemed to be lacking in a proper respect, politicians (like Joshua Morris) who had made jokes at Mrs Thatcher's expense, Booker Prize judges. (The Booker, thought Jeffrey, had recently become nothing more than a branch of Overseas Development.)

He glanced at a list of his evening engagements: Peter Stothard's and Andrew Neil's party, the Young Conservatives' Ball, and a late supper with the Lamonts. Should he try to heal the breach between Andrew Neil and

Lamont? Their feud was doing the Party no good whatever.

Jeffrey, who had been the youngest MP, but not for long, and the deputy chairman of the Party for a little while, considered that he had not done at all badly. He was, as Maurice Saatchi had once pointed out, the most prolific Tory novelist since Benjamin Disraeli.

Amaranth had hurried to the Grand and went into the crush bar at ten minutes after six to find Charles Harvey waiting for her. He had changed his shirt and was freshly shaved. He was still wearing his Old Carthusian tie. He had gargled with a powerfully pepperminted, snake-green wash, and, with a pair of tiny scissors he carried on his Swiss Army penknife, had cut the hairs in his nose. Whistling 'I'm in the Mood for Love', and rejecting the buzz of his telephone, he had prepared himself for the chase. It might well be Miriam asking him to ask the Chancellor whether she should buy or sell. Let her ask Dirty Harry instead.

David Swan joined them promptly at six-thirty. He, too, had his eye on Amaranth. She was at the age when many women are at their physical best: tall, thin, but shapely; smart, but not too dauntingly so; fragrant (a touch of Poison); and fun: she had mastered early on the necessary female skill of charity towards her suitors' jokes. Carole he found increasingly irritating. The simplest proposition seemed to call for endless repetitive explanation; her steaks had become increasingly rare, and, most tiresome of all, whenever they made love, be it after breakfast, lunch or tea, she would leap from the marital bed and turn on the vacuum cleaner, spending the next twenty minutes cleaning an already spotless house. David had come to associate the noise of the

Hoover with post-coital sadness. He would lie, exhausted among the twisted sheets, his head buried under the pillow, urging her silently to switch the damn thing off. Amaranth, thank God, looked like the sort of woman who had never seen a vacuum cleaner in her life.

It was in her honour that he, too, had shaved for a second time and puffed Carole's deodorant over his private parts. He knew only too well that he had something that Amaranth wanted very badly indeed – access to the Arden candidate's selection committee. He would have to pretend, however, that Carole was as keen as he was that Amaranth should have more than a fair crack of the whip. He could not take her to bed in his double, conjugal room, but, no doubt Amaranth had a single somewhere. David tried to work out just when Carole would return. It would be, he feared, too soon for comfort.

Amaranth introduced Swan and Harvey. The two had never met. When Swan heard that Harvey was at the Ministry of Transport, he tried to draw him out on the subject of motorways in Warwickshire, but the junior Minister in charge of roads said that this was not the time or place to discuss the subject.

Swan felt very much at a disadvantage, especially when Amaranth told him that she had promised to go to *The Times/Sunday Times* party with Charles, who had left them for a moment to have a quick word with Peter Riddell of *The Times*.

'I really think we should have a talk if you want to get adopted by our lot,' he said.

'What about lunch tomorrow?' Amaranth suggested. 'I'm going to try to speak in the debate in the afternoon, and I'll need my hand holding.' And in the meantime, push off – that was implied in her attitude, if not expressed in words.

Swan, who had not been invited to Grunte's party, or to Andrew Neil's, or to anyone else's, took himself into the Lanes where he ate a plate of fish, chips and Heinz tomato sauce and drank two pints of lager. Having looked gloomily into the windows of antique shops, and steered his way past lines of tipsy Tories, he returned to the Grand where a functionary manning the door noticed that he was not wearing a photo-pass.

Twenty heated minutes later he collapsed on to his twin bed, and turned on the telly. It was showing *Pretty Woman* and a good deal of Julia Roberts.

The Times/Sunday Times party was in a ground floor room of the hotel. *En route* from the crush bar Joshua paused at the palatial Gents. His neighbour at stall was Charles Harvey. They acknowledged one another gravely across a narrow divide. They had barely exchanged a word since Joshua had cross-examined Harvey some months ago – at John MacGregor's request – in search of Emma Kerr's killer.

Joshua, in order to be friendly, asked Harvey if he had heard of Clemenceau's remark about Lloyd George, made at the Paris Peace Conference after the Kaiser's War? 'Si je pourrais pisser comme Lloyd George parle!'

Harvey, nearly thirty years younger than Morris, did not really get the point, but with that courtesy for which the rising junior minister is rightly celebrated laughed generously in response. In return, he offered Morris Perry Worsthorne's comment on a speech made by a Liberal candidate at a by-election in the 1960s. 'All ham and no tongue.'

Harvey suggested Morris go on down to the party ahead of him, as he was waiting for a partner: he had no wish to take Rupert Murdoch's shilling, but he was happy to drink his champagne.

'My sentiments exactly,' said Morris.

The ballroom of the Grand, if that was what it was, soon filled with free-loaders. Peter Stothard, the editor of *The Times*, stood with Andrew Neil, his opposite number on the *Sunday*, to greet the guests. Stothard was flanked by his beater. They both hoped Joshua would write for their great papers. Morris replied that he would certainly do so, but only for money, and passed on, taking up a position in a corner of the room. A waitress offered him champagne or white wine. As a mark of the recession, about which the Chancellor had said only that morning 'in conference' that 'we could glimpse a bright light at the end of a long tunnel', the quality of the champagne had dropped a notch, while the white wine had every appearance of being a Muscadet. Joshua took from his hip-pocket a flask – a birthday present from Felicity, which she had sensibly filled with Mûre, a blackberry liqueur, the addition of which rendered any cheap white wine, fizzy or not, instantly palatable. Morris had learnt this aid to survival many years ago from Sir Fitzroy Maclean. It had saved both their public lives.

Joshua sipped and watched. Mrs Edwina Currie was exercising a basic charm. Mrs Virginia Bottomley, with whom half the Tory Party was secretly in love (Edwina hoped the other half was in love with her), was holding a small court, flanked by her husband, Peter. Virginia was everyone's favourite, a sweet woman whose schoolgirl looks appealed strongly to the over forty-fives. The catty among her sisters (and the hatreds that rive the small band of women MPs have to be experienced to be believed) called her Angela Brazil, but that did not stop her being the most popular girl in the school.

Judy and Douglas Hurd made an entrance, Douglas happily without that terrible mackintosh-overcoat without which no international conference report on the telly was complete. At Eton he had been known as 'Hitler Hurd', but events had mellowed him. The Hurds were swiftly surrounded by anonymous newspaper executives.

Amaranth Wilikins was pressed against the wall by Charles Harvey. She appeared to be raising no objection. Harvey, who had the reputation of a *coureur*, would run himself into more trouble if he were not careful. With Emma he had played with fire and narrowly escaped burning. It now appeared that he was an eager moth to Amaranth's flame.

Norman Tebbit, his blood pressure returned to near normal after the frustrations of debate, was exercising his somewhat malign charm over a group of columnists. Norman Fowler was no doubt preaching the virtues of greater European integration, while Bruce Anderson, a roving columnist, was talking to Sir Teddy Taylor, the discrepancy in height between them permitting Anderson to keep an eye open for bigger fish.

A waitress shoved a plate of cocktail bits beneath Joshua's nose. He took a boat-shaped piece of pastry filled with crab and proffered his glass for a refill. I'll give it ten minutes more, he thought, then I'll push off home.

He watched as Harvey called Kenneth Baker over to him in order to introduce him to Amaranth. They chatted for a moment or two and, as Baker extricated himself, he murmured, 'Venus toute entière à sa proie attachée. Racine.' Baker, at least, was one senior Tory who had read more than the occasional Archer.

Morris suddenly felt tired; the doctored wine was not giving him the uplift he needed. He slipped from the room and purchased a beef sandwich from the barman upstairs. It looked very good: the meat red, the mustard English, and the bread granary. He drove out of Brighton cheerfully enough, munching his sandwich, climbing the London road until he had breasted the Downs. He missed the excitement which was soon to shake the Grand Hotel.

Amaranth Wilikins and Charles Harvey left the party soon after Morris. It had been, thought Amaranth, a great success. Andrew Neil had been charming.

'Keep in touch,' he said as she said goodbye. He had even made a suggestion about a piece she might write on the role of women in the Tory Party, perhaps in the Government Whips' Office.

She had been introduced to Norman Lamont (very sexy) and afterwards Charles had been wonderful, guiding her from cab to restaurant, steering her around the menu ('the salt cod is quite delicious'), plying her with Vinho Verde and a glass of Setubal. He had held her hand while listening to her political ambitions, giving to them the same care he devoted to a Ministerial Statement in the House.

Grunte, he opined, was 'a pain in the bum', although he had been quite helpful over the matter of the new motorway route which happened to pass through his garden or, if not his garden, damn close.

'Didn't David Swan ask you about that?' Amaranth asked.

'Yes, but I was damned if I was going to tell him it had been OK'd. He's a developer in those parts and he's trying to get his finger in the pie.'

'What about Grunte's seat? It looks as if they're trying to get rid of him.'

'Safe as houses,' Harvey replied. 'If Grunte couldn't lose it, nobody can. We'll see what we can do. You've met Tom Arnold, he's an old friend. So is Jeffrey Archer.'

'Will you have a word with them?'

'I'll do what I can. Most of our women in the House are frightful old bats. We could do with a transfusion.'

As for Amaranth's speech, he told her what he had in mind and said he would sketch out something in greater detail by early next morning. Amaranth looked alarmed at first, then excited.

'We can rehearse it in the lounge at coffee time,' he said. 'You have five minutes to shake the world. You must do a Currie.'

They returned to the Grand Hotel, ascended together to Harvey's room on the second floor, drew the curtains and placed a bedside lamp on the floor. They were fumbling cheerfully, when the sudden excitement which brought so many conference-goers from their beds, frustrated further progress.

Carole Swan was back in the Grand Hotel around midnight. She was clutching her key and a small box of sticky chocolates which Grunte had thrust into an unwilling hand. She had not enjoyed the dinner. They had all been inhibited from plain speaking by the lavish hospitality, the fresh scampi with avocado had been too 'mucked about' for her taste, while that dreadful black man had insisted on telling her all about his times in and out of the ring with 'Big Frank' ('a lovely suit of clothes'), interrupting himself only to raise his glass of pink wine to Sir Ralph who had, in his opinion, 'done us proud'.

She could see that Paul Franklin had found the whole affair beneath him. And she had never had much time for Angela Cartwright, who, when it came to Grunte, tended to run with the hare, though it was plain enough that she had been put out by Grunte's placing Hyacinth on his right hand and had agreed with Carole afterwards that they would have little trouble finding the necessary fifty signatures. 'We'll trade the swine in for a younger model,' she had said.

As for that girl, words failed her. After a frightful red-headed youth with a beard had taken Hyacinth away to some dance, the party had broken up, though not before Grunte, who was tight, had made a speech about 'many years of close friendship . . . a happy ship . . . a united party' and much more of the same. Riding in her taxi Carole had passed Grunte, Burns and that tyke O'Farrell, walking noisily in the direction of the front. They seemed to be singing. She suddenly felt very tired indeed.

David heard her key fumbling in the lock. Switching off the bedside lamp, he leapt into position behind the slowly opening door. He was not often so skittishly lustful, but the combination of Amaranth and *Pretty Woman* had had their effect. As Carole's hand felt gingerly for the light switch, her husband grabbed her round the waist and buried his face in her neck, making growling noises as he did so. Carole's first, irrational thought was that she had entered the wrong room. Horror-struck, and then furiously angry, she let out a piercing scream and pushed her husband savagely away. David Swan fell backwards over a chair, clutching his knee in agony. Her scream, the crash of the chair, and his shouts of pain were followed by a moment's silence, and then by the ringing of an alarm.

Throughout the hotel, doors slammed, and feet could be heard pounding the length of corridors. Carole, who had fallen to the floor and was attempting to massage her husband's knee, looked up to see Kenneth Baker himself in a camel-hair dressing gown, flanked by two men with guns. Even ex-Home Secretaries were well protected. Baker, who had abandoned his spectacles, peered down at what was plainly a sordid scene of domestic violence of the kind he was familiar with only in statistics. He murmured, 'To be imprisoned in the viewless winds, And blown with restless violence round about the pendant world.' And then, to no one in particular, '*Measure for Measure*.' He then left the room bidding the Swans good-night.

John Gummer ran past the door, an overcoat over his pyjamas, carrying his famous pillow, the one with 'Not tonight, Josephine' written on it, and a small valise which he took with him ready for such emergencies.

The wail of alerted police cars filled the night air, Gerald Kaufman left the premises with the help of a fire escape, the fate of the Tory Party being no concern of his.

Ron Barton abandoned his vigil outside Charles Harvey's door. He had pursued the errant couple from *The Times* party to Brighton's only Portuguese restaurant and back to the lift in the Grand Hotel. But adultery was one thing, anarchy another. He made as swiftly as he could for the foyer.

Amaranth Wilikins travelled down to the foyer without Charles Harvey. She had dressed in a hurry. The clamorous bells had come too soon for both of them.

The Brighton Constabulary, whose marksmen had taken up positions from which they could command the Grand Hotel, was stood down after half an hour. The alarm had been quite definitely false. The revellers in the foyer, who included some of the more anxious in decorous nightwear, were shooed upstairs to bed by Alastair Goodlad, once the Party's deputy Chief Whip, whose butlerian rotundity made him quite admirably suited to the task.

John Gummer returned to his room.

The police, recognising Gerald Kaufman from the telly, seemed reluctant to give credence to his story. 'Shouldn't you be in Blackpool, sir?'

There was only one last contretemps before the hotel settled down to an uneasy sleep. Security on the door had reported a large black man demanding entry on behalf of a friend, a Sir Ralph Grunte, Member of Parliament, who was certainly in no condition to be in charge of a motor car. Grunte and his companion were ushered into a lift, and, as the door closed mercifully upon them, the strains of 'Eskimo Nell' could be heard as they were borne aloft by the soft hum of machinery.

The first full day of the Conservative and Unionist Party conference was finally over. 'More trouble than a load of kids,' was the view of an elderly sergeant of police.

Wednesday Morning

Norman Fowler, the chairman of the Party, was awakened early by the delivery of the national newspapers. They fell with a thud upon his bedside chair. The Conference was not just an affair, mounted at great trouble and expense, at which the Party's footsoldiers were given four days simply to kick over the traces. Some fun and a few games were certainly unavoidable (there are colleagues who always go too far), but that was not the point of the Party's annual seaside jamboree. It was a public relations exercise in which the Government and Party were shown to the media and the television viewer in as flattering a light as possible. Hence the portentous, and even fatuous slogan which towered each year in brightest blue above the rostrum. This year it was 'The Right Way Ahead for Britain'.

The Party's leaders were held up to the public's scrutiny; it was not the Party's fault that some, those with speech defects in particular, failed to receive the customary standing ovation after their speeches from an enthusiastic conference, or that others, standing some way up the ladder of promotion, were pinched for drunken driving. Fornication was inevitable; it was something of a relief that high unit labour costs had driven the boot man to extinction. Better an unshone shoe than a procession of the crippled, hobbling to their places in unfamiliar brown brogues in a very public breakfast room.

The Party conference would rise to its climax on the Friday afternoon when the Leader spoke. The conference would become a rally before which John Major must perform, reading from a thirty-minute script cobbled together by a squad of clever young men.

It had once been Chris Patten's task to help Mrs Thatcher as she worked through the night. She had had the tiresome habit of subjecting her speech-writers to a sixth-form question and answer session along the lines of, 'Tell me Chris, what do you mean by "liberty"?' and it was not until the welcome arrival of a cheerful Denis at two-thirty in the morning that she could be persuaded to go to bed. (Her late hours had, in fact, saved her life in 1984 when the Irish bombed the Grand Hotel.) However, John Major was usually in bed by midnight, thank God. But, although Margaret was now 'dead', she was not yet buried. Stricken with umbrage, she had spent the months since her destoolment sniping at her successor, travelling the world in order to raise funds for some foundation, and, in general, rocking the bloody boat.

Norma Major was terrified of her, but so were most people. The likelihood of her arrival at Brighton, the possibility of her speaking in the debate on immigration, and the nice problem of what to do with the old bat on the Friday afternoon (a vote of thanks? a place on the platform? a solo entrance?) – these matters were all now exercising Fowler's mind, the peace of which was not helped by the lead story in the *Daily Mail*: 'MAGGIE BRIGHTON BOUND'. 'Oh damn,' exclaimed Norman. A century ago she would have been sent abroad to govern India or Ireland. In the 1990s there was only the hope that her fires, so vigorously stoked up by the dispossessed, would begin to burn down of their own accord.

The *Mail* was firm in its forecast: the other papers only looked forward with relish to her eventual arrival. So far, it had been a very dull, even grey, conference. Charles Moore, in a leader-page article in the *Telegraph*, likened her descent upon Brighton to the Restoration of Charles II. There would be dancing in the streets. Like hell there would, thought Fowler. Why hadn't the piece been spiked? Where was Max Hastings?

Paul Johnson, the *Mail*'s 'hired gun', was recounting for the umpteenth time the glories of the Thatcher Years. The *Sun* led with an attack on the Sovereign for having asked the Bishop of Durham to a light lunch, but the rest of the papers made gloomy reading for the chairman. 'Lamont listless in economic debate'; 'Tebbit given cold shoulder by blind Tory' and 'Amess speaks up for Essex man' were some examples of their headlines. The reports of the political correspondents, who had all faxed their copy while still sober the evening before, were generally downbeat.

The afternoon's debate on 'Policy and Public Relations' promised, wrote Ian Aitken, 'to tap the well of a growing discontent'. Peter Riddell of *The Times* had written a piece about the Young Conservatives. It appeared that he had been thrown out bodily from a pub in Kemp Town called the 'Hedgehog and Hogshead' in the company of several YCs who had taken exception to three Asians drinking in the saloon bar. Riddell, who was a modest man, not given to cakes or ale, had, despite his shrill protests, suffered the same fate. His piece had clearly been written more in anger than in sorrow, the landlord's indiscrimination coming in for as much disapprobation as the racist high spirits shown by the Young Conservatives.

On that topic, Fowler found to his unsurprised dismay that several papers had 'profiled' the unspeakable Wullie Robertson. 'Is this the new face of the Tory party?' asked the *Mirror*. Garland, in the *Telegraph*, had drawn a cartoon of a kilted bare-arsed Robertson, blowing his trumpet, circling a walled city full of obvious Tories, labelled 'Jericho'.

Fowler tossed the papers on to the floor and went for a shower. It would be his task to hold Norma Major's hand, reply to the debate on public relations, and to steady the bloody Buffs. He should have stayed in the bosom of his family.

The Special Branch man standing outside Lady Thatcher's house in Belgravia noticed the arrival of a theatrical costumier's van. He had expected to abandon his post at 11 a.m. in time for an early pub lunch, but his colleague's arrival had been unexpectedly delayed. There was nothing about a delivery in his early morning instructions. He went up to the driver of the van and asked him his business.

'A box for her Ladyship,' was his reply, indicating a large grey box wrapped in string, the sort favoured by expensive tailors. 'Something for Denis, I expect.'

The policeman spoke into his portable radio and,

evidently satisfied with the response, took the box
himself, waving the van on its way. Bloody valet was
what he had become. Because his wife did not want to
move house he had turned down the job of guarding Ted
Heath in the Close at Salisbury; he had been given
Margaret instead.

In a small study off the hall, another policeman put the
parcel through an X-ray machine and then began to cut
the string. Lady Thatcher's post was still heavy, despite
her exile, and every packet and parcel was carefully
checked. As he cut, the door opened and the lady herself
swept into the room and, with an imperious gesture,
gathered up the box and carried it off.

'I know what it contains,' she cried, 'and the contents
are quite private.' Her tone bode no contradiction; it was
the voice so well remembered by all those who, over
twelve years, had sat at her feet in a thousand Cabinets.
At its timbre strong men had quailed; the bearers of
Military Crosses awarded for bravery above and beyond
in places like Italy and Burma had braced themselves in
anticipation of her terrible wrath. It was certainly too
much for two young constables with four 'O' levels
between them.

Upstairs in the best bedroom among the photographs
of 'Gorby', and Nancy and Ronnie, Lady Thatcher
opened the box and removed several items of clothing.
She took off her bright blue suit with the square shoulders, the outfit she had worn on the morning of her
departure from Downing Street, that dreadful day, when
betrayed by her Cabinet she had been persuaded
('against my better judgement, mark you') to vote for
John Major. What a disappointment he had turned out
to be! And so arrogant! She was irritated to find that one

essential item at least was missing, and made a mental note to have someone telephone for it immediately. Taking up a chair, she sat before the wardrobe's mirror, knees drawn up, her right hand outstretched.

She, too, had been invited to Jeffrey Archer's party at the Grand Hotel. Today she would travel by car to Brighton.

Later, two black bullet-proof Jaguar motor cars headed out of South London. Lady Thatcher sat in the back seat of the leading vehicle with her loyal biographer, Sir George Gardiner, MP, at her side. The driver and the large man in the front seat were both members of the Special Branch. The second Jaguar was the escort vehicle carrying members of her police bodyguard. Spirits in both cars were high, Margaret scenting battle, her guards taking what pleasure they could from the prospect of a day or two at the seaside. There were tired jokes about buckets and spades.

Margaret Thatcher had no tolerance for jokes of any kind, believing them to be a waste of time. She was about to wipe the floor with her enemies. Not unreasonably, given what had happened in 1984, Lady Thatcher had forsaken the Grand for the Hospitality Inn on the recommendation of an old ally, Sir Alfred Sherman, who had praised the pool, solarium, gymnasium and beauty salon. Although what use could dear Alfred have for any of them? she wondered. He was very plain and unathletic. Still, however difficult he had been in the good days, when they were all riding high, he was still most certainly loyal.

In Banstead, the black Jaguars stopped abruptly at a zebra crossing to allow three rastas and their large mother to cross the road. Lady Thatcher remembered the time in the late 1970s when she had gone on television and warned that people were afraid of being 'swamped' by immigrants. At the time, that old woman Willie Whitelaw had been excessively upset. She had been right of course. If only she had listened more often to her voices, how much better things would have turned out to be. And for Britain.

Her thoughts turned to Geoffrey Howe, for so long her most faithful lieutenant, and her right leg made an involuntary kicking movement. It was Elspeth who had put him up to it. Such ingratitude. She would take lunch at Gravetye Manor near East Grinstead (a 3 out of 5 in the *Good Food Guide*) where Peter Herbert, its owner, would see to it that she had two poached eggs on Bovril toast and a good, old-fashioned pudding.

Fowler joined Norma and John in the Majors' room. A cooked breakfast of the sort favoured by Mancunian commercial travellers was unanimously rejected. Over black coffee and croissants (Norma partook of a little black cherry jam) the Leader and chairman of the Tory Party took counsel together. Downing Street had originally put in a request for the Bridal Suite, only to discover that Jeffrey Archer had got in first. In consequence, they were a bit short of space.

They were soon joined by the Party's chief press officer. 'You know Margaret's on her way?' This piece of redundant information was greeted with silence. Norma said that she was going to spend the best part of the day as the guest of the Mayoress of Brighton – lunch in the Royal Pavilion – and then tea at the Marina. She, for one, had had her fill of oratory. John Major was giving lunch in a private room at Langan's to the French and

German ambassadors. 'Should I opt in or opt out?' The press officer laughed uproariously.

Hurd, who was entertaining members of the European Parliament to lunch at the Grand, murmured something to the effect that they would all meet Margaret soon enough, that evening at Jeffrey's great party: 'The three "Bs": Beluga, Bollinger and bullshit.' They agreed that John should let Margaret know that any intervention by her in the debate on immigration would be considered 'unhelpful', and should extend an invitation for her to sit on the platform on the Friday afternoon for the Leader's speech, sitting as far away from Ted Heath as it was humanly possible. With any luck they would not run across her during the day, although for press purposes both Major and Hurd would have to say how pleased they were to hear of her arrival.

'Who the hell was responsible for the fracas at midnight?' asked Fowler.

'Two of Grunte's constituents,' said the press officer, gathering his papers together. 'Wife mistook husband for someone else when entering her room. Perhaps she thought it was Grunte. The security people were very uptight about the whole business.'

David Swan woke painfully to a brilliant dawn and the distant sound of vacuum cleaners. Carole was already up and dressed. Tight-lipped, she told him that she was going back to Arden post-haste. She couldn't be expected to hang around with the press and everyone else knowing that she was responsible for last night's false alarm. Or, to be more accurate, that her husband was responsible.

'Why can't you read a book like everyone else instead

of watching dirty movies? I could have died. You are a filthy beast.'

David hoped silently that he would live so long. Aloud he said he would stay for another night and take her place on the constituency slate. 'Old mother Cartwright has always had a soft spot for me.'

'Do as you damn well like,' replied Carole, slamming the door. David Swan turned over and went back to sleep. There was lots of time before he was due to meet Amaranth Wilikins for lunch at the Black Chapati, 'where English eccentricity adopts oriental exoticism to produce something special', or so Jonathan Meades in *The Times* had said.

The early morning saw Brighton at its most brilliant. The sun glinted from the onion domes of the Royal Pavilion, James Joyce's 'lovely seaside girls' made briskly for shop and office, and the sparkling waves ended their cross-Channel journey by stirring gently the broken line of last night's jetsam. The Navy stood for ever on guard.

In his brother's flat in Kemp Town, Ron Barton, who had filed his copy in the small hours – 'Wife's greeting sends Tories packing' – had fried himself a pig's kidney, and was greedily rereading his copy. Unsatisfied, he helped himself to an old issue of *Penthouse* (his brother, a window cleaner, had kept every issue of the magazine) and, turning the pages at random, discovered Amaranth Wilikins spread languorously over three of them. That she was mother-naked went without saying. The captions spoke of 'Birmingham's rose-purple-coloured beauty'.

'Why rose-purple?' wondered Ron. 'She looks white enough to me.'

'Amaranth Wilikins, 26, is tired of being just a house-wife,' read the caption. 'She wants to become an international model. As far as *Penthouse* is concerned she's got enough on board to drive the Brummie bulls all round the Bull Ring.'

Nice turn of phrase, thought Barton. The magazine was dated September 1978, which probably made Ms Wilikins, prospective parliamentary candidate, somewhere in her forties. Ron slipped the mag into his plastic briefcase. Come in very handy, that spread.

The proceedings of the conference began each morning promptly at nine-thirty. By ten past nine the entrance and drive-way of the Grand Hotel had filled up with eager Tories, wearing their photo-passes with all the pride of the Old Contemptibles, conference agendas to hand. Michael Heseltine was surrounded by a small crowd of Tory ladies, the boldest of whom kept fingering the lapels of his suit. 'A lovely bit of cloth,' she later told her friends. She was from Bradford West.

Richard Ryder, the Party's Chief Whip, told his deputy, David Heathcote-Amory, that they should meet for coffee in the conference centre at half-time. 'We shall have something important to discuss.'

Under an Indian sun, the crowd moved briskly along the prom, chattering about the events of last night ('You would have thought she'd be too tired for that sort of thing') and hoping, with an optimism undimmed by experience, that the day's events would be as entertaining as they would be inspiring. John Patten was to reply to the debate on education and there was to be a debate on defence.

Joshua Morris, who was not expecting Felicity to join

him until late afternoon, determined to spend the morning wandering the streets of central Brighton. Parking was horrendously difficult, the off-street parking being given over to the Volvos, Rovers and BMWs of the conference-goers. He took a taxi the twelve miles into Brighton, and was dropped off at the Willett Collection, housed in the town's museum. For some years Joshua had nursed a gentle passion for collecting early Staffordshire pottery: not the Victorian mantelshelf dogs, or even the soldiers and sailors of the Crimean War, but the turn-of-the-nineteenth-century stuff, the square-based figures of gods and goddesses, busts of great men (few women), and resist lustre jugs.

He avoided the Lanes, that warren of alleyways linked by 'twittens', narrow passageways, and 'cat creeps', flights of connecting staircases, a roguish rip-off in his opinion, where antique shops sold junk, and jewellers, trinketry. Real life, he had read somewhere, had moved inland to the North Lanes, the 'alternative' Brighton around Gardner and Upper Gardner Streets, Kensington Street and Regent Street. That is where, or so he had been told, Brighton still offered a whiff of the cosmopolitan, esoteric atmosphere of the Left Bank in Paris or a hint of Berlin's former decadence.

The day was fine, but the gradients steep, and it was not long before Joshua ran out of puff. He sat in the window of a café and ordered coffee from a woman wearing a Campaign for Nuclear Disarmament badge. His conference photo-pass rested safely in his jacket pocket. It could have been a provocation. She seemed harassed and shop-worn, her greying hair tied up in a bun with a twisted elastic band. There was no hint of Berliner decadence about her, no echoes even of Juliette

Greco and *le quartier latin*. She spilt the coffee as she put it in front of him, apologised, and gave the table a cursory wipe. She was about as 'esoteric' as any woman in a telly soap advertisement.

For Joshua, at sixty-two, and suffering from a bad leg, distances had begun to take on an extraordinary significance. He would need to ring for a cab if he were to regain the Party conference in comfort. It had been forty years since he had first met Felicity; they had been students at the Sorbonne reading a course entitled 'Civilisation française', paid for by their indulgent fathers. She was eighteen, tall, dark and sweetly innocent. He was a year older, duffel-coated, thin and a little lame from an attack of polio. Together they had painted the town a decorous shade of palest pink, dancing at Le Bal Anglais, or was it Mimi Pinson, necking in other people's rooms, walking the streets of Paris, hand in hand during one timeless and unforgettable spring.

The following year, they had drifted apart – he to Oxford, she to sit decoratively in London art galleries. Thirty-five years later they had met again and, despite Felicity's husband and a brood of occasionally unsatisfactory children, they had fallen in love once more. For three-and-a-half years they had met twice or thrice a month, holidaying clandestinely together, clasping happiness against all the odds, basking blissfully in each other's company.

Smiling in anticipation of Felicity's imminent arrival, Joshua looked up to find Peter Worthington Evans at his table.

'Mind if I join you?' he asked.

Peter 'Worthy' Evans was a dull old stick but decent with it. A Tory MP and a member of the Government

Whips' Office, he, too, had fallen under the spell of the late Emma Kerr, but that was water under another bridge.

'I'm playing hookey,' he said. 'One can have too much of a good thing.' Joshua had a vision of a packed Party conference rising to its feet to applaud a black woman Tory trade unionist very much in the family way. There was usually one such every year. Two more coffees were brought to the table by the Campaign for Nuclear Disarmament.

'This will amuse you,' said 'Worthy' Evans, 'but I know you'll keep it under your hat.' Joshua promised to do so. Richard Ryder, the Chief Whip, and his deputy had been asked by John Major to appoint a woman in the Whips' Office. Like Paris himself, Ryder was deciding to whom to give the apple. 'It lies between Edwina Currie and Emma Nicholson, with Dame Elaine Kellett-Bowman a rank outsider.'

Joshua, who had been in the Commons for over twenty years, knew only too well that there had never been a woman in the Conservative Whips' Office. Major, who before the election had been the subject of adverse newspaper comment for not having put a woman in his Cabinet, had felt compelled to make a move. The whips, however, would not take kindly to a woman set among them. Their common room had the feel of a changing room at a minor public school. And that was not all, said Peter Evans.

'You know the trouble we've had over the years with MPs' secretaries?'

Joshua, who had had a series of secretaries, one of whom had married John Biffen, said that he did.

'There is a long history of MPs,' said Evans earnestly,

'separated from their wives, who are left behind in the constituency with little to look forward to save the Mayoress's tea party, falling in love with their secretaries.'

Joshua nodded. Paddy Ashdown, it appeared, was only the most recent of a long line that stretched back way beyond Sarah Keays and Cecil Parkinson. MPs did have the opportunity for dalliance, away as they were from home for the best part of the week – and for more than half the year. Joshua did not think that 'Worthy' Evans was the sort to stray, but then he had never met his secretary.

'They're going to be recruited centrally from now on, that is by the respective Whips' Offices,' said Evans. 'It will be my task to see that we employ a reliable sort of woman.'

'The sort you could take home to mother?' Joshua started to laugh. My God, he thought, Edwina Currie a whip, and his own secretary given the once over by 'Worthy' Evans.

'They will be highly qualified, of course,' said Evans, 'but on the plain side. We have an example to set.'

'When I was at school,' said Joshua, 'the housemaster made it his business to cast his eye over the cooks, maids and bottle-washers. He had two criteria: age and a remarkable plainness. We had little scope for passion.'

'Not a word to anyone about what I have told you,' warned 'Worthy' Evans. 'Tony Newton, the Leader of the House, is to make an announcement about it when we go back next week.'

They left the café and hailed a passing cab. They failed to notice Ralph Grunte. He was on his way to Roedean in another cab to fulfil an engagement to speak to the girls of the sixth form. He had been asked to speak some months ago on the subject, 'A Woman's Place'.

Amaranth crossed her silken legs and waited impatiently for Charles Harvey to show up. The lounge of the Grand Hotel was almost deserted, save for a tiny man perched on a bar stool, who seemed to spend much of his time muttering into his hand. The excitements of the previous night had left her jaded but unsatisfied and now her stomach churned in uneasy anticipation. She had received a note that morning while breakfasting at 'Mon Repos' from Sir Charles Webb-Bowen no less, telling her that she would be called upon to speak third in favour of the motion: 'That this Conference believes that better public and press relations would enable Government and Party to get its message across to the public more effectively.'

She would be given four minutes before the lights. Four minutes to stand before 7,000 of her peers, to say nothing of the thousands of invalids, shift-workers and bored housewives who might well be tuned in to BBC2. Could she seize her chance? What the hell could she say? Where was Charles?

She sighed with relief when he hurried in, carrying various paper bags marked 'Bits and Pieces' and 'Bijou'. When Amaranth looked discreetly at the contents, there was much giggling. Then Harvey took several sheets of paper from his pocket, the contents of which he read quietly to her. They finished their coffee, and Barton watched as they went upstairs to Harvey's room.

Amaranth descended alone at twelve-thirty, pink and pampered, and called a cab to take her to the Black Chapati in Circus Parade.

★ ★ ★

Angela Cartwright jammed her befeathered tweedy hat on her head. She had bought it on a trip to Munich with the League of European Women. Urging the Malcolms, Kevin and Janet, before her, and with Paul Franklin in tow, she set out, as she put it, to 'beard the chairman of the Party in his den'.

She had written to Chris Patten well before the election seeking an appointment while at Brighton to discuss several matters of importance. At the time Patten had been sitting in his Smith Square office, gently smoothing the bags beneath his eyes. He had discovered when reading *A Burnt-Out Case* the sentence, 'The pouches under his eyes were like purses that contained the smuggled memories of a disappointing life'. He had felt depressed. The election was looming: the chances of his holding Bath slight indeed.

The Party chairman had rung the area agent in Birmingham, who had put him in the picture. 'They're after Grunte's blood,' the agent had said, 'and I don't blame them.'

During his time as Party chairman, many constituency officers had been to see him on a similar errand. Their 'Member' was either too old, or, in one case, too young. He or she was too 'left wing' ('not in tune with the wishes of the rank and file') or, and this was very rare, too 'right wing' ('fails to move with the times'). He had either supported Michael Heseltine in his leadership bid ('disloyal to dear Mrs Thatcher') or had failed to turn up to a multitude of constituency functions, wine and cheeses, bring and buys.

One MP had consistently not only drawn the raffle but won it, pocketing the prizes which included, said one shocked party member, 'a Wedgwood vase'. Another had a wife who rivalled Mrs Proudie in the intensity of her opinion and the strength of her will. And yet another had been caught *in flagrante* with the wife of the Association's Treasurer ('on a snooker table in the Club. You can imagine how we felt'). As in every case the recalcitrant MPs had been chosen from a list of several hundred aspirants by the very persons now so aggrieved, Patten was not inclined to give much weight to their judgement.

Mrs Cartwright and her little band of the disaffected were shown into his hotel room by the new Party Chairman's secretary, a formidable woman who had, in her time, served both Cecil Parkinson and Norman Tebbit. She had even taken John Gummer under her wing. She went, as it were, with the job. Norman Fowler waved the group to a half-circle of uncomfortable chairs.

He had to admit that the charge-sheet read out by Angela Cartwright did contain some remarkable offences. Her feather bobbed up and down in indigna-tion as she talked, and Fowler, who had no wish to gaze into her eyes, found himself flinching instead at the sight of Paul Franklin's bright yellow socks. The Malcolms, Kevin and Janet, were clearly overcome by the sight of Norman Fowler in the flesh, and sat silently together, sucking boiled sweets.

The list of sins, venial and otherwise, was long, but not so long as to come as a surprise. Fowler had taken the trouble to have a word with Richard Ryder in advance, and the Chief Whip had shown him a copy of Grunte's confidential file. Most of it was humdrum enough, a Young Conservative rogered here, another there. There was also the famous time when Sir Ralph had kissed

Mark Fisher, Labour's front bench spokesman for the Arts, on his bald pate at the end of a drunken speech in the House.

'And if Carole Swan were here,' said Mrs Cartwright, adding a *petits four* to a long meal of wrong-doing, 'she would be able to tell you about what he did to her daughter Grace. And within the portals of the Palace of Westminster. Purple, she was, for weeks.'

'Wasn't Carole Swan the woman who raised the alarm last night?' asked Fowler.

Mrs Cartwright made a face and said, 'Such appetites,' in a disapproving tone of voice. Franklin guffawed. Janet Malcolm went pink. There was no doubt that Grunte was altogether too much of a bad thing, but it was not the Party Chairman's task to get rid of him. He asked them to put their complaints in writing and have a word with the area agent, and bade them good-day. Christ, what a shower!

Joshua Morris submitted himself to the first of the day's body-searches. He allowed himself to be groped by motherly women crammed into uniforms of the kind which once might have been issued to the Croatian National Guard, and entered the ante-hall of the conference centre with a quite irrational lifting of the spirit. There was much noise. A large board was covered with 'urgent' messages. 'Will Mrs Edwina Currie ring TVS?' 'Will Sir Nicholas Fairbairn ring his acupuncturist?' 'Would Lord St John of Fawsley ring the Queen Mother?' (That last one must be a joke.)

Huge piles of every newspaper and magazine were being offered for sale. Notice-boards flourished with handbills advertising some lunchtime meeting, rally or lecture. Norman Tebbit and Cecil Parkinson were speaking at a meeting of the 'Conservative Way Forward', a group of irreconcilables whose toast was to the Queen over the water. Joshua thought he might go, if only to relish their discontents. The ante-hall was never empty, however worthy or exciting the debate might be. There must be a steady proportion of grass-rooters who never listened to a single word of the conference proper, spending the mornings awash with coffee, lunchtime with lager, and tea with Typhoo. Everyone seemed to know each other; the four walls resounded to the brayings of renewed insincerity.

Camera crews and their front men cruised the available space looking for celebrities to interview. BT salesmen pushed mobile phones. A floodlit Teresa Gorman was holding forth about women; despite Mrs Thatcher's long rule, it appeared that the party discriminated outrageously against them. A junior hospital doctor was telling Virginia Bottomley of the long hours he worked in casualty. Gerald Kaufman, as usual, had not a good word to say for anybody or anything.

Joshua found a seat and watched Hyacinth Scragg being put through her paces. She was wearing a checked calico dress of the sort worn by Annie before she got her gun. She had good reason to look very pleased with herself. A caterpillar was thrust beneath her nose and a woman interviewer began the interrogation.

Was it true that she had been one among others who had put up bail for Wullie Robertson? Hyacinth, who looked dumbfounded, denied the charge. 'As far as I am concerned . . . ' she began.

The interviewer, who should have kept her mouth shut, interrupted to ask whether or not Hyacinth had been with him at the Young Conservatives' Ball. 'Yes and no,' mumbled Hyacinth, to whom the news of the arrest and incarceration of the chairman of the YCs had just come as a surprise. She had glimpsed him afar only a moment or so ago. 'That's a real politician's answer,' said her tormentor, grimly.

'He took me to the dance, it's true,' said Hyacinth, her temper showing, 'but I ditched the ginger swine as soon as I possibly could.'

'You dropped him for the Prime Minister.' It was not a question, there was no smile. Hyacinth, happily unused to the ways of the more unscrupulous telly interviewer, promptly stuck a roll of paper she had been carrying into the broadcaster's eye, thus bringing the proceedings to a close.

Joshua rose to his feet and applauded noisily. The crew looked pleased enough, the camera man muttering something to the effect that the bitch had it coming. Joshua grabbed Hyacinth by the arm – she had been looking as if she were about to attack her victim's other eye – and steered her away.

'Well done, but don't push your luck,' he warned her. Hyacinth was soon surrounded by well-wishers, and Joshua left her to be spirited away, this time by TV-AM.

He found another seat, and waved Tim Boswell to sit next to him. Boswell, middle-aged and wearing heavy spectacles, was Morris's whip, responsible for his moral welfare, political views and time-keeping. He was large and good natured, which was, perhaps, just as well.

'What's this I hear about the dreaded Wullie?' Joshua asked.

Boswell took an adjacent seat and sucked in his lips with professional disapproval.

'Bugger got himself pinched late last night for disorderly behaviour, charging through the streets yelling "Up Yours Delors" and "Britons awake" and other such inflammatory and ridiculous nonsense. Personally, I blame Norman Tebbit. Robertson spent most of the early hours in the nick getting sober. He wasn't the only one picked up by the police. A girl from Essex and a YC from Aldershot were also put in the bag.'

The Party's whips affected Second World War slang. Forty years ago they would have all been half-colonels in Intelligence. 'The chief agent was awoken at six in the morning; he had to ask John Wakeham, you know how good John is at this sort of thing, to quit his room at Topps Hotel (he won't stay in the Grand for all the tea in China and who shall blame him?) and pop down to Kemp Town and arrange bail. Cost the party three hundred quid and a good deal of vile publicity to come, no doubt. Personally, I think jail's the best place for him. The very idea of Robertson MP for some Godforsaken seat in the Lowlands makes my blood run cold. We've enough trouble with our Scottish Members as it is.'

Ralph Grunte had been pleased to receive a letter from the Headmaster of Roedean; yes, it was a head*master*. It appeared, or so his secretary told him, that a bloke had been given the job of presiding over England's most famous girls' school. Must be a rum cove, thought Grunte. Some people have all the luck.

For a moment he thought he smelt a rat; could it be one of Marjorie's 'little jokes'? The Gruntes had gone their own ways for years, but Marjorie had a taste for practical jokes. After one of Ralph's more painful foolishnesses, she had once persuaded a lover to telephone Grunte pretending he had a message from Downing Street. 'Ring PM's private secretary soonest.' It had been the early evening of the day after polling day, 1983. Grunte, who affected never to have sought office – 'too many people dependent on me, dear boy, wheels of commerce and all that' – would have been only too delighted to accept the seals of any office.

Now it was far too late for a red box and a black Rover. The Roedean letter seemed genuine. Could the writer take advantage of Grunte's undoubted presence in Brighton for the Party conference? Would he speak to his sixth-form girls on the place of women in politics, or on any other subject he wished? Would he care to stay on for a bite to eat? Greatly looking forward to his acceptance, the pleasure of his company, and more besides. Grunte, not altogether convinced of its provenance, showed it to Marjorie over supper (gammon and pineapple, and a bottle of Soave). Her first reaction had been to laugh, but her second thoughts were more sombre.

'They must be mad. Why you? If you must go, for God's sake turn up sober and keep your hands to yourself. They're a toffee-nosed lot. Wasn't Lynda Chalker once Head Girl?'

Grunte had not the faintest idea whether she had been or not, but the invitation seemed genuine enough. La Chalker was not his cup of tea anyway. Grunte had written back to say that he would be delighted, and to expect him at mid-day. Would there be room for his Roller? There would.

The Roller, however, had developed some fault and had been left in the hands of the Grand Hotel's garage mechanic. Miffed, Grunte hailed a cab and instructed the driver to take him gently to Roedean. 'We are in no hurry.' He took his seat carefully in the back; only Hitler and his ilk sat in the front of chauffeur-driven motor cars. The police presence seemed, if anything, to be even more oppressive than yesterday (the Tory Party had become acutely aware just how much its security was costing the poll-tax payer); perhaps there was trouble brewing. But the bright sun and blue sky with a dusting of high-flying clouds teased Grunte back into his usual state of mindless euphoria. The sea breeze was strong enough to mould the skirts of passing women, and Grunte, who could remember little of the events of the night, save that he had spent a good deal of money feeding the faces of his party faithful ('Pity about Hyacinth'), and that he had been seen back to the Grand after a drink or two by Leroy Burns ('Grand fellow, must see if I can't find him another Sierra'), gave thought to his pending performance.

He had meant to ask his research assistant to sketch something out for him on 'A Woman's Place' or some such subject, but the silly girl's talents did not encompass putting pen to paper. He had forgotten how many women MPs there were ('too damn many'), and, as with the majority of his age and class, he had gone through life deaf to the quackings of feminists. Grunte's views were not untypical: there were too many blacks, buggers and uppity women, all of them reading the *Observer*. So powerful had these embattled minorities become, that decent chaps like him had been forced upon the defensive.

There was certainly nothing oppressed about Marjorie, who not only slept around the Midlands circuit, but had a controlling interest in his finances. Once asked many years ago by a visiting American Congresswoman what it was like having a woman leader, Grunte had replied that it was like being at home all day, a *bon mot* that had earned him his place in 'Sayings of the Week'. At the Copper Beeches, Warwick Road, Arden, a des. res. with flagpole in landscaped garden and garaging for three motors, Marjorie had picked the curtains, ordered the colour schemes, hired the gardener and packed two large freezers with ready-cooked meals for two from Marks and Spencer's. Grunte was struck by a twinge of self-pity. If anyone was oppressed, surely it was he?

Roedean stands high on the cliffs to the east of Brighton on the coast road which leads inevitably, as all roads do, to Peacehaven. The school is a complex of large, red-bricked barrack blocks, which had been taken over during the war (happily unoccupied) by the American Army. The site was certainly bracing; the flower beds faintly municipal. As the cab wound its way to what, the driver assured him, was the administrative block, Grunte noticed a sports field full of girls doing gymnastics. They were all dressed in green knickers and white vests.

The cab drew to a halt, and Grunte, who was ten minutes early, let the meter tick away as he watched the girls bending and stretching to the commands of a whistle-blowing games mistress. He supposed they were all about fifteen or sixteen. The girl nearest to the car, noticing the fixity of his stare, responded with a discreet V sign. Affronted, Grunte urged the driver onwards, and determined there and then to abandon any idea of making a formal speech and to encourage questions from the girls instead. It was an easy way out, but one which could make for a far more enjoyable session.

The Headmaster, who had written so fulsomely, was not present. He had been called conveniently to London. The invitation had been meant not for Sir Ralph Grunte, but for his colleague, Sir Ralph Howell, a Norfolk Tory of the old school whose granddaughter was in the fifth form. This alarming error had been spotted by his Deputy when it was too late to do anything much about it. She had telephoned Lynda Chalker at the Foreign and Commonwealth Office to ask her opinion of Grunte, but the alumna had been abroad, organising the delivery of powdered milk to Ethiopians. Of Grunte, little was known, and the entry in *Who's Who* was gnomic, to say the least. He had been the chairman of the Party's backbench Europe committee until he had been ousted, with the help of the whips, by Sir Norman Fowler. The fact that he had once been the President of the Midlands Motor Traders' Association, and was a director of Harry Greenway plc, was not considered to compensate sufficiently for Sir Ralph Howell.

'You'll have to make the best of it,' were the Headmaster's last words on leaving that morning to catch the 9.22 to Victoria.

The school smelt of cabbage, perspiration and Mansion polish with a discreet top dressing of Rochas' 'Femme'. The absence of noise placed it happily in the private sector. Grunte, who had been made very welcome indeed, noticed a table in the corner of the Headmaster's study, laid for four persons.

'You will join three of the senior staff for a light luncheon, after your speech?' There were two bottles of Australian cabernet on the table. Penfold's Reserve. Could be worse. Grunte asked his hostess whether there were any press present, and seemed relieved to hear that there most certainly were none.

'The girls,' she trilled, 'are all yours.'

A second glance at Grunte had been enough to arouse the Deputy's suspicions. The checks of his three-piece suit were large and loud enough to be migraine-inducing, and the tie, although defiantly striped, was not one she recognised. But it was hard to tell in the Tory Party, nowadays. He had two pens in his top pocket, and a red handkerchief rammed up his sleeve. His voice, although commanding, carried a Midlands twang, and there was a distinct smell of alcohol, blended with Old Spice. Sir Ralph Howell would have induced confidence, even in schoolmasters; there was something a bit dodgy about Sir Ralph Grunte. He might have stepped out of John Osborne's *The Entertainer*. She decided not to offer him a gin and tonic before his performance. Let the celebrations begin once it was safely over.

The forty or so girls, dressed in mufti to mark their status as sixth-formers, stood up on the arrival of the speaker and his escort. After a flattering introduction, culled from Grunte's CV (which he, in turn, had written for Conservative Central Office), Grunte said how delighted he was to accept their kind invitation. His wife, Marjorie, had been in Bunwell House at Cheltenham Ladies' College, and she was no lady. This brought a titter, although not from the 'chair', who had herself been educated by the successors of Miss Beale and Miss Buss. Grunte then asked them whether they had heard the one about the Norwegian woman who had bought her son three shoes, having been told he had grown a foot; a sally which was met by universal groans. The speaker grinned good-naturedly, and said as they were all clearly so smart, he would sit down and invite their questions.

'I can't promise to answer them all but I'll do my best.'

The first girl to get to her feet was plain and heavily bespectacled.

'Monica?' said the 'chair', at the same time passing a scribbled note to Grunte: 'Jenkins – her father is a Nobel Prize winner.' It meant nothing to him.

'What,' demanded Monica, 'is the Government's policy towards science? Are we doing enough to enable us to compete in the world?'

Grunte, who had no idea what the Government's policy was, or even if it had one, charmingly admitted to his ignorance and invited another question. He had learnt early on that it was better not to flounder; a simple admittance of ignorance was much to be preferred to any amount of flannel. And, he was an old enough hand to know that nobody else in the room wanted to know the answer. Monica was a pain.

A black girl with an Afro haircut then asked what was Grunte's attitude to the Third World. Were we doing enough to bridge the gap between rich and poor? Grunte, who had little time for the Third World, said that as far as he was concerned, most of it seemed to have moved to Birmingham. At this there were distinct signs of unease.

The 'chair' moved swiftly to his rescue, bowling him what she thought to be a slow ball. Did Sir Ralph think Party conferences were worthwhile?

Grunte said that by and large most people had a jolly time, although there was, perhaps, a shade too much speechifying. He, for one, slept through most of the afternoon sessions in order to be at his best for the partying which took place every evening. Few of us go to bed sober, he pronounced. Of course, the conference was not what it was. In Margaret Thatcher's time – he wished that she were still at the helm – the party could always look forward to a damn good Leader's speech on the last afternoon. 'She was the only man in her Government,' he concluded to a room full of raised eyebrows.

'I know a limerick about Mrs T,' said a red-haired girl with freckles. 'Would you like to hear it?'

The 'chair' hurriedly intervened. 'No, Amanda, we would not.'

Now Grunte knew a limerick or two, having been regaled at supper (Safeway's chicken stroganoff with frozen beans) by Marjorie, who had a fund of the milder ones. 'Have you heard this one?' he asked.

'There was a young lady called Gloria
Who was had by Sir Gerald du Maurier,
A few other men,
Sir Gerald again,
And the staff of the Waldorf Astoria.'

There was polite laughter. The 'chair' remained stone-faced. Encouraged, Grunte essayed a second one.

'Said the Duchess of Alba to Goya
Please don't forget I'm your employa,
So he painted her twice,
Once dressed very nice,
And once in the nude to annoya.'

There was more laughter. The 'chair', hoping to break the sequence (and to discourage Amanda) asked for a question on art. Who, for instance, did Sir Ralph consider to be the leading British artist of the twentieth century? Grunte knew several piss-artists, but thought better of naming them. Brushing aside the straw, he solemnly recited a third limerick:

'My dear Mrs Ormsby Gore
I really can't do any more.
I feel quite ill,
You're not satisfied still,
And look at the time, half-past four!'

At this there was a loud outburst of laughter, and everyone looked at a girl sitting at the back, who, scarlet in the face, ran out of the room, sobbing. 'That,' said the 'chair' grimly, gathering together her papers, 'was Priscilla Ormsby Gore.'

Grunte's apologies, 'my dear lady, I had no idea,' caused much hilarity and more unrest. Amanda, ginger, pink and cheerful was on her feet again. 'Have you heard this one, Sir Ralph?' she asked. There were cries of 'oh no' from her neighbours, but Amanda was not to be deterred. The 'chair' sat with her head in her hands.

'I tell you in the Welsh town of Abercwmboi [the accent was bogus Welsh]
'There's a fuck that you're bound to enjoy.
Dilys Rees is the grind,
And up your behind
Comes the nose of her corgi named Roy.'

The 'chair' slammed the lid of her desk and, grasping Sir Ralph by the arm, propelled him from the room. 'That's more than enough,' she cried, leading the speaker to lunch.

The Deputy Head poured them both a very large gin and tonic.

'I deserve this,' she said.

'So do I,' Grunte agreed. It wasn't as if he had asked for a fee, he had gone to the school for nothing, out of the goodness of his heart.

They were joined for lunch by the geography mistress, whose name he had not caught, and the games mistress, whose whistle-blowing prowess he had earlier admired. A Miss Nancy Smart. They showed the Australian red no mercy. He told Miss Smart the girls she drilled so magnificently ought to be included in the Royal Tournament at Earl's Court, he, for one, being heartily sick of sailors dismantling and reassembling guns.

They started with avocados and a French dressing, and finished with a plate of cold roast beef, and a hearty salad. Lots of fibre. Grunte, who suffered from diverticulitis, had to watch his diet. The Deputy Head held forth at some length on subjects such as the national curriculum and the iniquities of Bridget Plowden, whoever she might be.

She was interrupted by a tapping on the window. It was Amanda who, beaming like a Cheshire cat, wiggled her fingers at Grunte in a familiar greeting and waved what looked like an autograph book in his direction. Miss Smart sprang to her feet, left the room and sent her packing.

'That girl!' she sighed on her return. 'She's a real menace.'

The Deputy Head, a charitable woman, did not demur. 'She is, I must confess, the daughter of the

Bishop of Shrewsbury. As for that limerick of hers, I have heard her tell worse. I can only suppose she gets them from her father.'

They polished off the Australians with a piece of Double Gloucester and the three women saw him off. As his cab departed the gates of Roedean, a handful of girls, including Amanda, raised a ragged cheer. 'I haven't laughed so much since Grandma caught her tits in the mangle,' was the verdict of them all.

Ron Barton sat by a corner table in the Black Chapati in Circus Parade, New England Road, watching Amaranth Wilikins take lunch with David Swan. Forty or not, she was a good-looker. Jim Lester, a portly Tory MP, who was partly hidden by a pilaff, could not take his eyes off her. Barton sneaked another look at his copy of *Penthouse*. On one of the three pages a nude Amaranth had been photographed playing croquet. 'In at the first putt', the caption read.

Ron had rather hoped that she would be lunching with Charles Harvey, with whom she had appeared very thick while taking mid-morning coffee at the Grand.

The table, Barton had learnt, was booked in the name of David Swan. A telephone call to the Grand confirmed that the Swans, who were from the Forest of Arden and thus constituents of Sir Ralph Grunte, had a double room on the first floor. Barton did not care for Indian food and ate sparingly from the vegetarian buffet. He wished that he could have listened to their conversation, but he would not have made much of it if he had been sitting at the next table.

Swan asked Amaranth if Harvey had given her any information about the new motorway. She laughed.

'What do you want to know for?' she asked.

He hesitated, and then told her frankly that he was interested from a financial point of view. As a developer, it was important that he should know the exact route which it was to take. It would make a big difference to property values in the area – some would go up, some would go down.

'I'm interested in making money too,' Amaranth said.

'Well,' Swan ventured, 'I might be prepared to pay for a copy of the plans.'

They were just finishing their lunch and Barton chose this moment to walk over to their table. He heard Amaranth say, 'If I lay my hands on the plans, David, I won't let you have them. I'll put them up for auction.'

Barton wondered, what plans? Swan looked furious, and Barton intervened.

'Mrs Wilikins, I believe? I'm Ron Barton of the *True Brit*. I'm told you are about to make your maiden speech this afternoon.'

Amaranth, who had been showing signs of boredom, flashed Barton her selection-committee smile. Swan gave him no such greeting.

'Be kind to me after my speech?' she pleaded. 'It is very much a maiden.'

Barton told her that he would be sitting ringside along with a photographer. 'Would you be interested in going exclusive?' he asked. He explained that were her speech a success, she would be paid well for comment and pictures provided they were exclusively for the use of the *True Brit*. 'But you'll have to wow them in the aisles. Take care.'

Barton saluted (he had been the smallest soldier in the army), and took a cab back to the conference, closely followed by Amaranth. She dropped a sulky David off at the Grand Hotel. Not only had she been unhelpful from a business point of view, but the prospects of inveigling her into his empty bed did not seem rosy. She had told him she was promised that evening to Charles Harvey, who was taking her to Jeffrey Archer's party. Charles was 'a sweetie' and had been so very helpful.

And so very busy building Britain's roads, Swan said to himself. Lunch had not altogether been a waste of time. Amaranth had repeated enough of what Harvey had told her about the motorway to make it worthwhile telephoning his partner in Arden to make local inquiries. And even if Harvey had written just about the whole of Amaranth's damn speech, she would, were it to be successful, be more in need of his favours than Harvey's.

He had told her of that morning's meeting between the local Tories and Norman Fowler. 'We will have no difficulty in getting the fifty signatures we need for a Special General Meeting. The task then will be to kick Grunte out. And then, my love,' he added meaningfully, 'if you play ball, I can help you to a very safe seat.'

Spouse-less in Brighton, he managed to catch up with Angela Cartwright in the foyer of the Grand Hotel. Without a photo-pass hanging from his left lapel, he was uncomfortably conspicuous; his identity had been checked three times since Amaranth had dropped him. Large men in plain clothes and short haircuts had wanted to know his business. Property, he had told them. It had not been enough.

Mrs Cartwright somewhat reluctantly gave him her blessing. 'I don't know, I'm sure, what you two were up to last night, and it's none of my business, but it's a great pity that Carole has packed her bags,' she said. 'We needed her at our meeting with the chairman this morning. He was very obliging. My next port of call is the area agent, if we can get any sense out of the poor old boy.'

Carole had left her photo-pass with Angela, who, taking it from its plastic cover, crossed out Carole's name, substituting that of her husband.

'I hope it will do,' she said doubtfully. 'If I were you, I would go to the conference centre itself and ask to see someone in security. We don't want to lose you, too.'

David said he would do just that. Was there anything else he could do? She knew where he stood over Grunte. Angela looked at him doubtfully, seemed to change her mind, and then thought better of it.

'Hyacinth seems to have gone mad. Something on the local news about her poking some television woman in the eye, to say nothing of her dancing the night away with John Major. You would think he had better things to do with his time. Keep an eye on her. If she is not watched like a hawk she will be in trouble of some sort before you can say Jack Robinson.'

News of the Conservative Party conference at Brighton took up the greater part of Wednesday's 'The World at One'. James Naughtie's North British voice, heavy with East of Scotland rectitude – a characteristic he shared with both John Smith and Gordon Brown – warned his listeners that the road ahead for the Tories was a rocky one. Lady Thatcher had left her home in Belgravia for Brighton, where she had promised 'a little plain speaking', a threat which had, according to Naughtie, 'brought a frisson of excitement to the town'. (She was, actually, at that very moment congratulating Peter Herbert, the owner of Gravetye Manor, on 'the most delicious, old-fashioned, English, scrummy, hot pudding'; as ever, she had placed the emphasis on all the wrong words.)

The platform was faced, warned Naughtie, with a difficult afternoon. The Government's low standing in the polls meant that the debate on policy and public relations, which was to be replied to by Norman Fowler, the chairman of the Party, would no doubt release a flood of anxiety and complaint. Tories rarely challenged Party policy as such. If policies had been misconceived, or even unpopular, it was the Party's press and public relations advisers who were told to pull up their socks. The message had not been put across properly.

There was some speculation by the estimable political correspondent, John Cole, (brought back by the BBC for the conference) about the role Lady Thatcher might play. His Protestant voice told the nation that Lady Thatcher might speak in Thursday's debate on race, for that was what it was really all about or, on the other hand, she might be asked to take the chair for John Major's Leader's address on the Friday afternoon. She was keeping her cards close to her chest, and her powder dry. Before leaving London that morning she had spent time at the hairdresser's. What was certain was that she would put in an appearance that evening at Jeffrey Archer's great party; the one social event in the Brighton calendar which was quite definitely not to be missed.

Jeffrey Archer was then interviewed by Sue MacGregor. The Great Novelist was uncharacteristically coy, denying that he intended to greet his guests dressed as Louis XIV.

'I have a black list,' he told Ms MacGregor, 'and you are on it. You will not be welcome at my party.'

When asked who would be welcome, Archer replied, 'La crème de la crème', and that his lucky friends would be plied with Krug and shepherd's pie. 'We shall all have a jolly time.'

Would Margaret Thatcher be coming? She most certainly would. 'I have a lot of time for Margaret.'

Naughtie asked John Cole whether he had been invited to what was clearly the party of the century, and Cole replied gravely that he had. But he was not going dressed as William of Orange.

Wullie Robertson's arrest and release on bail was made much of. There was a brief recording of an interview with him conducted earlier that morning in front of the Kemp Town nick. He was practically incomprehensible. Lord Wakeham, who had come with the necessary cheque, had muttered something about boys being boys, and that Robertson would do well to go to his hotel and sleep it off. It appeared that Robertson and a few of his YC friends had spent the small hours of the morning in Regency Square banging on doors and shouting 'Britons awake'.

The Young Conservatives involved, intoned Naughtie, a strong note of disapproval in his voice, were mainly Scottish West Coast, former members of the Federation of Conservative Students, a body so high on lager that even Mr Norman Tebbit had been obliged, when Party chairman, to disband them. There had been something about Harold Macmillan being a war criminal. It was believed that they were to stage yet another demonstration at the Party conference, this time during tomorrow's crucially important debate on immigration.

Indeed, at that very moment, Robertson, who had spent the morning since his release drinking black Nescafé in an attempt to clear his head, was handing out drafts of speeches which he wished his mates to make in that debate.

'Stand in front of a mirror and rehearse them,' he instructed. 'If we put ten names in to speak against the motion, even that poor bugger Webb-Bowen will have to pick one of us. Remember our slogan: "No nignogs in Noddy Land".' Robertson had once been to Stirling Polytechnic.

Joshua Morris lunched with two journalists, Simon Hoggart of the *Observer*, and Christopher Hudson of the *Telegraph*. Political scribblers were usually better value than politicians, most of them being irreverent and much better informed. It appeared, to Joshua's surprise, that a Cabinet Minister was about to announce the break-up of his marriage in favour of life in France with another man. His name was not yet a household one, but, even so, Joshua was certainly astonished. Were they not given enough to do? Did they have time for dalliance?

The Cabinet seemed to him to have a reputation of worthiness verging on the dull. He still had difficulty remembering the name of the Secretary of State for Scotland.

The three had lunch at Al Duomo in Pavilion Buildings, the sort of Italian restaurant where the waiters threaten their customers with giant pepper mills. But it is hard to pick a quarrel with pasta. Their conversation consisted almost entirely of gossip of the kind that, if only it could be bottled, would have an instant sale.

The Government's motion on its press and public relations was to be moved by a District Councillor from Saffron Walden. Hoggart said that Saffron Walden was surely the current wife of Brian Walden, a joke which he later attributed to James Fenton. Hudson asked whether they knew the difference between an Essex Girl and the grand old Duke of York? They did not. The answer, said Hudson, was that the Duke had only had ten thousand men.

They shared a bottle of Barolo, then made their way back through the Lanes to the Conference Hall and stood on the sea-front opposite the entrance, watching the arrival of the Great and the Good.

Leroy Burns was rebuking a demonstrator, who had arrived to take part in a rally to be held the next day against racism and the National Young Conservatives. Morris said that he was 'glad Burns is on our side'. Race was, in the Tory party, the great unmentionable.

'Sex is taken in its stride,' he said, 'and the days when an MP's career would have been ruined by divorce are long past. "Mucky" publicity in the tabloid press is considered to be an embarrassment, but providing a separation is undertaken discreetly, the response of the local Party is usually "sad, but not surprised".'

It was well known that political life played havoc with family life. Religion, continued Joshua, warming to his subject, played no part at all. Even Canterbury's Tory MP was a devout Roman Catholic. Death was treated with a certain deference, although the passing of a sitting MP was regarded either as a blessing in disguise ('never liked him') or, if the Party was unpopular, as a confounded nuisance, a by-election inevitably leading to exposure, expense and humiliating defeat. 'Death in harness is the Liberals' best friend,' he said.

But race was the subject about which many party activists felt most strongly. Conservative clubs, the financial mainstay of many a local party, discouraged the membership of blacks, and the Saturday night prejudices of the Party's working-class supporters would appal an *Observer* reader. Hoggart agreed: hence the rise of 'Essex Man'. The marshes of Essex, he said, were so right-wing that even the newsagents were white.

The Party line was easily enough understood: we should control immigration (for that read 'black' immigration) even more strictly in the interests of those Black Britons who were already British citizens. Equality before the law, certainly, but last in for God's sake slam the door. Despite the underlying racism of so many, a deliberate effort had been made to attract the ethnics into the Party, if only to deny their votes to others. Hence John Taylor's unlucky candidature in Cheltenham, with all its resultant difficulties, and the arrival on the stump of several Asians, many of whom sounded more Sandhurst than Sandhurst itself.

Morris, Hoggart and Hudson agreed that the afternoon's debate on press and public relations would be a doddle as far as the platform was concerned. Wool would be pulled over seven thousand pairs of eyes. The one to watch would be tomorrow morning's debate on the Government's immigration policy. What if Margaret were to speak? Or Tebbit?

The trio stood, their backs to the sea, noting the return from large and jolly lunches, of such tyros as Sam Langford ('nasty bit of work'), Eric Forth ('I've got spurs that jingle-jangle') and the beautiful Amaranth Wilikins ('a real goer').

Having been groped by the Croatian National Guard, the friends parted company, the press to their pens on the platform's left hand, Joshua to sit among the delegates of his local Party. What pleasures, he wondered, did the afternoon hold in store?

Wednesday Afternoon

Seven thousand Tories took their places, to the urgent encouragement of Sir Charles Webb-Bowen, for what would be, he assured them, a debate of great importance to the Government and Party. Despite winning the election, 'we are not as popular as we should be,' he proclaimed; a truism which met with some ungrudging assent. There was a faint cry of 'And whose fault is that?' but it went largely unremarked. One advantage of so large a hall was the inability of all but the most vocal heckler to make himself heard.

The chairman solemnly read out the terms of the motion (chosen beforehand by Central Office) and announced that it would be moved 'by Mr Enderby, who is the chairman of the Saffron Walden District Council and a farmer; and seconded by Mrs de Crespigny, who is a magistrate and a mother of two. She comes from Cirencester.'

A posse of the Party's agents took up position behind a group of Young Conservatives who were threatening to unfold a banner. There was a moment's consultation between Webb-Bowen and his minder, that led the chairman to announce that an amendment had been tabled which, he said, would be moved after the proposer and seconder had spoken, by Ms Amaranth Wilikins. The moving of a meaningless amendment, or a request to 'oppose' the motion, are devices used by the cunning to get themselves called upon to speak.

The noise, which had been post-prandial in its intensity, rose in anticipation. Would the boat be ever so gently rocked? Webb-Bowen, peering over his half-spectacles, urged the hall to 'settle down'. John Major flashed his Brixton smile, John Gummer put away his Jackie Collins novel and Norman Fowler, whose task it was to reply to the debate, fixed his face into an expression of thoughtful concern. He had decided upon an announcement to the effect that the Party was to sack its advertising agents.

Councillor Enderby had all the fluency of a life spent in the lower reaches of local government. He took hold of the rostrum with both hands. 'We all know the Government's policies to be right, to be in the national interest.' Here he paused but the applause was not immediately forthcoming. Undaunted, he continued. 'Our policies are both necessary and courageous.' Joshua knew from long experience that 'courageous' meant deeply unpopular; he had lived through the poll-tax fiasco. Still there was no audience response. Undeterred, Councillor Enderby raised his voice. 'We will win through.' No one much seemed to think so.

Then came the inevitable change of tack. 'We have an admirable Prime Minister [scattered applause], a great Foreign Secretary [no discernible applause] and an inspired Secretary of State for Trade and Industry.' (Here Michael Heseltine, smoothing back his mane, got to his feet, thereby prompting a steadily growing cheer.) 'We have the men,' cried Enderby, 'we have the measures, we have the message – but we cannot put it across! Central Office must carry the good news from Aix to Ghent!' (Ghent? thought Barton. He must mean Kent.) 'Our well-paid spin-doctors must get off their backsides, Mr Chairman, and give us the tools with which we can finish the job.'

His amber light flashing, Enderby quickly gathered together his papers and made for his seat, only to be surrounded by newsmen. There was a warm round of applause for him and much head-nodding by old women of both sexes. We must get our publicity right. Did you see our frightful party political broadcast? We are no match for Walworth Road. We are lucky to have won the election.

Mrs de Crespigny ('Creppiny, Mr Chairman,' she corrected him irritably) said much the same thing, but took longer to do so. Her voice was very 'Cotswold', her 'fs' became 'rs'. She had, it appeared, been out on the knocker, 'like all of you, ladies and gentlemen', an activity which seemed to meet with universal approval. To go out on the knocker was party activists' jargon for canvassing, a thankless task usually carried out at night with the aid of a failing torch and a broken pencil. It was an activity closely related to 'knocking up'. It enabled the committed to track down the less committed, and to identify 'the enemy'. As an Orficer of her Association, she knew the value of keeping in touch.

Joshua wondered whether the sight, uninvited, of so tweedy a magistrate at one's rarely opened front door was such as to give confidence to the rural labouring classes. But she was a cheery old sort, if a shade old-fashioned ('I am old enough to be your mother, Prime Minister' had gone down rather well), and when she finally shuddered to a halt, having gone through at least two red lights, she was rewarded with much applause. The Malcolms said she reminded them of Margaret Rutherford.

And now it was the turn of Amaranth Wilikins. She floated demurely to the rostrum, pausing *en route* to give Sir Tom Arnold a peck on the cheek. 'You are sweet,' she murmured. The photographer from the *True Brit*, alerted by Barton, took a picture 'Beauty and the beast'. It might make a cover for *Private Eye*. Her dark blonde hair and serpentine figure drew the approval of Sir Charles Webb-Bowen himself. He welcomed her warmly to the microphone, 'one of the more promising younger women members', and warned her of the amber and red lights. 'After five minutes, my dear, the amber; after six, the red.' He did not look as if he meant it.

The platform, which had become rather glazed during Mrs de Crespigny's harangue, came to life. This was no constituency battle-axe. Michael Portillo ran a Spanish comb through his boot-black hair. Gummer put away his book. Peter Lilley came down to earth. Amaranth was wearing what appeared to be a blue-black overcoat with square shoulders, the skirts of which came down to the knee. Power dressing, noted Joshua cheerfully, who had heard of Amaranth but had not been introduced. Let's hope she is as good as she looks.

Councillor Enderby and Mrs de Crespigny had made speeches that were as inoffensive as they were predictable. Those who had been obliged to pay for their own lunches had managed to keep awake; those who had been the beneficiaries of hospitality of one kind or another, had dozed gently, helped by the lights and the warmth of so many. At the sight of Amaranth Wilikins there was a deal of coughing, a shuffling of feet and a perceptible rise in the level of attention. Ron Barton, who had had a word with his editor at his regular table at the Savoy Grill, had been told he could pay five thousand for an exclusive if he thought her to be worthwhile. Mr Gordon Greig of the *Mail* turned up a fresh page in his notebook, and Mr Chris Moncrieff of the Press Association, who could sleep standing up, opened a parrot-like eye. He could smell copy.

Amaranth asked sweetly for the Conference's attention. She was not going to say or do anything that would make John Major's task more difficult: the Cabinet, here she indicated them with a sinuous wave of her hand, was the most brilliant since Herbert Asquith's and, as for Central Office, and she looked directly at Sir Charles, who was mopping his brow, they were good men and true who strove mightily in the interests of the Party, and for precious little reward. My God, thought Joshua, what next?

'I'm going to turn my fire on our opponents, the Labour Party,' said Amaranth a little smugly, 'and what is more, I have something up my sleeve.' At this, she slowly removed her jacket-cum-coat. She was swathed from neck to knee in what appeared to be a 'coat' of many colours. Those in the front stalls, and in particular the press, could make out that she was wearing beneath her multi-coloured top layer a flesh-tinted body stocking.

'There are seven strands to Labour's policy,' said

Amaranth, 'just as Salome wore seven veils. I will remove my veils one by one, as I demolish, in turn, the proponents of these cardinal precepts of what today passes for Socialism in the People's Party.'

In the gallery, Charles Harvey's fingers remained painfully crossed. Amaranth had wanted to call Asquith, 'Anthony'.

'First,' she said, slowly unwinding a scarlet chiffon scarf some three feet in length, 'we had Neil Kinnock. A garrulous Welshman who could not see a beach without running along it. Did we want him to run Britain?' There were cheerful cries of 'No'.

Robert Atkins, once the Minister for Sport, shouted, 'One down and only six more to go.'

'Next,' said Amaranth, above a swell of noise and twisting to unravel a tartan scarf, 'we will dispose of the new Labour leader John Smith, and his promises to spend more of our money and not to raise taxes.' Amaranth stood apparently bare-breasted before the multitude. Janet Malcolm slapped her hands over Kevin's eyes, Mrs de Crespigny asserted a total disbelief, and Lord Whitelaw was gently helped from the platform.

My God, thought Joshua, she looks like the figure-head on the *Cutty Sark*.

Webb-Bowen, who had raised his gavel, let it fall back gently into place. It was more than his life was worth to bring an end to such a performance.

'Next,' said Amaranth, who had let drop the first two scarves on to the heads of the assembled press men, 'we have Gerald Kaufman, all vinegar and no chips.' At this there was much unkind laughter, and cries of 'More, more'. Amaranth twirled about, and a lemony yellow scarf fluttered on to the head of William Rees Mogg.

Amaranth's midriff was revealed to the multitude. Nestling in her belly-button was what appeared to be a large diamond. At this Wullie Robertson's band struck up, several yobs having armed themselves with tin trumpets. Amaranth quelled them with a glance. The hall fell totally silent, and John Gummer was distinctly heard to say that he could not stand much more of it.

The sequence, which included Gordon Brown, Robin Cook, Bryan Gould, and, as a finale, Clare Short, was triumphantly concluded. To a chorus of whistles, Amaranth stood before the party like Rider Haggard's She-who-must-be-obeyed. Once she had stripped, her body suit became more obvious, and there was a general release of breath.

'What a cheek!' cried Angela Cartwright. Grunte thought her a damn fine woman. Norman Fowler made hurried notes to his speech in reply. With a pretty wave Amaranth donned her jacket, acknowledged her applause and, blowing kisses to the crowd, stepped lightly down from the rostrum.

She was promptly grabbed by Ron Barton. 'Five thousand keeps your mouth shut. Follow me.'

Sir Charles had great difficulty in restoring order. 'Quite incredible,' he kept saying. 'Remarkable.'

He had to be urged by his minder to call another speaker. 'Sir Teddy Taylor,' he shouted, only to be told that Taylor had done his stuff the day before. 'So sorry,' said Sir Charles. 'Sir Trevor Skeet MP.'

Joshua, who had made for the exit in search of a cup of tea, noticed Edwina Currie standing by the door. She was tight-lipped. There were tears in her eyes and she was looking far from pleased. 'What a bloody nerve!' she cried. At last she had been totally upstaged.

Trevor Skeet struggled to make himself heard against the din. A throng of newsmen, accompanied by their photographers, left the hall in pursuit of the vanished Amaranth. She had been spirited away by the Poison Dwarf. The British press, yellow and lily-white, thrives upon competition, and a striptease at an otherwise dullish Tory Conference was just what the newsdesk ordered. The cry went up for more pix. Sir Robin Day searched a long memory for some event remotely comparable, and could only come up with Edwina's famous threat to handcuff herself to the rostrum until hanging was brought back. He had insisted on the whole sequence being shown again and, indeed, it was to appear, more or less in full, that evening in every national television news bulletin. The Dimblebys had been at a loss for words. David had been shocked; Jonathan, who was altogether the more worldly, found the spectacle to have been immensely diverting. 'For a moment or two, she had me fooled.'

Delighted by Amaranth's success, Charles Harvey ran down two flights of stairs and plunged into the press room behind the platform. MPs were usually made to feel welcome; they were always good for a comment ('Outrageous,' says senior Tory MP), or a piece of gossip. He saw Amaranth pinned in a corner by a tiny man who was waving a piece of paper under her nose, while a bevy of journalists tried to attract her attention. Harvey elbowed his way through and, grasping Amaranth by the hand, pulled her away from Ron Barton, and escorted her out of the room.

'You promised,' cried Barton, following, and clinging to her other arm.

Harvey thrust him aside and, with a gallantry which

began even to him to appear to be excessively foolish, given the time and place, dragged Amaranth from the clutches of the mob.

'Mrs Wilikins will give a press conference at four-thirty by the escalators. In the meantime she has nothing to say to any of you.'

'What's it to him?' asked the guardians of our freedom. 'Has Harvey a piece of the action?'

The debate ended on a predictable note of anti-climax. Other publicity seekers had had their thunder stolen. Norman Fowler who, as is customary, devoted the first part of his reply to saying something nice about the speakers ('Amaranth Wilikins does not need me to gild her lily. I look forward to her performances on the Government's front bench') then attacked the Labour Party, sacked the Party's advertising agency, and called for still greater efforts from the Party's rank and file.

'You, at least,' he cried, 'care for the future of our great country. You are the Party's ambassadors at large,' and more of the same. The platform's motion was easily carried, as amended, though no one knew what the amendment was, and the bulk of the hall filed patiently out in search of cups of tea and a Bath bun.

It was unanimously agreed by the platform that if Amaranth had carried Salome's platter as well as the seven veils, Jeffrey Archer's head should have been on it.

Joshua left before the end of the Party Chairman's speech, and took a cab the twelve miles out to Wenlock Manor. Felicity was expected to arrive around five o'clock, having driven from Herefordshire. The cab drove steadily out of Brighton on the London Road, and then, at the summit of the Downs, turned left down a long lane. The October trees showed no sign of autumn and the fields were being ploughed for winter wheat. The sea was a Cambridge blue. Wenlock Manor was a small Georgian country house, which had been sold as a hotel twenty years ago. It was run by a French couple; he cooked, she sat out front and waited at table, a pretty daughter handed out the keys. Joshua Morris had told them of Felicity's impending arrival, and ordered a light supper at seven to be eaten in their room. The hotel food was too good to miss; if they were peckish later, they could tuck into Archer's shepherd's pie. There were no messages for him at the desk. He had taken care to tell no one save Felicity where he was staying.

Joshua removed his jacket, lay on the bed, turned on the telly but cut the sound. Amaranth was ridding herself of 'Gordon Brown'. 'A Scotsman who flatters only to deceive,' he remembered her saying. She'll be all over tomorrow's papers, he thought, and drifted off to sleep.

He was awakened by Felicity, who whispered into his good ear: 'In the beginning was the Word, and the Word was Aardvark.' The first word in any good dictionary, she explained. She was a headmaster's daughter.

She unpacked her suitcase, explaining that she had, on this occasion, brought none of her 'little delicacies' with her. 'Coals to Newcastle, the food's far too good.' She took off her dress and shoes and lay beside Joshua on the narrow bed. They kissed, and Felicity fell fast asleep, tired from her journey. Joshua held her for half-an-hour, dozing contentedly. It had been three weeks since they had last met. It was an unsatisfactory relationship, but their meetings made up for infrequency by their intensity. At five-thirty they made gentle love; then Felicity ran a bath. Joshua opened a bottle of House Champagne and set a glass of it on the edge. 'We shall get a better bottle, no doubt, at Archer's soirée.' Felicity wondered whether attendance was compulsory, but Joshua explained that, as he was writing a column for next Sunday's *Observer*, it would be as well to look in. A tap at the door announced the arrival of Madame L'Hermitte who, pushing a trolley before her, announced loudly enough for Felicity to catch, 'Madame, je peux servir?' Supper consisted of a tomato salad, a plate of stuffed mussels, and a square of Pont L'Évêque. There was a half bottle of Pinot Gris.

Felicity, wrapped in her daughter's dressing gown, took a seat. 'God, I'm hungry. Tell me, darling, tell me about the Conference.'

'We have a new star,' said Joshua. 'She's Amaranth Wilikins. Dishy-looking blonde of about forty. Did a strip-tease on the rostrum. Seven veils, each one a Labour Party stalwart. Had everyone fooled for a time, but she was wearing a body stocking. Old Webb-Bowen nearly had a stroke.' Felicity asked Joshua what he knew about Amaranth. 'Not much. Married but divorced. Robin Day told me he had seen her lunching yesterday with Ralph Grunte – it's rumoured that she's after his seat. I'm sure he's after hers.'

At the Grand, David Swan fastened his amended photo-pass to his jacket and set off briskly towards the conference centre some two hundred yards away. The mid-afternoon sun was still unseasonably warm, and there were children bathing in the sea. A train of donkeys, led by an Indian, trundled past, and cheerful Jewish widows went in search of patisseries. Two antique dealers went by, holding hands. Swan bought a lunchtime edition of the *Standard*, only to find a picture of an angry Hyacinth Scragg confronting a half-blinded lady interviewer. 'Major's midnight partner makes her point', was the caption. Perhaps Hyacinth would be a better bet than Amaranth?

At the sight of his mutilated photo-pass, the Croatians summoned, after some comment between themselves, a senior officer, who listened with growing impatience to Swan's explanation as to the means whereby he had come by it. 'You say this is your wife?' The functionary seemed unconvinced. 'She has packed off home, and your local Party want you to take her place?'

David said that was indeed the case.

'Out of the question,' was the reply. 'All passes have to be issued by Central Office.'

'In that case,' argued David stubbornly, 'take me to whoever it is represents the National Union in this building.' Swan had made half-a-million by the time he was thirty, he had chaired the Planning Committee of the Arden District Council for the past ten years, and he was not the sort to give in easily. He made his way into the building, the security officer in tow. The woman behind the National Union desk broadcast a message for the Party's chief agent and, after ten minutes or so, a harassed man with an unlit pipe introduced himself.

'What's the trouble?'

David explained all over again, saying that as a member of the executive council of the Forest of Arden Conservative Association, he had been conscripted by the chairman, Mrs Angela Cartwright, to take his wife's place on the constituency delegation.

A cunning glance came into the functionary's eye.

'Are you by any chance Irish?' he asked. David said he was not.

'What is the name of your Member of Parliament?'

'Sir Ralph Grunte, and has been for as long as I can remember.'

A message was then broadcast asking Sir Ralph Grunte, Member of Parliament, to please come straightaway to the administrative desk in the lobby, as 'a matter of urgency'.

Grunte, who had hugely enjoyed Amaranth's performance, was drinking a cup of tea, laced with brandy from his flask. 'I must ask that young woman to speak at one of my supper clubs. Damn sight more fun than Angela Rumbold.' At the sound of his name, he swallowed his tea, excused himself and, followed at a step behind by Leroy Burns, made his portly way down to the lobby. He spotted the Party's chief agent (whom he did not like) together with a woman, and a man who looked like a car park attendant. They were surrounding David Swan, one-time Mayor of Arden, the father of the bruised Grace, and the author of the offensive letter in the *Arden Recorder* calling for his de-selection.

The chief agent asked Grunte whether he was prepared to vouch for a Mr David Swan, who claimed to be a member of his local Party.

Grunte looked Swan in the eye. 'Never set eyes on the bugger,' he said. 'Lock him up.' He moved on, having scarcely broken pace. Leroy added, 'Yeah, piss off,' and the two stately figures were lost in the crowd.

A struggling Swan was summarily ejected, helped on by a boot up the backside on the part of the Party's chief agent. 'Bloody Irish.'

When he got back to his room at the Grand Hotel, he

spoke urgently to his solicitor with a view to bringing a private prosecution against the Party's chief agent for assault and battery. It had not been easy for him to gain readmission. The security people in the foyer were even more officious.

'It's the Archer party tonight,' they told him. 'We get the riff-raff barging in.'

Idly, David leafed through the list of functions, pleasures and invitations which Carole had left on her bedside table. He would have to find something to do. The West Midlands Area Tories, to which organisation Arden belonged, were holding a dance to the music of the Majorettes, but David did not fancy being enveloped in clouds of blue tulle. There was a Bow Group party at the Metropole, but he had no wish to listen to all those sixteen-year-old merchant bankers with Gummer glasses. Swan had no view as to the rival merits of the narrow as opposed to the wider band of the Exchange Rate Mechanism. Perhaps he should have done, as interest rates determined his profitability.

On the table was a list of the Arden delegation together with their hotels. The Malcolms he could do without. Angela Cartwright would learn of his humiliation soon enough. Leroy Burns he never wished to see again, and Paul Franklin with his bicycling and innumerable kids was a right ponce.

But there was Hyacinth Scragg. He rang her hotel, and after a long wait she came to the phone.

'Hyacinth, it's Dave, David Swan. I'm on my tod. Carole's gone home to mother.' He paused, waiting for a giggle, but none came. 'Would you care for a bit of supper, and then we could look in at the Area Ball. I know I'm not John Major, but I'm better looking.' He was in his prime, and had not long ago given up playing Rugger for Dudley.

Hyacinth took a long time to respond. 'I'd like to go to English's and have lobster,' she said at last. 'I've never had lobster.'

'You're on,' cried Swan. 'Pick you up at seven.'

He showered, changed his shirt, and, pulling out the bedside table from between the twin beds, kicked them together. The lovely Hy would pay for her lobster thermidor. As long as no one blew up the bloody hotel, that is.

John Major shaved carefully for the second time that day. The French Ambassador had been elliptical, the German hearty. Douglas had spent much of the time explaining to the table the intricacies of the plot of his next novel; Leon Brittan had been rather short with him. It was to be set in Brussels.

John asked Norma, who was putting on her paint, what she thought of Amaranth Wilikins's performance; his question, expecting approval, received the reverse. The blokes had enjoyed it, but most of the women, including Norma, had thought it cheap and unhelpful to the cause. 'I expect she will be at Jeffrey's party,' said Major. 'She'll be carried in inside a cardboard cake.'

'If so, don't bring her near me,' was the reply. 'And don't leave me alone with Margaret. She'll want me to give her money for that wretched foundation of hers.'

John Major had forgotten all about Margaret. Perhaps she too would leap from a passing cake? At seven-thirty the Prime Minister was expecting Kenneth Clarke and John Patten, together with silly old Webb-Bowen and his minder. Thursday morning's debate on immigration was 'giving cause for anxiety'.

At seven, the Majors switched on the end of the news to listen to 'Conference Report'. They lay side by side, doing their relaxation exercises – deep breathing and total muscular relaxation from the feet up. Norma had picked up the idea from a little woman in Brixton.

'Conference Report' carried an electric charge which had been lacking from 'The World at One'. The platform had won a comfortable victory in the afternoon's debate on policy. A blonde Tory had stripped and received a standing ovation from a minority of her audience. Lady Margaret Thatcher had turned up in Brighton.

'I'm full of fight,' she was reported to have said upon her arrival at the Hospitality Inn. 'I know what's best for Britain.' She had had her hair done and was wearing blue.

The arrival in the town of what was described as 'massive police reinforcements' was put down to the possibility of demonstrations by blacks against Wullie Robertson's Young Conservatives. 'The front,' John Cole reported, 'is stiff with po-lice-men.'

His Celtic tones were complemented by those of Jim Naughtie himself, who had set up shop in an attic room of the Grand, but who had been spending much of the 'happy hour' between six and seven trawling for 'vox pop'. He had spoken with Norman Tebbit who, when asked his movements that evening, said he had discovered in Hove a pub called the 'Earl of Essex' where he was going for a noggin. After that he would attend upon Jeffrey Archer, who had once been his deputy chairman. 'Not the happiest of times.' He had not yet made up his mind whether he would speak in Thursday's debate on immigration. After Tuesday's goings on, he frankly did not give a Castlemaine XXXX for his chances of being called to the rostrum.

Cecil Parkinson told Sue MacGregor that he no longer had a part to play in the affairs of the Tory Party. Things were not what they used to be, he lamented. His autobiography would be published on the fifth of November. Its title *Leading Man*. Would he tell all? 'All that Lady Thatcher will let me.' He hoped to run into her (Sue) later at Jeffrey Archer's grand party. 'We shall be first among equals,' he told her.

'Cecil Parkinson,' said Ms MacGregor, 'has not yet lost his touch.'

There had been some dispute among the BBC's team of reporters as to who should interview Ms Wilikins. In the end, Naughtie pulled rank, and took on the task himself.

Amaranth was still on a high. She had changed back into her blue suit in the ladies' loo. Her seven veils were much in demand; one had fallen into the hands of the Party's Wessex Area Treasurer who had undertaken to make it a prize in the Christmas draw.

In the few hours since she had brought the house down she had been interviewed by three tabloids, Sky Television and by Tony Howard for 'Newsnight'.

Ron Barton, who had received a bollocking from his editor ('where was yer, you prick?') had been given instructions to raise the offer to £10,000. 'A thousand words of her life story, and from what you tell me, Ron, we got the pictures. Good lad.' The editor of the *True Brit*, who had been raised at Kelvin Mackenzie's knee, was the possessor of a mercurial temperament.

Amaranth had received good advice from Charles

Harvey about the interviews. 'Remember when you meet the press, to say that your speech was all in fun, and that you are really a serious person. If you are asked why do you want to become an MP, say this: "A mixture of ambition and service; ambition is, of course, the engine of the public good. As for service, it is not for me to give value to the two halves of my equation." Smile a lot. If they ask you if you read, tell them your favourite writers are Hardy, Thomas Love Peacock and Iris Murdoch. They will have read none of them. If they ask you what wing of the Party you belong to, say it is your intention to sit prettily on the fence. Be nice about John Major, Douglas Hurd and Michael Heseltine. If they ask you about Margaret, look sad and say how much you once admired her. Got it?'

Amaranth said that she had. 'Charles, I am so very grateful.'

Now Naughtie told her: 'You were not only the belle of the ball, but the star of the show. Do you always take your clothes off when you speak to Conservatives?'

'Not in public,' breathed Amaranth. 'I simply wanted to draw attention to the nonsenses in Labour's policies. I was perfectly decent. I was wearing a body stocking.'

Naughtie read out a statement made on behalf of Dame Margaret Fry, a past chairman of the Party's National Union. 'I hope the example set by Ms Wilikins will not be permitted to lower the tone of this conference. We are not here to have a good time.'

'Indeed we are not,' said Amaranth hastily.

Would Amaranth be going to Lord Archer's party, along with *la crème de la crème*?

'If you'll take me, James,' said Amaranth, her laugh

124

tinkling like so many distant cow bells. 'I must go and change.'

The penultimate interview was with Sir Marcus Fox, a doughty Yorkshire man, known to his enemies in the Party as 'the last of the summer wine'. Fox was the chairman of the back bench 1922 Committee and could always be relied upon to come to the aid of the Party, especially midway through an election. When Margaret finally foundered, some hoped that he had gone down with the ship, but here he was as buoyant as the Vicar of Bray. 'A lovely lass,' he said in warm Northern tones, reminiscent of an ad for John Smith's best bitter. 'She'll go down a treat in Shipley.'

'Does that mean you are giving up your seat in Parliament, Sir Marcus?' asked Naughtie.

'Not yet, bha gum,' was the reply.

Naughtie had been filling in time. 'We have tried, but without success, to persuade Lady Thatcher to come to the microphone,' he said. 'The conference is waiting to discover what it is she intends to do, now that she has finally arrived in Brighton.'

It so happened that Lady Thatcher was, at that very moment, engaged in a nasty altercation with the security men on the door of the Grand Hotel, having, in the excitement, forgotten to wear her conference badge.

'Don't you know who I am?' she had demanded imperiously of a recently conscripted Bengali. 'Take me to your leader.' She was rescued by James Spicer, a vice-chairman of the Party, and led blinking into the foyer. Naughtie thrust a microphone under her nose.

'Have you anything to say?' he demanded.

'Not to you, young man,' she shouted, 'but I will certainly have something to say to John Major.'

James Naughtie promised more from the Hotel later that evening. 'We shall all be going to Jeffrey Archer's party.'

Full of mussels and topped up with Pinot Gris, Joshua and Felicity drove down into a twilit Brighton. They could not make up their minds whether they would like to live there. Hove was elegant, Brighton racy, and Kemp Town struggling, but there was something louche about the whole place. 'It must be fearfully packed during the summer months,' said Felicity, 'and in October stuffed with politicians.'

When they reached the Royal Pavilion, 'the prettiest building in England', they were stopped by two constables.

'Round you go, sir and madam,' they were told. 'The front is impassable. There's a bloody riot going on, the town is crammed with nigs, er blacks, and they are looking to sort out the Young Conservatives. All very nasty. Most of the force have drawn shields and batons, and I've no doubt we're in for a long night.'

Joshua spun the Rover, locked its doors and drove swiftly back to Wenlock Manor.

'Thank God, we've missed Archer's party,' said Felicity. 'If you put your foot down, we could be back in time for pud.'

Lying together in bed with crème brûlée and champagne to hand, the only light coming from the soundless telly, curtains left open to the soft night, they talked over old times. Joshua quoted Lord Rochester on the 'bitch Paris': 'Where man may live in direst need, but ne'er lack land to set his seed.'

'You weren't in direst need,' said Felicity, 'you got

thirty thousand francs a month, which was more than I did. Thirty quid. And you didn't succeed in planting your seed in me. I was too well brought up. Three years at Cheltenham in the late forties.' And she added, 'It was probably just as well. Someone only had to look at me later on for me to get pregnant.' Between them the lovers shared eight children, neatly divided between them.

'We can criticise our children,' said Felicity, 'and we certainly do, but we can't blame each other for their failings. How very nice.'

By ten they were fast asleep in each other's arms, and so they missed, not only Jeffrey Archer's party, but pictures on the telly of an angry Lady Thatcher, an indignant Jeffrey Archer, a statuesque Amaranth in chiffon, all against a background of racing cars, billowing smoke and licking flames.

The party was already in progress when the riot took place. The guests – John and Norma Major, Margaret Thatcher, sundry Cabinet Ministers and a collection of the more respectable 'hacks' – were given champagne and plates of shepherd's pie. 'In Alistair McAlpine's day,' said John Cole, who was chatting to Amaranth, 'we were given lobsters.'

'I haven't seen anything of Jeffrey Archer,' Amaranth said. 'Doesn't he come to his own parties?'

'He's outside in the corridor,' Cole told her. 'Patrolling. Turning away gate crashers.' One or two back benchers had had the temerity to chance their arms and had been severely dealt with. He gathered that the diary editor from the London *Evening Standard* had been physically removed by Jeffrey himself.

The shepherd's pie was followed by waiters carrying plates of nibbles; nuts, crisps, salted crackers and more champagne. The host, who had joined the party by now, told his guests how good Krug was.

Amaranth was joined by Charles Harvey, who had accompanied her to the party and had been circulating among his colleagues. He said he had heard a rumour that Margaret Thatcher was going to be made Governor of Gibraltar, 'but I'll believe that when it happens.'

The hum of conversation was interrupted by Richard Ryder, who called for silence for the Prime Minister, and John Major had just started a short speech of thanks to their host, not only for his hospitality, but also for his creativity, when there was a thunderous noise of shouting and breaking glass outside.

Those who could moved to the window and looked with shocked surprise at fires, fed by municipal deck chairs and the contents of thousands of bin bags, blazing along the Promenade. Police, drawn from several county forces, were trying to separate two opposed rioting mobs.

Some two hundred Young Conservatives, reinforced from London and elsewhere, had marched along the front with racist banners ('No Nignogs in Noddy Land'), led by a piper in full Highland dress. The procession had been broken up by a large number of black youths from Lewisham, Deptford and Brixton, waving Ethiopian flags.

Kenneth Clarke watched from the window as the police got mixed up in the brawl. Someone suggested he should go out and read the Riot Act, but he declined. Jeffrey Archer declared that he would go out on his balcony and address the mob. 'They will listen to me,' he said. Had he not travelled to parts of Kurdistan where no white man had ever trod?

Lady Thatcher said she would stand at Jeffrey's side. 'They will certainly listen to me.'

They were both dissuaded with difficulty, Michael Heseltine pointing out that not only would they be the targets of missiles but so, too, would be the windows of the hotel.

John and Norma were escorted out of Jeffrey Archer's Bridal Suite and back to their own and since it was not safe to leave the hotel, Lady Thatcher accompanied them, as she wanted to talk to them about the progress of her Foundation.

John Cole said that he was going to take his camera crew down into the foyer but, before he could do so, the Bridal Suite was invaded by the survivors of a defeated army. The Young Conservatives had turned their backs on the enemy, broken through the police cordon and forced their way into the hotel.

Jeffrey Archer bravely attempted to remonstrate. For his pains, he was pushed without ceremony into the adjacent bathroom and a chair back wedged firmly beneath the handle of the door. His cries went quite unattended.

Wullie Robertson, who was bleeding at the nose, was carrying a banner wrapped around a pole, as if it were the regimental standard of the Gordons. He waved it around in a manner that threatened to do someone a serious injury. His cohorts fell upon the champagne and what was left of the shepherd's pie. Several, standing on the balcony in full view of the crowd, taunted their enemies below. At this juncture the Party's chief agent suggested to the invited guests that it would perhaps be better to withdraw.

Hyacinth was as good as her word. The lobster served to her at dinner with David Swan was her first but, judging from the way she let the butter run down her chin, not her last. She loved English's: all those fishermen's nets and scallop shells, surly elder waiters and large platters of steamed fish. She ate a lobster and a half, filling in any gaps with slices of brown bread and butter.

Hyacinth was what David Swan's mother would have called 'a bonny lass' and David was beginning to think so too. He bought a bottle of Frascati (a wine which does not travel much beyond Rome) and they finished with crème caramel, cognac and several cups of coffee.

Although they were eating early in the evening, English's was already full of Conservatives demanding in patrician tones that the bones should be removed from their Dover soles. Michael and Anne Heseltine were at either end of a large table of their constituents; attending to the annual ritual whereby the faithful are rewarded for a year spent addressing envelopes and running bazaars. Hyacinth thought Anne Heseltine was very dishy and wondered where she had her hair done.

Later they talked about the rest of the Forest of Arden delegation, agreeing that Angela Cartwright was 'a pain in the bum' and Franklin was creepy, while the Malcolms were the world's biggest bores. 'They only make love on the twenty-ninth of February,' said Hyacinth, 'and then only when it rains.'

But when it came to Grunte, they disagreed. Despite Swan's abuse, Hyacinth stuck up for him. She thought he had 'a heart of gold'.

David told her that he had been thinking of working hard to get Amaranth Wilikins selected as the Conservative candidate for Arden in place of Sir Ralph.

Hyacinth exploded. 'Are you crazy?' she demanded. 'That tart? Not one woman on the committee would vote for her. We all think she did the Party a great deal of harm with her strip-tease.'

This set David thinking. If Amaranth was not going to be accepted as the candidate, and if she refused to co-operate with him over the new motorway, and if she rejected his amorous advances, what was the point of pursuing her? He must, however, find some way of persuading her not to brag to the other members of the delegation about his suggestions.

'Perhaps you're right,' he told Hyacinth. 'She's a bit of a liar, I know. For instance, Charles Harvey has tipped her off about the new motorway but she pretends she doesn't know. I think she's going to cash in on it.'

'There you are then,' said Hyacinth.

The night was still young and at this point David suggested that, as Carole had pushed off home, they should go back to his room at the Grand and watch television. Hyacinth, who thought that David was quite good-looking although rather old, wondered what she had to lose. It could not be her virtue. She had lost that on top of the Yardley bus at the age of twelve. It was either the Grand or an early night.

They walked away from the front past a late-night shopping complex where a tipsy David bought Hyacinth several small presents. He slipped his arm around her waist and, with growing anticipation, they entered the Grand through its rear entrance, thereby missing the riot. The lift stopped at the first floor where they glimpsed Jeffrey Archer saying goodbye to a departing guest.

'I do like a good Jeffrey Archer,' said Hyacinth. 'I get them out of the public library.' David kissed her on the mouth. He much preferred Jackie Collins.

Once inside No. 23, David turned on the telly. David Attenborough was crawling up behind two copulating lions.

'BBC 2,' said Hyacinth. 'Let's have ITV.'

David took two quarter bottles of champagne out of the mini-bar, and collected two tooth mugs. Hyacinth, who was developing a taste for it, knocked hers back in two gulps, while David Swan gathered his strength for the assault. The night was young and Hyacinth ('call me Hy') uncommonly beautiful.

A key turned in the lock, the top light was switched on and the errant Carole stood on the threshold, her suitcase in hand.

'Hello,' she said, defensively, 'I'm back . . . ' There was a total silence, interrupted by Hyacinth who smoothed down her skirt, grabbed her coat, and peevishly demanded, 'Where's my chocolate teddy bear and my new knickers?' She found the bag containing the several gifts on the bedside table and, with a cheery 'goodnight all', left the room. She was followed five minutes later by an angry Carole, suitcase in hand, who was to find that she was unable to quit the hotel until midnight.

David, who had been given a piece of her mind, returned sadly to a state of detumescence and made do with David Attenborough who at least was living vicariously. Good on him.

★ ★ ★

Amaranth and Charles Harvey left the party before the disturbance. *En route* to his room they met only Roger Freeman, the Minister for Public Transport, and thus a ministerial colleague of Harvey's, who was on his way to Archer's party. He wanted to tell Charles, that he had, at last, been on a bus in Brighton. They were not very comfortable, he complained, and inclined to take 'one' way past 'one's' destination; but cheap, none the less. Harvey suggested, a shade abruptly, that Freeman might now try the tube.

Their love-making, which was protracted and energetic (Amaranth was afraid she had cricked her neck), continued until midnight, and she slept soundly until seven o'clock next morning.

Thursday Morning

It was reported on TV-AM that there had been forty arrests as a result of the riot, but it was not known if any charges would be brought. Two policemen had been admitted to hospital along with Wullie Robertson with a broken nose.

The Home Secretary was interviewed. The police had been magnificent, Kenneth Clarke said. 'Lore'n orda' must be maintained at all costs, and the riot, if that was what it was, had been swiftly contained. He murmured something to the effect that youth must be served, 'John Donne', but the interviewer did not take him up on his quotation.

What was the Tory Party going to do about its Young Conservatives? Had the Home Secretary seen the offensive banners carried by the Party's youth wing? What effect would last night's regrettable occurrence have upon the morning's debate on immigration, to which Mr Clarke was expected to reply?

The Party chairman would decide later that day on

what course of action to take pertaining to the Young Conservatives: the morning's debate would continue as planned. 'Nignog' was not a phrase that came readily to his lips. It was not in vogue in Nottingham. What was its derivation?

When told that Robertson's condition in hospital was 'stable', Clarke replied with a flash of humour that the news was better than expected. 'Wullie,' he mused, 'was not as balanced as one might like.'

The Grand had a wartime look to it, security having been reinforced. Municipal workers were dousing the remnants of the street fires that had burned so brightly the night before. Ash blew along the front, driven by a brisk morning breeze.

At nine o'clock sharp, the party chieftains met in John Major's room. They had slept badly. The riot, particularly the part the Young Conservatives had played, had occupied the media to the exclusion of everything else, save for Amaranth Wilikins's 'exhibition'.

'We are in danger of turning into some seaside vaudeville,' was the view of the Prime Minister. Graver even than usual, he was wearing one of his greyer suits. Fowler, who had fallen into bed at four in the morning, agreed; if this morning's papers were any guide, the Party conference had given the appearance of a night-club crossed with a football riot. The platform's comfortable victories in debate, over Europe and party policy and PR, had passed almost without comment.

Lady Thatcher had arrived breathing fire and smoke, and had, so far, given no undertaking as to her silence in the debate on immigration. John Gummer was despatched to discover her intentions. Lamont told how she had gone round the dining room at breakfast handing out brochures about her Foundation. 'We must keep alive the sacred flame,' had been her message. There was much adverse comment.

They then held a discussion about the riot. The news from the Brighton General Hospital was that Wullie Robertson was resting comfortably, his injuries were relatively light and he would be released that afternoon into the custody of the Secretary of State for Health. The police were contemplating bringing charges of riot and affray.

It was agreed that John Major, departing from precedent, should 'say a few words' at nine-thirty, and announce that the national YC executive and officers were to be disbanded à la Tebbit.

Kenneth Clarke would reply to the debate on immigration and promise stricter controls on all immigrants, whether Bantu or Bulgarian. 'Now,' murmured the Home Secretary, 'is the time for all good men to come to the aid of the Party.' He was wearing a newly purchased pair of suede shoes.

As the meeting broke up the conversation turned to Archer's party. 'I wish,' said Douglas Hurd, with all the authority of a member of Pop, 'that Archer would not go round his wretched parties asking if one wanted "some Krug". "Some champagne" might be passable. But I, personally, was taught to say "wine". We all know that the stuff costs sixty pounds a bottle.'

Margaret Thatcher was sitting up in her double bed at the Hospitality Inn giving dictation to two secretaries. Had not Winston done as much when he was Premier during Hitler's War? The Great Man had risen late, attended to his correspondence while still in bed, lunched and dined extravagantly well (which she certainly did not) and stayed up half the night, much to the chagrin of his generals. Late hours had probably contributed hugely to Alanbrooke's disenchantment with Our Great War Leader. As much might be said for members of her cabinet. It was not usually until two o'clock that Denis could persuade her to go to bed.

George Gardiner and Alfred Sherman sat in an anteroom ready at an instant to do her bidding. Denis Thatcher, who was knocking golf balls into cups, was at the same time rehearsing his speech, to be delivered at lunch that Thursday to the Hove Rotary Club. It was entitled 'Can Britain recover her former glory?' He, too, had his doubts.

John Gummer was announced, but Margaret Thatcher listened with scant patience to his supplications. It had been a mistake on her part to appoint him chairman of the Party in the 1980s, the twin conditions of the appointment being, as she remembered, the removal of his 'dreadful' beard and the dropping of the 'Selwyn'. She told him that she had no intention whatsoever (here her voice rose in pitch) of addressing the Party conference on any subject what-so-ever. For fourteen years she had delivered the Leader's speech on the last afternoon of the conference; she was too old a hand to speak from the floor. She would, as John Major knew, take her place on the platform on the Friday afternoon as was her due. Until then her sole performance would be as guest of honour that evening at the Eastbourne Conservative Club, where she had been asked to unveil a bust in commemoration of Dr Bodkin Adams.

Gummer having been summarily dismissed, a lugubrious George Gardiner tapped on the door and entered carrying a large parcel, marked 'urgent', upon which Lady Thatcher fell with cries of pleasure.

'Out, out,' she shouted. 'We must have a modicum of privacy.'

Amaranth's hosts at 'Mon Repos', having remarked upon her unslept-in bed, speculated cheerfully as to the identity of her partner. Couldn't have been a member of the Cabinet, they agreed. Judging by their recent performances, they were all living on their memories.

She returned in time for breakfast. 'Muesli, dear? And have you seen the papers?' asked the younger of the two men who ran the boarding house. 'You're all over them.' She was told to sit tight while he went round the corner to the newsagent, returning with an armful of print.

The 'heavies' all carried more or less the same picture of a statuesque blonde, at first sight naked, standing on the rostrum, her arm outstretched in the direction of Sir Charles Webb-Bowen, whose incredulous, even leery expression, was later to be the cause of much hilarity. The *Mail* had indeed captioned the picture 'Take as long as you like, my dear, the floor is yours'.

She was on every front page, save for the *Independent* which carried a picture of the Queen Mother (Amaranth was on page 2). The political correspondents had all been carried away. Michael White of the *Guardian* likened Amaranth to Venus rising from the foam, Bruce Anderson to the spirit of enterprise, while Lord Wyatt of Weeford, who had been sent to Brighton for the *Telegraph*, wrote that he had been 'captivated' by a performance which by its daring and originality had brought an otherwise dull Tory conference startlingly to life. What a filly! A star is born, was his conclusion.

The tabloids were even more generous. *Today* had her on the front page, in full colour. 'Tories unveil secret weapon', it claimed. The *Star* carried three pictures of her scattering her scarves upon the heads of cheerful spectators: 'Ex TV Weathergirl sends the barometer rising'. To Kelvin Mackenzie, the *Sun*'s editor, Amaranth was the Tories' page three girl.

The *True Brit* had all the usual pictures, but there was a sinister announcement. Tomorrow, it said, our ace reporter, Ron Barton, will bring you exclusively Amaranth's life story written by the new Madonna herself. She was under the impression that Charles had put the kibosh on any exclusive agreement with Barton, and most certainly nothing had been said about her writing her life story.

What had he found out about her? There were secrets she would prefer to keep to herself.

Overwhelmed by her publicity, Amaranth finished her breakfast, and set out for the Grand and Harvey, doing her very best to subdue a worm of doubt. She felt a little like the sorcerer's apprentice.

The guests of the hotel were picking their way gingerly along the front towards the conference centre. The weather had turned a chill grey, and a brisk wind scattered the ashes of half-a-hundred fires. The sea was the colour of slate. Amaranth had to struggle against the tide. If she could not find Charles in the hotel, she would be obliged to seek him within the conference building.

She was stopped by the man behind the desk, who had no difficulty in recognising her. Despite the fact that she had not registered, there was a sheaf of messages. She took them into the almost deserted coffee lounge. They were peremptory in tone, flattering in derivation.

'Please ring Features Editor, the *Sun*', and 'Get in touch soonest with BBC's Newsnight', and several more of the same.

Ron Barton sidled up to her, and, without as much as a by your leave, took a seat, placing his dictaphone between them as he did so.

'Pity you didn't accept my offer of five grand. The editor would have doubled it, if you'd played ball with me. Now you're all over the bloody papers. No hope of an exclusive.'

Amaranth, who felt her temper rising, asked about the trailer in today's *True Brit*. 'Who says I am writing the story of my life? Are you paying me for that?'

'Not a sou,' was the response. 'I've got the pictures, lovely pictures. As for the rest I can make it up. Our library girl has been through our cuttings and there is quite a lot about you. And Mr Wilikins has been very helpful. You made an enemy there.'

At the words 'lovely pictures', Amaranth remembered the 'spread' in *Penthouse* for which she had received £500 all that time ago. 'What pictures?' she asked, her face colouring. Would they come back to haunt her now?

Ron Barton looked her up and down. Amaranth, who was wearing a navy blue skirt, matching blazer and Hermès scarf, felt uncomfortably naked. 'We all had a good view of you, yesterday,' said Ron, 'but not as good as it could be.'

He took from his plastic executive briefcase photostats of the three-page *Penthouse* spread. 'A bit raunchy for a family newspaper,' he said, 'but I expect we'll manage somehow.'

Amaranth burst into tears, and leapt to her feet. 'You

little shit,' she hissed. She lunged at Barton who ducked. Ron was looking pleased with himself. With those pix and the copy he would concoct, he would be in line for a handsome bonus.

A large woman of formidable appearance, who had been passing the open door of the coffee lounge and whose attention had been caught by Amaranth's evident distress, came over to them. She asked if anything was the matter. Could she be of any assistance?

'Is this man being a nuisance to you, my dear? He seems to spend his time hanging around the 'otel.'

It was Mrs de Crespigny. 'I've been sexually assaulted!' cried Amaranth. 'This little swine put his hand up my skirt and groped me. He hurt.'

Her distress was obvious. 'Get the police,' cried Amaranth. 'I want him arrested. I will prefer charges.'

At the word police three security men and an elderly constable left their post in the hallway and entered the lounge. They were confronted by Mrs de Crespigny.

'Orficer,' she said, 'I sit on the bench in Cisister. This young lady has been assaulted sexually by that beastly little man.' She pointed at Ron Barton who was no longer looking pleased with himself. 'I insist you take him into custody. He is a menace to all decent women.'

The elderly constable shooed away the two security guards, and locked the door. Amaranth was sobbing wildly, Barton was fiddling with his dictaphone, and Mrs de Crespigny was standing between them, her hands on her hips and her legs placed firmly apart. Her shoes were very sensible.

'There is far too much of this sort of thing,' she cried. 'In Gloucestershire there is a positive epidemic of it.'

The constable took out his notebook, and asked if

anyone had witnessed the incident. It appeared that Mrs de Crespigny had not actually seen Barton's snake-like right hand thrust itself up Amaranth's navy blue skirt. 'I was just passing the door, orficer. But see for yourself, the poor woman is evidently very distressed.'

'Name?' said the policeman to Amaranth and then took down her particulars.

'And you, sir?'

'I'm Ron Barton and I'll have you know that I am the Roving Correspondent of the *True Brit*, the newspaper with an even bigger circulation than the *Sun*, and I never laid a finger on, or up, the lady. She's making the whole thing up.'

Amaranth cried loudly that she was not. 'I'm sore,' she said. 'He deliberately set out to hurt me. And simply because I refused to write my life story in his bloody rag.'

Luck enters into all things, and here Ron Barton was unfortunate. Some police make quite a tidy income ringing up their contacts at the bottom end of Fleet Street whenever they have a customer of public interest. How else could it be so swiftly known that a prominent member of the Royal College of Acupuncturists, say, had been picked up during the night and pinched for drunk-driving? There is no agreed tariff, but money most certainly changes hands. It so happened that the local station was still waiting on the *True Brit* for recognition of a tidbit passed on to that paper six months ago about a rural dean and a lady elephant-tamer. They had been told, once too often, that 'the cheque is in the post'.

'Do you wish to prefer charges, madam?' asked the constable. Amaranth said she most certainly did. 'In that case I must ask you both to come down to the station with me. You will, of course, travel in separate cars.'

'Shall I accompany you, my dear?' asked Mrs de Crespigny, and the two women left the hotel together. Barton, who wanted to telephone his paper, was told he could do so later, 'in the nick'.

Amaranth sat in the back of the police car with Mrs de Crespigny ('Nora, my dear'). In the front, beside the driver, sat a woman PC. Amaranth, who was by now terrified by her audacity, asked her what would happen next, and was told she would be asked to make a statement, and possibly be examined by a lady doctor. 'Then off you go. We are obliged to send the details to the Crown Prosecution Service, and in six months' time we shall know whether we can prosecute. Take an hour or so of your time, this morning. You'll be back in time for dinner. By the way,' added the WPC, 'I thought you were terrific at the conference yesterday. My sergeant wondered whether you might be available for one of our benefit nights. But I suppose you will be too busy.'

Mrs de Crespigny said there was no question of Mrs Wilikins performing before the Sussex Constabulary. 'I've never heard of such a thing.'

Once at the Prince Albert Street police station, Amaranth and her escort were taken to a small, comfortably furnished room where they were interviewed by a woman detective. With a feeling that the die was cast, Amaranth put her signature to the statement alleging sexual assault on the part of one Ronald Barton. She was asked to step next door where she was cursorily examined by a female Indian doctor who offered no opinion.

Mrs de Crespigny ('Nora Champion de Crespigny is my full name') wrote to the effect that she had been passing the lounge at the time, and was a witness, if not to the actual assault, then to Mrs Wilikins's evident distress. 'He would not have been such a fool as to do it in front of witnesses.' The WPC agreed. It would have been most unlikely.

Amaranth and Mrs de Crespigny summoned a taxi and were taken back to the Grand.

Ralph Grunte woke late in his room on the top floor of the Grand Hotel, and broke wind. He had not retired to bed sober, but then he rarely, if ever, did. At the House of Commons he could at least rely upon one of the whips to put him in a cab, and pay the driver. This chore fell, more often than not, upon his area whip, the unlucky 'Worthy' Evans, who was owed a tidy sum. Evans kept a note of his expenditure in a little black book which he presented to Grunte at the beginning of each Summer Recess.

In his constituency, the pressures of being nice to people, opening fêtes, and being one of the lads had driven Grunte to seek the comforts of alcohol – that necessary anaesthetic without which politics would soon become intolerable. The duties which fell to Worthington Evans at Westminster became Bill O'Farrell's responsibility in Warwickshire, while at Brighton he could always rely upon Leroy Burns.

What I need, thought Grunte, telephoning room service for 'a proper English Breakfast' and a newspaper 'small enough to read in bed', is a bit of nooky. He had picked up the phrase from his teenage secretary. 'Nook and Cranny.' Slap and tickle, we used to call it. A beguiling vision of Roedean's Amanda doing physical jerks in her underwear, touching her toes and running on the spot was interrupted by the telephone. It was Angela

Cartwright. Grunte braced himself for remonstrance and rebuke.

'I am very worried by Hyacinth Scragg,' she said. 'I feel that I am, as you might say, *in loco parentis*.' Grunte felt relieved that the responsibility was not to be thrust upon him. He already had an interest in the lovely Hy.

'I know I can rely upon your discretion, mum's the word,' his constituency chairman continued, 'but all the publicity she has been getting has gone to her head. Dancing at all hours with John Major and attacking that television reporter – the poor woman might easily have lost an eye.' (Grunte settled down comfortably and glanced at his *Daily Mail*; Angela never used one word where three would 'suffice'.) 'And that's not all. Carole Swan has just rung me from her lovely home to tell me what happened last night in the Hotel . . . '

Grunte, whose attention had been momentarily distracted by the sight of Amaranth on the front page, switched his attention back to the telephone. He held his breath. The saucy sod. Not content with blackguarding him in the columns of the local rag, him and his silly daughter's bum, the one-time Chief Citizen of the Borough had been up to no good with a girl young enough to be Grace's sister, and in the Grand Hotel, and at a Conservative Party conference of all places. His enemy had been delivered into his hands.

'And we're supposed to be the Party of the family,' said Grunte, piously. 'I am most grievously shocked, and so too, will be John Patten.' Mrs Cartwright said she was, too.

Grunte seized his chance. He was well aware of the forces operating against him, and he knew that Mrs Cartwright, as chairman of the Association, carried enormous influence. If she could be won over, his seat was probably safe. And the old thing wasn't really that old . . .

'Angela,' he said, 'you and me, we've not always seen eye to eye recently, but we are friends. Come and have a spot of lunch with me today, at the Hospitality Inn at one o'clock. Just the two of us. With any luck we can straighten out Hyacinth, David Swan, the swine, and any other little local difficulties.'

Mrs Cartwright said she would be only too delighted.

Joshua Morris looked down his calendar of events, carefully prepared for him by his secretary. Under 'Thursday', he read of only two engagements: his treat, that is, the lunch he was giving at English's Oyster House at one o'clock for six of his local party, much travelled Salopians upon whose goodwill, patience and forbearance he had long relied; and (here his heart fell) the National Society of Agents' dinner at the Metropole Hotel. This annual event lacked gaiety, being viewed by Ministers and MPs alike as a necessary chore where political shop would be the most attractive item on the menu.

Felicity could not easily attend the lunch as her status was indeterminate; and she had no wish 'to break bread, or even to take wine' with the Party's local professionals.

'I shall come into Brighton with you, and then drive to Battle to visit my brother. I will be back at the Grand at ten.'

'I'm sorry you're not coming to the agents' dinner,' said Joshua. 'It's the stuff of politics.' He told her that when Ted Heath was Prime Minister, Mrs Sarah Morrison had been appointed a vice-chairman of the party with a brief to turn Ted into a human being. They had attended the agents' dinner at Blackpool, and Sarah, sitting way below the salt, had noticed with alarm that Heath was silent. She scribbled on her napkin the words, 'For God's sake say something', and, having folded it carefully, passed it up through the guests to the Prime Minister himself. Ted opened it, wrote, 'I have', folded it and passed it back to her. Margaret and the Prime Minister had had no such trouble. Lady Thatcher never drew breath, while John Major was a good listener.

Joshua made a note of Felicity's brother's telephone number just in case, and joined the queue of conference goers as it shifted sullenly forward step by step. The Croats had apparently been put on red-alert. Amaranth was the subject of much comment. One matron declared that if Ms Wilikins – the accent was on the Ms – came looking for a seat in Camberley she would receive short shrift. Her husband, who was wearing a Sapper tie, reluctantly agreed.

Hyacinth Scragg, escorted by a camera crew, director and producer, was let through the barrier with scarcely an attempt at scrutiny. There was a murmur of disapproval. Her hair had been done in the salon at the Grand (paid for by TVS), and she was wearing what looked like a gypsy costume. The TVS producer had had the idea of asking Hyacinth to play the role of 'guest interviewer' and had spent an hour or so that morning, showing her something of how it was done. 'Don't let them rattle on; when you have had enough, smile sweetly, say "many thanks" and we'll switch off the lights.' She got the hang of it quickly enough. This was fun; with any luck she could say goodbye to facials, mud-packs and manicures. Tim Renton, once the Minister for the Arts (in any other country save Britain his title would have been Minister of Culture), thought Hyacinth would have made an admirable Carmen. His blood, though thin, was still capable of being stirred.

'My God, what next?' asked the Camberley matron whose sandy, pine-fringed garden produced nothing quite as exotic. 'Is she going to dance?' Her husband, taking his cue, murmured that nothing would surprise him nowadays. The Party conference was in danger of becoming a music-hall.

One old dear was doing her knitting. She was sitting on a shooting stick.

Once inside the building Joshua was surprised to see Enoch Powell sitting alone in front of a cup of coffee. He had aged: his toothbrush moustache, which once might have led the reconquest of India, had turned quite white. He sat gazing into space, his unblinking stare which had compelled Harold Macmillan to shift him in Cabinet so as to avoid what he took for continual rebuke, unbroken by the throng that pressed about him. Had he come to prophesy rivers of blood?

Morris could never make up his mind about Enoch. Was he a great man robbed of political success by his own misjudgement, or a pedant who should have stuck to his texts? His turning up at Brighton had, given the occasion of the debate on immigration, an almost vulture-like quality. Had he come to gloat? Were he to be called in the immigration debate Joshua would most certainly abandon the bookshop where he planned to spend at least part of the morning.

In fact, the great debate, like most 'great debates', was something of an anti-climax. Instructions had gone out from on high that the boat was not to be rocked, and

Margaret Thatcher was as good as her word. Enoch Powell sat hunched and brooding, breaking his silence only to pass the time of day with John Biffen. Norman Tebbit had, it was said, returned to a board meeting in the City. Even the bulk of YCs were absent from the hall. Their disbandment was announced, almost *en passant*, by John Major, and the squads of stewards had little to do, save to crick their fingers and steal glances at their copies of the *Daily Mail*.

The mover of the platform's motion (welcoming the courage with which the Government was facing the problem of transnational migration) was, perhaps, a shade patronising. His well-meaning attempt at being nice to Black Britons amounted to little more than the recital of a catalogue of sporting achievement. At the mention of 'Big Frank' Bruno, Leroy Burns got to his feet and forced a round of applause. John Taylor spoke well and got a standing ovation.

The debate was wound up by the Home Secretary who was at his most Clarke-ish, punching the air with his fists and pushing back a lock of hair à la Heseltine. Yet it was not an unsuccessful attempt to bring out the best in his audience. The vote was taken just before eleven o'clock, and only a scattering of frayed cuffs were raised in opposition.

Joshua Morris left the hall and stood in line for a cup of Gold Blend.

Sir Charles called for order as the hall emptied and promised the residue a 'lively debate' upon the Health Service. Webb-Bowen had about him that healthy gloss which derives from subscriptions paid annually by Coutt's banker's order to either BUPA or PPP. Mrs Virginia Bottomley would reply to the debate.

The new Secretary of State for Health gave the hall that shy smile which had, in the past, turned so many Surrey knees to water, and caused the audience to pay intense attention to every spoken word. But not on this occasion.

As she spoke, a note was passed to the platform by one of the pretty Central Office girls whose continual mounting of short steps served to titillate elderly conference husbands. It was passed unopened to John Major who wrote, 'That we should live so long' upon it and handed it to his neighbour, Norman Fowler. 'A matter for you, Norm,' he whispered. 'See if you can find out what's happened. He's probably signing copies of his books. Try Waterstone's.' Fowler left the platform.

Joshua had taken his cup of coffee to a corner seat in front of a television set on which Martyn Lewis was calling the shots. Lewis was handed a piece of paper which he scanned with some evident perplexity. He then announced to the watching nation: 'It is reliably reported from the Conservative Party's conference in Brighton that Lord Archer has disappeared. He has not been seen since the events in the Grand Hotel last night when, following upon the riot in the streets outside the Grand Hotel, a mob of Young Conservatives forced themselves into his room, where he was holding his conference party. There is talk, as yet unconfirmed, that the police have received a ransom note. We shall keep you in touch with developments.'

Lewis was heard to turn to his producer and protest that the message must be 'a bloody joke', but he was swiftly reassured.

'It is no joke,' he told the watching millions. 'Archer has gone walkabout.'

The news of Archer's disappearance spread like a stain across the body of the conference. The camera crews, who had been lazily patrolling the ante-halls in search of someone to interview, even Mr Ivor Stanbrook, were stung into action, and Hyacinth and her team who had taken up position on the open roof of the building, sent messengers below in search of people prepared to comment. The roof terrace was the most favoured spot for television interviews, the roofs of Brighton, the sea and a bright sun usually adding to the holiday atmosphere of the conference jamboree.

Joshua Morris could not be said to be suffering from *schadenfreude*, if the definition of that word is pleasure at the misfortune of one's friends. Nevertheless, he felt guilty at the rise in excitement that followed strongly upon the news. Those to whom he spoke found the whole affair to be at best a stunt, thought up by the Great Novelist in order to publicise, if not a book, then a fund for a worthy cause such as the Kurds, or at worst a tiresome distraction from the proceedings of the conference.

'We have had enough trouble with that Rushdie feller,' was the view of one tweed jacket, 'without having Archer go missing.'

The political correspondents had all returned to their common-room below stairs where they sat before their portable word-processors and spoke urgently with their editors. As the debate on immigration had passed without untoward incident, a spot of excitement was doubly welcome. But who on earth would pinch Archer? The hacks hung around the television monitors and the tapes waiting for the latest news.

'Perhaps,' said the diary editor of the London *Evening*

Standard, who had been ejected from Archer's party the night before, 'the bugger is sleeping it off?'

Charles Harvey returned to the Grand Hotel where he was joined by Amaranth. 'What the hell's going on?' she whispered, as she was hushed to silence by the crowd in front of the television set on which appeared the stricken face of Margaret Thatcher.

'Jeffrey Archer's been kidnapped. Haven't you heard?'

Margaret Thatcher was being interviewed on top of the conference building by a young, and rather frightened-looking girl with a mop of black hair and gypsy ear-rings, who on inspection turned out to be Hyacinth Scragg.

'I am making this appeal to Jeffrey's captors,' said Lady Thatcher, 'whoever they may be, in the name of all lovers of English literature.' At this there was a raucous laugh from the back of her hotel audience. It could have come from the distinguished historian and former MP, Sir Robert Rhodes James.

'Jeffrey,' Lady Thatcher continued, 'has made a unique contribution to letters. It is outrageous that his captors, these evil men, should not only have the gall to seize him from his hotel but also to demand a ransom for his safe return. I am pressing upon the authorities, and upon the Home Secretary in particular, that every step is taken to bring the perpetrators of this vile act to justice.'

Hyacinth interrupted to ask which of Mr Archer's many books was her favourite? She received a withering look for her pains.

'I have never been able to make up my mind whether or not I preferred *First Among Equals* to *The Day of the Jackal*. They were both quite excellent.' Lady Thatcher's voice rose an octave. 'What I will say, however, is that few people have done more for the Conservative Party, and, incidentally, for me, than has Jeffrey Archer. He has taken the word to nearly every constituency in the country.'

'Flogging his bloody books,' said one curmudgeon.

'Shh!' cried someone else. 'It's no laughing matter.'

'How much are his kidnappers asking for?' said Hyacinth who, despite the distraction of an earpiece down which her producer was shouting instructions, was quickly catching on.

'Ten million pounds,' was the reply. 'We must find the money.' Lady Thatcher appeared to be almost on the verge of tears. 'We must find the money,' she repeated.

Hyacinth then reminded the former Prime Minister that in the past she, for one, had had no truck with terrorists. 'Had she now changed her mind?' Lady Thatcher tore the tiny mike from her lapel and, tossing it back at Hyacinth, turned smartly on her heel.

The picture changed to an anxious-looking John Cole. He was even more Protestant than usual. The nation which had, over the years, got used to his accent, found him harder than ever to follow, so moved was he by the unexpected turn of events.

Not only had the Press Association received a ransom demand from an organisation calling itself 'The Friends of Le Pen' ('J. Archer will be released on the payment of ten million pounds in used notes, details of the "drop" to follow'), but other nefarious bodies were muscling in. The IRA claimed that an active service unit was operating in Sussex, and that a 'video' of the unhappy Archer pleading for his release would be made available later in the day.

The editor and staff of the *Guardian* had issued a statement to the effect that 'fiscal rectitude' demanded that no Government money should be forthcoming, while the *Sun* had announced that it was opening immediately a fund to meet the cost of Jeffrey's liberty. 'He is,' said Kelvin MacKenzie, 'the Dickens *de nos jours*.'

'The conference of the Conservative Party has been dogged,' said Cole, 'by the most extraordinary events and happenings. Ms Wilikins has brought the house down by taking her clothes off. The national chairman of the Young Conservatives, who had been arrested by the police, is in Brighton General Hospital nursing his injuries after last night's riot. And now the former deputy chairman of the Party, and confidant of Prime Ministers, has been kidnapped.

'What,' asked Cole, 'will happen next?'

Gerald Kaufman was then interviewed. He said that he had been in politics for forty years, but he had never known anything like it. It was not at all like a Labour Party conference. A film-buff, he likened the Tory conference to a cross between *A Night at the Opera* and *Monkey Business*, 'with John Major playing Zeppo'.

Amaranth had more on her mind than the disappearance of Jeffrey Archer. She tugged at Harvey's sleeve and begged him to take her to lunch. Harvey, who had now decided that his association with Amaranth was more of a liability than an asset, shook his head.

'Not possible, I'm afraid,' he said. 'I haven't got time for lunch today – an important committee.' What he did not say was that Miriam, his wife, had telephoned that she intended to join him in Brighton. His lack of sympathy added to Amaranth's distress.

'I must talk to you,' she said. 'Let's go up to your

room.' He shook his head again and said he could manage to give her ten minutes in the bar. There she told him all that had befallen her that morning, even revealing the existence of the *Penthouse* pictures.

To her dismay, he was even colder than before. A false accusation, even against Barton, he insisted, would put an end to any hopes she had of a political career. Given the fact that there were no witnesses to the actual assault, it was Barton's word against hers. 'Unless the feminists get behind you, the Crown Prosecution Service will probably do nothing.'

She might have turned the tables temporarily on Barton, but there was no guarantee that the paper would drop his projected life story together with the compromising pictures. They would not go down well at Conservative Central Office, or, to be more specific, with Sir Tom Arnold. The *True Brit* thrived mightily on outrage, and even a charge against one of its own reporters could be presented as an occupational risk suffered by those who devote themselves selflessly to the discovery of the truth. 'I am afraid,' he concluded, 'you have over-egged your pudding.'

At this Amaranth broke once more into tears, and angrily accused Harvey of giving her bad advice. 'I'm in a real mess,' she said, 'and I have also lost ten thousand quid which Barton said he would pay me for an exclusive. As it is he's got the lot for nothing. And what I haven't told you is that I'm in deep trouble. Financially.'

Harvey, whose instinct for survival had been finely honed and knew it was time he disengaged, was even more alarmed when she stood up and said, 'I'm going to write a piece about what goes on here for the *Daily Mirror*. I've got nothing to lose.'

With which parting shot, she turned on her heel and walked back to 'Mon Repos' where her hosts opened a tin of lentil soup. 'So very sustaining,' they said.

'We are all famous,' claimed the elder of the two. 'From now on we shall sell "Mon Repos" on the basis that Queen Elizabeth slept here.' They were kind, and the younger one filled her a hotty. She was clearly in need of a spot of 'shut-eye'.

Amaranth, curled up beneath her eiderdown, began to regret bitterly her performance of Wednesday afternoon. Publicity must be taken in small doses, and should be favourable. She had feelings of panic. The newspapers, which she had opened that morning at breakfast with such glee, now appeared threatening and censorious. What was worse, the prospect of three pages of photos of her stark naked displayed across the *True Brit* was almost too much to bear. They would be sniggered over by the lubricious (Ralph Grunte would love them), and her chances of being adopted as a prospective Conservative candidate seemed over. There would always be someone at the back of the meeting who would rise to her feet, a yellowing copy of a tabloid-newspaper in her hand.

Amaranth had gambled and she had lost. And Charles Harvey had ditched her. She cried herself to sleep.

Harvey, for his part, having retired to his room, called room service for a salt-beef sandwich. Pretty women were all very well, but not if they were liable to appear mother-naked across the pages of the tabloid press. He was, after all, a junior minister ('a coming man') and vulnerable to the Nigel Dempsters of this world. Amaranth was clearly what Miriam would call 'a high-risk investment'.

He was due to take his place on the conference platform that afternoon as his boss, John MacGregor, would be replying to the debate on the future of the railways. Bring back the old Great Western.

Exhausted by his midnight exertions, he too fell asleep.

Joshua Morris hurried along the front, plunged into the Lanes and entered English's Oyster House to find his Salopians sitting down to lunch. He made his apologies. The restaurant was one of Brighton's oldest, all fishermen's kitsch and rickety lobster pots, and it did not appear in the *Good Food Guide*. But what it served, it served well. And there is never much fish in South West Shropshire.

Joshua had kept up his friendship with the bulk of his Party activists who were, on most occasions, only too happy to leave 'politics' to the Member. It was an old-fashioned viewpoint, long vanished from the Marches of Essex and the urban constituencies. He ordered four bottles of Cloudy Bay Chardonnay and the party plumped for large Dover sole 'on the bone', minor surgery being one of its several pleasures. Peas (frozen), chips (too crinkly) and bottled tartare sauce combined to make a splendid lunch.

No one seemed to care overmuch about Jeffrey's fate, his guests having more in common with the Archers than with Archer. Miss Ethel Jones, who was the postmistress at Onibury, read nothing except the rustic novels of Mary Webb ('I've read *Gone to Earth* forty-three times, and seen the film more times than I can remember'). Joshua had enjoyed the film. It had been shot in Shropshire while he was at school at Shrewsbury. Jennifer

Jones had played Hazel Woodus. Mrs Annie Morris from Cheyney Longville was the last loyal reader of the novels of Francis Brett Young, fat, blue volumes with gold pears on them, all about goings-on in the West Midlands set in the early part of the century. His mother had had the set. Joshua's chairman, a Ludlow solicitor, read Trollope. His agent, however, had not really progressed beyond Rider Haggard.

They all agreed that Archer's books were, like most modern novels, full of sex, intrigue and violence, an opinion which Joshua acknowledged, knowing it to be only partly true. Intrigue, yes, but precious little sex and violence. They were not the sort of books Enoch Powell would find salacious.

As they were tucked away in an alcove, Joshua could 'say a few words' over the coffee. Besides the usual pieties, he told them the story of Monsignor Ronald Knox having a busman's holiday taking care of a church in Normandy. The services were, in those days, conducted in the vernacular, but confession proved very difficult indeed, so thick was the parishioners' accent, and so basic Knox's French. He coped by the use of this simple tactic. He would listen with care, and interrupt at intervals with the words, gravely uttered, 'Vous avez, avez-vous?' It had worked a treat. Joshua wondered if his Anglican Salopians had got the point.

Joshua left English's Oyster House in the company of his guests. He had been presented by them with a book, a first edition of *A Night in the Snow* signed by the author himself, the Rev Edmund Donald Carr. It was very civil of them. The slim volume is a favourite in Shropshire, being the account of a terrible twenty-four hours spent on the Longmynd by a parson in January

1865. He recounts, besides his other adventures on the mountain, the 'agonal phenomenon' in which, at times of great distress, the events of one's life, well or mis-spent, pass swiftly before one's eyes. A Tory Party conference had something of the same effect upon Joshua.

Rather than be jollied along by Sir Charles ('Welcome back, ladies and gentlemen, I hope you have all lunched exceedingly well'), Joshua went to the travelling book-shop where he hoped to find that his own most recent book, *A Short Life of William Cash*, had enjoyed a sale. He was surprised to discover that the taller Fiona was busily engaged in draping the front of the bookshop with strands of black crepe paper while the shorter was sitting at the back of the stall, snivelling. They had set out on display their entire stock of Archery in what they must have intended to be a posthumous tribute to the author.

Was Jeffrey Archer dead? They believed so, having been told so by a passing journalist, 'and he was on *The Times*.' Joshua said that meant nothing and, as for Archer, he had not heard as much. He expected that Jeffrey had nine lives. The smaller Fiona essayed a brave smile.

No, there had been no sales of his book.

Ralph Grunte followed Angela Cartwright, who was wearing that terrible Bavarian hat, into the Brasserie at the Hospitality Inn. It was not as expensive as La Noblesse, but he had already spent at least forty pounds feeding Mrs Cartwright's face on Tuesday evening. They left their coats at the desk, and as his guest went next door to the 'little girls' room', Grunte gave the bloke behind the counter a tenner to lose that 'blasted' hat.

'Tell her it was given to someone else after lunch by mistake.'

Greatly heartened, he opened the menu and masterfully ordered for them both. Tomato soup, cutlets and *pommes frites*. He asked the wine waiter to bring him a bottle of Penedes. No need to spoil the ship.

'Angela,' he said, 'has anyone ever told you what a damned handsome woman you are?' Mrs Cartwright had to admit that no one had done so for a very long time. Her husband, Bert, certainly had not, but he was no oil painting himself.

'Now, Ralph,' she said, tapping him on the back of his hairy hand, 'don't be a naughty boy.' She had suddenly become as arch as the old Waterloo bridge. Grunte attacked the wine savagely, taking care to keep Angela's glass filled to its brim. Why will she sip it like a bird in front of its bath? At this rate he would be pissed and she would be still sober.

John Wakeham, who was passing by, was grabbed by Grunte who insisted on introducing him to 'my constituency chairman'. Wakeham, who was partly hidden behind the smoke of his large, Cuban cigar, said how honoured he was, and how considerable was Grunte's contribution to the Party. 'We wouldn't be the same without Ralph,' he said, and moved magisterially towards the door.

Angela was clearly chuffed. She was about to proffer an olive branch, and tell him that the de-selection issue was going to be dropped, when Grunte leant across the table and told her that for a long time he had wanted to do something for Bert, to put a little business his way. Would her husband care to make an appointment to see him at Grunte House? He had need of the services of another qualified accountant. 'And I've heard Bert's good at his job.'

Angela beamed with pleasure and said she would give Bert the message. A reticent woman, she was even induced to mumble something about times being difficult and the recession biting 'deeper' than they had feared.

For Grunte, it was now or never. He could either consolidate his victory by taking her hand and holding it, a gesture which could lead to a difficult afternoon of dalliance (there was no doubt that, whatever the wine might be telling him, Mrs Cartwright was very plain indeed), or, were it to be gracefully acknowledged and the hand tactfully removed, it would still be game, set and match to Grunte. Ever the gambler, Grunte seized Mrs Cartwright's hand and squeezed it. Angela, looking intolerably coy, promptly squeezed it back. She made no move to take it away.

Grunte ordered two brandies and, having knocked his back, they left in the Roller for the Grand Hotel. Angela did not even remember to collect her hat.

Hyacinth Scragg, telly interviewer-extraordinary, was busy fending off the not altogether unwelcome attention of her producer, a youngish man in a denim suit with his hair tied up in a pig-tail. It was badly in need of a shampoo and set. He was called Angus. They were in the saloon bar of the 'Earl of Essex'.

'Margaret eats interviewers for breakfast,' he told her. 'Remember poor Robin Day. Knighted him one day, wouldn't let him get a word in edgeways the next.'

Angus's hand kept resting on her Romany bottom. Hyacinth pushed it gently away, and asked for a roast beef sandwich and a glass of best bitter. She had already been promised a fee of a hundred quid for her exploits, and there had been hints, dropped by Angus, of more work to come. 'TVS,' he said, 'is not long for this world, but we could use a fresh face and a quick wit.'

The crew were all very matey and jokes were tossed around freely. The sound man claimed to have heard the phrase 'early to bed and early to rise' regurgitated in Brussels as 'early to bed and up with ze cock'. Angus's hand returned to its resting place. What was Hyacinth doing this evening?

'I am being made Miss Young Conservative by the Birmingham Tories. They want me to be in the ballroom of the Metropole at nine o'clock.'

'We will be there,' cried Angus, 'in the line of duty.'

John Major called for beer and sandwiches in his modest suite, and summoned his 'crisis team' to attend upon him. Something must be done about Archer. The team included his private secretary, his press chief, Gus O'Donnell, who had replaced 'dear Bernard', and John MacGregor, who was wearing a new kilt that had arrived in the post that morning from The Scotch House in Knightsbridge, a store which is a favourite of the Americans and Japanese. He had borrowed a dirk from Sir Nicholas Fairbairn. Besides the Leader of the House, Tony Newton, Kenneth Clarke and Norman Fowler were also in attendance, together with John Gummer (in case of any errands), and the Head of the Special Branch. Norman Lamont had been sent for 'as a matter of urgency', but he was believed to be lunching at Manleys, a very superior restaurant some fifteen miles away.

'There is a lobster salad side to the Chancellor,'

observed Clarke, who had, at least, read Strachey's essay on Cardinal Manning.

John Major said, 'We shall need his signature on the ransom cheque.'

Fowler was quite downcast, fate having conspired to turn the Conservative conference into a bear-garden. First Amaranth's dance of the seven veils, then the YC-inspired riot and the arrest of its leading lights, and now the mysterious disappearance of Jeffrey Archer, upon whom the party had come to rely, if not for advice, then at least for refreshment. Gummer asked brightly whether it might not be possible to arrange an exchange, 'as had been done at the height of the Cold War', but the silence which greeted his suggestion discouraged him.

'We could offer Ralph Grunte, I suppose,' said Major, 'but they would want something more in part exchange.'

Major sent Gummer out to the kitchen in search of Branston pickle. Then the Prime Minister, turning to the Head of the Special Branch, asked him to brief the meeting. Where was the Great Novelist, who was holding him and what did they want?

Thursday's 'World at One' was specially extended to sixty minutes. It was, as everyone later agreed, Jim Naughtie's finest hour. Lady Thatcher's tearful appeal for Jeffrey's safe return 'in the name of literature' was duly repeated, an item that was followed by a brief studio discussion between Melvyn Bragg, Malcolm Bradbury and Germaine Greer as to Archer's place in the Pantheon. It was agreed that Archer was the sort of writer who enjoyed fame and fortune only in his lifetime, and that he would leave nothing for posterity.

'He was lucky enough,' opined Bragg, 'to have

invented his own football pool.' His use of the past tense was ominous.

Naughtie, his voice vibrant with emotion, described how he had enjoyed the author's hospitality only the night before. He had been 'a generous host' and the Krug (which was a peculiarly expensive brand of champagne, not much drunk in Scotland) had flowed like water from a Highland spring. The unwarranted intrusion of drunken Young Conservatives, fearful for their lives, had been described in his hearing as 'a diabolical liberty' by none other than Norman Tebbit himself. He understood that Archer had been locked in his own lavatory, and nobody had set eyes on him since.

Mr John Smith, the leader of the Opposition, yet another Scot, was then asked to comment upon the financial implications of the ransom note. Should the Treasury pay, or, if not, the National Heritage Foundation? Did the whole episode not demonstrate the need for a National Lottery?

Smith was his canny self. He did not believe for one moment that Archer had been kidnapped. 'It is some stunt, thought up by Central Office to distract attention from the need to devalue the pound.' 'The Friends of Le Pen' did not exist – outside, that is, the ranks of a few misguided Young Tories, many of whom he had to admit were Scots. The IRA was just making mischief, and he had every sympathy with the call by the *Guardian* newspaper for fiscal rectitude.

'After the events in Brighton this week,' he concluded, 'politics is clearly too serious an activity to be left to the Tories.' It was the verdict of the Manse.

A further item on the programme was supplied by Ms Sue MacGregor, who was standing at the barrier of platform three at Brighton Station. Three dark-blue police buses had drawn up in the station yard, and some sixty young people, carrying an assortment of cheap suitcases, ghetto-blasters and cans of Foster's, were shepherded on to the platform by a squad of policemen. They were led by the bearded figure of Wullie Robertson.

The Young Conservatives, whose disbandment had been announced by John Major that morning, were being 'entrained', to use the police terminology, and were headed, not for Victoria where their entry might have been anticipated by their enemies, but for Clapham Junction whence they would be permitted to make their own way home.

Robertson had no comment to make save to say that the fight would go on. Empty beer cans were tossed in the direction of Ms MacGregor, who was forced by the barrage to take refuge in the station-master's office. 'They are travelling', she was told, 'in a sealed train.'

Thursday Afternoon

Thursday was Heseltine's day. Throughout the seventies, in office and out, Michael Heseltine's conference speech was the event of the week. In the eighties, especially after his resignation from the Government over Westland, he had been banished to the conference 'fringe', where he spoke to large and enthusiastic audiences. In the nineties, back in office, and respectable once more, he had again taken the Party in hand.

Having lunched well, the Tories made for the conference hall in search of inspiration. Michael was always good for a bit of uplift. Save, that is, for Grunte, for whom it was too late, for Amaranth, who was recruiting her strength, and for David Swan, who was out on a limb. Janet Malcolm had retired to her bed with a cold, and Kevin was reading to her.

Mrs de Crespigny, who had 'lunched out' on the events of her morning ('I never did have much time for journalists'), marched a band of her fellow Party members in the direction of the conference, studiously ignoring the jeers of a scattering of youthful demonstrators. 'We should bring back National Service' was Mrs de Crespigny's view.

The first debate of the afternoon was ostensibly about Trade and Industry, but such niceties as sticking to one's brief had long been disregarded by Michael. His task was to raise the roof, to rally the faithful and to confound the Party's enemies. This he generally managed to do in a thirty-minute performance. Joshua Morris had once referred to him as 'Mussolini being played by Robert Redford'. Other, more perceptive political journalists, had written that Michael knew instinctively just how to find the clitoris of the Tory party. It was for that reason perhaps that there were no empty seats in the House.

There were, however, some notable absentees from the platform. John Major, Norman Fowler and Kenneth Clarke were not in their places. The political correspondents, who usually cluster at the base of the platform in reserved seats, had also disappeared. It was reliably understood that Major, Patten and Clarke were to hold a press conference in the Grand at four o'clock to pay tribute to Jeffrey Archer. Not for the first time in his life would Michael Heseltine be left playing to the gallery.

In their small suite at the Grand Hotel, Norma and John Major lay side by side on the twin beds. Norma's advice as to total, creeping relaxation, was being put into practice. Lie still, close your eyes and, beginning with the big toe, progressively relax every muscle until the back of the neck is reached.

Norma was already fast asleep; John was stuck halfway, riven, as he was, by the twin anxieties of Archer's disappearance and Margaret's bloody-mindedness, not to mention the rumours that were reaching him about

Amaranth. And he could not even rely on Fowler to take the press conference called for four o'clock. At lunch he had said that Jeffrey's parties had been wrongly described as Bollinger, Beluga and bullshit; they were 'Krug, krap and kedgeree'. This suggested that the chairman of the Party might not be able to rise to what ought to be a solemn occasion. After all, Jeffrey was no joke.

In an ante-room a clever young man was sketching out the first draft of a statement to be made to the press. He had a first in Greats and had never read an Archer in his life, but he had been taught to cope. Major went through the form in his mind: the Home Secretary would open the proceedings with an account of the outrage; Tim Renton, rather than Peter Brooke, would say a few words putting Archer 'in the frame'; and he would go in to bat last.

It was all very tiresome, not least because of the need to work on his Leader's speech, due to be delivered in under twenty-four hours. What with one thing and another, this year's conference would long be celebrated in song and story.

The three o'clock news on Radio 4 was all about Archer. There was still no news of his whereabouts. Yet another ransom note had been received from a group claiming to be holding the author; this time it was the Animal Liberation Front. Sinn Fein promised to release their video at five o'clock. There had been no further word from 'The Friends of Le Pen'.

Wullie Robertson, interviewed at Clapham Junction, claimed to know nothing whatsoever about Archer's disappearance. Gerald Kaufman had maintained that the whole thing had been got up by Michael Heseltine's enemies within the Party who were anxious to distract attention from his speech that afternoon. The headmaster of Wellington College had denied that Jeffrey was an old Wellingtonian. 'We had several Archers, but certainly not that one.' Debbie Owen, the literary agent and wife of David, had paid a charming tribute to her erstwhile author. The BBC would be going over live to the Grand Hotel in Brighton at four pm when there would be a press conference.

The bulletin had taken on a solemn, almost funereal note: were the worst to have happened, no doubt Sir Michael Checkland, the director-general of the BBC, would order the playing of martial music.

Ron Barton had been given the second-class treatment at the police station. After a twenty-minute wait, during which he had been ignored by the station sergeant, who had none of the qualities of the late Jack Warner, Barton was asked to make his statement. The room smelt of vomit, masked by Dettol.

'You're one of them scribblers, are you?' he was asked. 'In which case we'll make a better than usual job of it.'

Ron dictated a statement to the effect that he had been conducting an interview with Mrs Wilikins, and that the assault did not take place. 'I told her we were going to print some pix of her in the pink in the paper tomorrow, and she just went ape.'

He let it be known that news of his 'arrest' and statement would doubtless appear in the *True Brit*, along with the names of his investigating officer.

'Make a habit of putting your hand up women's drawers, do you? You're about the right height. Some people have all the luck,' was the response. He was then charged and released on bail. He asked whether he could telephone for a taxi.

'Who do you think you are?' he was asked. 'Beattie with her bloody phone card?' He left the police station and, after a longish wait, hailed a passing cab.

When he arrived at his brother's house in Kemp Town, he found that his fax, which he had taken the precaution of bringing with him, had spewed out a roll of paper long enough to be featured in an Andrex advertisement on the telly. Some of it was unsolicited; much was from the office of the editor of the *True Brit*. Its tone, which could never have been described as 'cultivated', became more demotic as message followed upon message.

A spy at the *Sun*, who was anxious to join the *True Brit* as its Court Correspondent, had tipped off the editor of the *Brit* that the Brighton police had 'come up with the goods' on his star reporter. A telephone call from 'Charlie' at the station had told of an incident in the lounge of the Grand Hotel in which Barton had been accused of having 'fumbled' none other than the same Amaranth Wilikins whose pictures were that morning in every paper. Barton, loudly protesting his innocence, had been charged with an offence, and the Crown Prosecution Service would decide whether to prosecute.

Kelv, warned the spy, would make a meal of it. There was never any love lost between those two. And Ron was known to have funny little ways. The *True Brit* stood to bring the tabloids into disrepute – that was Kelvin Mackenzie's view.

In consequence, the editor of the *True Brit* was demanding to know what the hell was going on? Was

Ron 'on the job', or was he still indulging in his 'filthy habits'? The burden of the message was that Ron should fax the life story of his victim 'soonest' with no mention of what had happened at the Grand.

Ron's brother, whose day off it was, had been driven to distraction by the continual bleeping and whirring of the fax. He had just decided to go out and try to find Ron when his telephone rang. It was the editor speaking from his regular table at the Savoy Hotel (he was never without his mobile phone). He had just been told, over his omelette Arnold Bennett and a half bottle of Pol Roger, that Jeffrey Archer was missing. The story of the year and where was Ron? Up the skirts of some Tory.

'What the hell have you been up to?' his brother demanded when Ron arrived.

Ron told him to piss off. It had been a ghastly day and he felt he had to have a rest before he faced the world. He went to bed and when he woke up more white fax paper had emerged from the machine.

The *Sun* had got wind of Barton's scoop – the *Penthouse* pictures – and had been making mischief. The copyright of the pix was the property of one Bob Blackstone who had, since he had run his airbrush over Amaranth's private parts, got God. He had become born-again, and was the 'pastor' of a charismatic church in Hemel Hempstead. He had no wish whatsoever for his name to be printed on the three-page spread, and, to his credit, was unwilling to sell anything to the *Sun*, or anyone else. He had destroyed the negs. The reproduction of the *Penthouse* pages alone would be difficult to do, and Bob Guccione, the mag's owner, was a hard man to cross.

The *True Brit* might have to make do with a rehash of

Thursday's pictures. 'In which case,' said the fax, 'we'll need a bit of spicy copy from you, Ron. The best you've ever done.' Its tone was menacing. There was a post-script. 'Daisy in Sports sends her love and says she will bake you a cake with a file in it.'

Sod Daisy.

David Swan was in two minds; should he return to Warwickshire to face an angry Carole, a penitence which would involve days of silence, pursed lips and slamming doors, or should he hang around the conference, taking in the delights of the town? Brighton had a reputation for pleasures of all sorts. A fellow Mason in Warwick had been an officer in the town's vice squad, and his stories were enough to make your hair stand on end.

David stared at a leaflet pinned to a notice-board in the foyer of the Grand announcing that Miss Hyacinth Scragg was to be crowned Miss Young Birmingham or something that evening at the Metropole. (He wondered what she had done about her knickers.) It won't be long, he mused, before Hyacinth drops the 'Scragg' in favour of something more up-market: Fairfax or Mountjoy.

He had begun to regret that, out of pique at the way Amaranth had treated him, he had transferred his amorous attention to Hyacinth. Perhaps he should have persevered. There was still the question of how much she knew about the motorway to be answered. Business before pleasure.

He spotted Peter Worthington Evans standing talking to the security staff at the door. At school he had been Pete Evans who lived in or near Sparkbrook. He had been what his son would have called a 'train spotter'. It was just possible that he would know where to find

Amaranth. Evans did, because it is the job of the whips to know everything. 'Try "Mon Repos",' he said. Now he was a Member of Parliament he did not seem too eager to talk about old times.

David asked in the hotel for directions to Gardner Street and 'Mon Repos', and set out briskly in search of Amaranth. Summer was paying what was likely to be its last visit to Brighton, the sun having broken out from behind the bank of French clouds, and the sea was seething with white horses. HMS *Bournemouth* steamed slowly by, ever alert against the remote chance of an Irish sea-borne landing. Could she help find Jeffrey Archer? David had great faith in our brave boys in blue. Navy blue.

A hand suddenly descended upon his shoulder, and a deep Brummie voice behind him requested a few words. It was Leroy Burns.

'Dave,' he said, 'you're not thinking of writing any more of them letters?'

Swan disengaged. 'What letters?'

'You know what letters. Like the one you wrote to the *Recorder* asking for Ralph to be given the order of the boot. Pinching your daughter's bum, and all that. I just thought I'd tell you that I'm thinking of putting pen to paper myself. About you playing around with Hyacinth. Got rumbled by your missus up in your room at the Grand Hotel. Right, man?'

Leroy paused; he was very large and very black. 'I don't blame you, like. Hyacinth would fit nicely in anyone's bed. But I'm telling you to lay off Grunte in the meantime. "Ex Mayor tumbles teenager." Lovely headline in the *Recorder*.'

David Swan, scarlet in the face with anger, said nothing in reply.

'And there's another thing. Ralph knows and I know all about the tricks you're up to – and your friends. Trying to get rid of him and give his seat to that Wilikins tart. We'll go to any lengths to stop that – I mean it.'

David still said nothing. Turning on his heel, he made off rapidly in the direction of Gardner Street. A misspent youth in Burslem and Brum, taken with the fact that he was at least four stone lighter than Burns, urged caution. He would ring his solicitor. Threats and menaces. The *Recorder* would be unlikely to print such a letter for fear of libel, but news of its existence would soon become known. Whom had Carole told?

Leroy Burns, who had once gone ten rounds with the young Bruno, made his stately way back to the conference. He had done his bit for old Grunte. That was one bout 'good ole Leroy' had won on points.

The owners of 'Mon Repos' politely denied David Swan entry. Ms Wilikins was asleep and could not be disturbed. Come back later, or ring after four o'clock.

At the stroke of four from the town's many clocks, the younger of the partners woke Amaranth with a cheerful 'cuppa'. 'This will please you, dear,' he said, handing her a copy of the mid-day edition of the London *Evening Standard*. Peter McKay had written very sweetly about her in his column. 'We need fun in our politics', and more in that vein. Amaranth had the looks, and the nerve, to succeed in what was still, despite everything, a man's world.

The tea, the kind words and a hot bath revived Amaranth somewhat. Her temperament, which had been described by the headmistress of her direct grant grammar school in the Potteries, as 'mercurial', responded to the good news. She would put on her paint and return to the lounge of the Grand Hotel. Sod Charles Harvey. Maybe David Swan could turn out to be a better bet.

Five minutes after David had set out to find Amaranth, Carole Swan entered the Grand Hotel for the third time in a week. Despite her lack of a photo-pass, she was waved cheerfully through the security and greeted as an old friend by the man at reception. 'Good to see you again, madam,' he said. Your husband, she was told, has just gone out. His face was quite straight; Carole's was quite pink. She had been responsible, after all, for Tuesday's late-night shambles.

'You will be leaving us tomorrow?'

Carole, who was not without spirit, said that if all went well, she certainly hoped she would.

The Brighton conference had so far turned out to be a great disappointment. Thanks to David's bad behaviour she had spent most of her time on the road, having driven the better part of 800 miles in four days. Anyway, she preferred Blackpool, where she had gone on holiday as a child. Last year she had left David at home and spent several happy afternoons riding the trams for which that windy city is famous. And she had eaten a stick of Blackpool rock.

As she stood in front of a battery of lifts waiting for one of them to respond, the door opened and a flustered Angela Cartwright stepped out, looking rather like Shirley Williams pulled through a hedge backwards. Carole had never seen La Cartwright looking so dishevelled. And she was not even staying at the Grand, so what had she been doing on one of the bedroom floors?

'Hallo,' said Carole. 'I thought you were staying at the Queen's?'

'I've lost my hat,' Angela Cartwright spluttered. 'It's all Grunte's fault.'

Carole had a mental picture of a greenish tweed trilby with a cock's feather in its band. 'How is Grunte?' she asked. It was not really a question demanding an answer. She had simply been taken aback.

'The old swine is drunk and disgusting,' was the reply. 'And what's more, he can't get it up.'

Carole stepped hurriedly into the lift and pressed the button. At this rate it would not be long before she would be back on the road again to Warwick, having seen precious little of the Party conference. She had dined with Ralph Grunte on the Tuesday night at La Noblesse but had not enjoyed the occasion. She had been attacked by her husband when she returned exhausted to her room, and had been, in consequence, the unwitting cause of what could have amounted to the evacuation of the hotel. She had spent most of Wednesday on the road, only to find David groping that Hyacinth Scragg in their bedroom. She had arrived in the nick of time, or had she?

It now appeared that Angela Cartwright, whom she had always considered to be beyond sex, or, at the very least, temptation, had been persuaded into bed by Grunte. God, how that woman blew hot and cold. First she wanted him out then she wanted him in. Carole, who was a simple woman much given to jam-making, cactus-rearing and the local Women's Institute, where the quality of her Victoria sponge gave rise to much comment, felt that politics was getting beyond her.

What was more, she now regretted having told Mrs Cartwright of David's misbehaviour with Hyacinth Scragg. The woman could not be trusted. And where was David? He evidently had not checked out. His clothes were hanging in the cupboard and his pyjamas were underneath his pillow. Carole made sure her door was locked – she had no wish for David to return with some other woman in tow – got into bed and fell asleep.

Angela Cartwright took a taxi to the Hospitality Inn, and retrieved her hat, but not before a very nasty row indeed had taken place. Faced with the manager, an obsequious Swiss, the cloakroom attendant had been compelled to admit that 'a fat gentleman' had paid him to lose it. He had promptly given the hat to the woman who looked after the Ladies lavatory. She was a stout German who had received the gift, not only as a token of hoped-for love, but as a reaffirmation of her nationality. She would have it cleaned, spruce up the feather and wear it that Sunday to the Lutheran church. She was very loath indeed to part with her acquisition.

Mrs Cartwright had threatened to involve the police, the manager had snatched the hat away from its new owner (it was as well that Angela could not speak German), and sacked the cloakroom attendant on the spot. It had all been most unpleasant. She left the Hospitality Inn shaking with rage. The excitements of the afternoon had made her feel quite unwell.

Of one thing she was certain, Sir Ralph Bloody Grunte was for the high jump. She would call a meeting of the Party's delegation for the next morning, and start up the process of de-selection. But could she carry the meeting with her? Of whom could she be sure? Paul Franklin would be solid, she supposed, and very possibly the Swans. Hyacinth Scragg could not be relied upon. That black bruiser was quite hopeless, and the same probably went for the agent, Bill O'Farrell. She was not certain about the Malcolms.

She returned to the conference hall, where Michael Heseltine was still responding to his standing ovation. Invitations to attend a meeting at the Queen's Hotel for ten o'clock tomorrow (Friday) morning were left on the conference ante-room notice-board. Grunte would rue the day he had tried to make a fool of Angela Cartwright.

Joshua Morris did not feel in need of enthusiasm. A full-frontal Heseltine speech could be an exhausting spectacle, and mass hysteria, however skilfully induced, and in whatever cause, is not a pretty sight. He felt he no longer had the stamina for it. Instead, he took a cab half-a-mile down the front into the stuccoed palaces of Hove, and walked slowly back along the front towards the Grand Hotel. He passed the glories of Regency Square with its pretty balconies, a square now home to an underground car park. The air was soft, and the municipal gardeners had covered the frequent beds with autumnal tints, among which were yellow, white and bronze chrysanthemums, melancholic blooms which the Chinese associate with death.

He determined to ring Felicity in Battle to try to persuade her to come back to Brighton in time to have dinner together. He would duck the agents' dinner, and go to the Grand; they could eat at leisure, talk over old times, and watch the world go by. So far, at this Party conference, if at none other, there had been few dull moments. He found a telephone box. Felicity agreed readily, and they arranged to meet at seven-thirty in the foyer.

Once inside the hotel – the security seemed if anything to be even more severe – Joshua went into the ballroom where the press conference was being held. An officious attendant refused him entrance on the ground that he was not press, but he was easily convinced when Joshua produced his press pass. 'Terrible news, Mr Morris,' he said. Joshua, not certain what exactly the custodian had in mind, agreed that it most certainly was. It was a little past four o'clock and the Home Secretary was already on his feet. He was wearing a black tie and seemed to be threatening retribution. He concluded by saying something to the effect that the light had gone out of the world when Byron died, adding, 'G.M. Young.'

He was quickly followed by Tim Renton, who attempted a eulogy of sorts, although Joshua had a strong impression that Renton, an old Etonian who had been Margaret Thatcher's last Chief Whip, had only a nodding acquaintance with Archer's oeuvre. He concluded by making a reference to the very real possibility that, in happier times, Archer would have been a candidate for the Nobel Prize.

'For chemistry?' said someone. There was a suppressed giggle.

John Major smiled his appreciation of Tim Renton's brave try, but made no effort to get to his feet. In truth, he was none too happy with the draft of a speech provided by his private office. It had not seemed somehow to have struck the right note.

Clarke invited questions, and John Walsh, the literary editor of *The Sunday Times*, got to his feet.

It was at this moment that Jeffrey Archer's head and

shoulders appeared round the ballroom door. The sequence was caught on camera – Archer's initial expression of incredulity, the consternation of the platform, and the hilarity of the assembled hacks. Tim Renton fainted clean away. It has become a television 'classic', continually played and replayed, particularly at Christmas. As a piece of film, it rivals the men on the moon, the assassination of JFK and the best of Morecambe and Wise.

Archer, faced with a mass attack of reporters and cameras, promptly disappeared, and ran upstairs to the Bridal Suite. As he took the stairs two at a time (Archer had run for the 'Varsity and Great Britain in his day), he was heard to shout that it had all been a dreadful mistake.

The younger members of the press pursued the author to the doors of his suite only to find the entrance barred by beefy Securicor men. The older, and those who had lunched rather well, clustered around the platform party.

Major had left by a rear door. Clarke was tight-lipped, claiming that 'he had work to do'. Only the revived Renton, colour returning to his cheeks, was prepared to meet the press. He had no explanation for Archer's reappearance. 'You must remember, we only feared the worst.' Asked to account for the author's disappearance for the best part of fifteen hours, Renton reminded his audience of the mysterious circumstances surrounding the whereabouts of Agatha Christie in the 1920s.

'Had she not been to Harrogate?' he asked. 'Was the mystery ever revealed?'

The Grand Hotel was peppered with pundits, who, standing before their television crews, gave the good news to a nation of book-lovers. There was much excitement. Gerald Kaufman said it had all been got up for the press, a 'typical Tory stunt'. The *Daily Mirror*'s political editor claimed that the Conservative conference had become a seaside vaudeville in which naked women vied with missing pop-novelists in search of the public's attention. Had the Party nothing to say to the unemployed? In comparison, last week's Labour Party conference at Blackpool (during which Roy Hattersley had been tarred and feathered by a band of socialist women led by Clare Short and Glenda Jackson), had been like a vicarage tea-party.

Lord Rees-Mogg opined that the 'goings-on' threatened to bring politics into disrepute, while Lord Wyatt of Weeford, who was dressed for Goodwood Races, said that he had enjoyed himself hugely.

Lady Thatcher was reliably reported to be 'beside herself with joy'.

'He who was lost, hath been found,' intoned John Cole, who had, in his youth, attended very Protestant services indeed.

The Tory Party conference reaches its apogee between the hours of eight and ten o'clock on the evening of the last full day. The fringe of meetings is still well attended. Tory doctors, lawyers and accountants all meet and elect each other into office for another year. The Tory Reform Group looks to a more liberal future, the Monday Club back to when the 'coloureds' knew their proper place.

'The Friends of Margaret Thatcher' meet in a Kemp Town basement in order to plan the counter-revolution. Ted Heath entertains a select company of journalists to dinner at Manley's. The Prime Minister dines with the officers and executive committee of a Tory 'area'. This year it was the turn of the Conservatives of Wessex.

But these are minority interests. The great majority are either at table or in their cups, ready to dance the night away, or to spend hours rekindling old friendships with the flammable help of political gossip.

Felicity arrived at the Grand Hotel at seven-thirty to find Joshua in the bar, talking to Charles Harvey and a woman who turned out to be Mrs Harvey. Miriam had, for once, deserted her brokers in favour of a night with her husband. She wore a choker of pearls (real?) and a little black dress, and she smelt rather too strongly of scent – 'Jolie Madame'. Felicity thought her to be a tough cookie. They disengaged and went to sit in two corner seats of the principal lounge, a position from which they could watch the world and what they hoped was his wife.

'What do you think of Harvey?' asked Joshua.

'Accipitrine.'

'What on earth does that mean?' he asked.

'Hawk-like, predatory, too smooth and a shade dangerous,' said Felicity.

Joshua never ceased to be pleased by her love of words. He told Felicity that he and Harvey had had a chat before Miriam joined them, and that Harvey had been very frank. It was common gossip, after Amaranth's performance as Salome, that he had been on what might be described as intimate terms with her, and naturally he hoped that she would be discreet.

It now appeared that they had had a row, and Amaranth was threatening to go public. She had tried to pump Harvey about a new motorway for which he had some ministerial responsibility.

'Why did she want to know?' Felicity asked.

'Lord knows. She might have had some business interest, Harvey thought. Apparently, she's broke and she said she thought she might write about the conference in the *Daily Mirror*. The inside story.'

Carole Swan went by, wearing her pink. Joshua drew Felicity's attention to her. 'The woman who set the alarm bells off on Tuesday night – mistook her husband for an intruder. Oh, and look. There's Amaranth herself.'

'The party's piece of skirt,' said Felicity. 'She's overdressed.'

She was wearing an off-the-shoulder dress, was looking preoccupied, and was clutching a sheaf of messages in her hand.

'The media,' said Joshua. 'This morning she was hot property, although I suspect that Archer's resurrection has knocked her off her perch. And it was not as if he were in the tomb for three days. Would you as a member of the executive committee of the Leominster Tories [Felicity was a keen attender of Party meetings, cooking delicious stews and serving them to hungry Tories in her large, cold house near Croft] choose her as your prospective candidate?'

'I rather approve of Peter Temple-Morris,' said Felicity, 'although he is, like you, a bit left-wing. But were he to be kicked upstairs, would I pick Amaranth? Certainly not. She's too glam for a Tory MP, and she would play havoc with all you old things in the 1922 Committee. You need to be cosseted, loved and polished, not driven to distraction by a tart. It would be Emil Jannings and *The Blue Angel* all over again. She would have you all crowing like so many cockerels.'

Joshua went to the bar for champagne cocktails. He had no regrets at having abandoned the agents' dinner. It was not as if he had been asked to perform at it.

The two Dimblebys introduced themselves to Amaranth and, sitting on the twin arms of her chair, proceeded to entertain her. Amaranth, distributing her favours equally, as if watching Wimbledon, seemed much cheered by their attentions. A waiter gave her a message which, with a charming apology to her guests, she read. Having done so, she crumpled it into a ball, tossed it in the general direction of a waste-paper basket, looked at her watch, and got to her feet. She excused herself and disappeared into the night. The Dimblebys went over to the bar where they began talking to Robin Day.

'Do your "Shropshire Sherlock" stuff, Joshua,' hissed Felicity. 'Go and pick it up.'

Looking rather sheepish, Morris did as he was bid. No one seemed to notice. On his return he smoothed the paper open and together they read:

Hope I haven't sneeped you. Meet me for a drink in the bar at the Hospitality Inn at eight to show there's no ill feeling.

The message was typewritten and unsigned.

'Sneeped,' said Felicity. 'Such a good word. Onomatopoeia.' It was the headmaster's daughter again.

'Yes, but what does it actually mean?' asked Joshua.

'Pissed off,' retorted Felicity, 'offended. I should know, I had a mother's help from Staffordshire who was always that way, and usually said so. "Lobby" is another local word. Means a sort of stew. A mess of pottage.'

Joshua looked at his watch. 'Talking of which, let's dine,' he said. 'I have booked a window table but I'm told all is peaceful outside. No rioting tonight.' They moved into the dining room, stopping to have a word with the Howes on their way.

'There's more to the Archer story than meets the eye,' said Geoffrey. 'He's to tell all on the nine o'clock news.'

A corner table in the window of the restaurant of the Grand Hotel was the favourite position of the political voyeur. Look to one's left and the light of the westering sun flattered the passers-by, of whatever political persuasion, touching them with the gilded band of health. Small clusters of the photo-pass-bearing classes stood talking about events: the reappearance, so far without explanation, of Jeffrey Archer after all that terrible fuss at lunchtime; Michael Heseltine's speech ('I admit he's good but I do wish he would have his hair cut' was the view of the woman from Bradford), and the generally alarming nature of the conference so far.

There were about twenty policemen, and a procession of black Rovers disgorged or collected the leading lights of the Tory Party. Peter Brooke, the Minister for Fun, dressed in the colours of Chelsea, trotted past blowing his referee's whistle. He was followed by a car with a mounted television camera. The Chancellor in full evening dress left the Grand to be driven to some important function along the coast. With that flippancy which could one day prove to be his undoing, he told Hyacinth Scragg and TVS that, if he looked cheerful, it was because now the prodigal son had returned, the Treasury would no longer be obliged to kill the fatted calf.

'Were there other lights at the end of the tunnel?' asked Hyacinth.

Lamont looked inscrutable. 'We must,' he said, 'wait and see.'

Felicity and Joshua, having decided that temperance was by far the most overrated of the virtues and greed the most worthy vice, ordered dinner. Between them they had over seventy years' experience of dining out. 'In large hotels stick to simple dishes that have not been mucked about, and trust that the chef knows a good butcher,' was Felicity's advice. She was writing a cookery book but had not yet been able to find a publisher. Each of them ordered whitebait, and Joshua an underdone rump steak with onion rings, and a green salad. They ordered a bottle of Toro Gran Colegiata '86.

'When broke or in doubt,' pontificated Joshua, 'order Spanish red and white from Alsace.'

To the right the diners could survey the remainder of the tables and, as the wall between the dining room and the foyer was made of glass, keep an eye on all the comings and goings within the hotel itself. It seemed that everyone who was anyone was on parade.

Lady Thatcher, who had been having a few words with John Major in his suite ('I insist that Ted Heath mount the platform tomorrow for your speech before I do. I was Prime Minister three times longer than he was.') came down the stairs and passed out of the hotel under heavy escort. She had a curiously unattractive, bustling walk, and she stopped every so often to receive homage from an old acquaintance. It was a regal progress. A small, bald equerry carried her umbrella. There was no sign of George Gardiner.

'She's going to Eastbourne,' said Joshua, 'something

to do with unveiling a bust of some doctor or other.'

Between the whitebait and the steak (Felicity rarely ate more than one course) Hyacinth and her telly-crew struggled past the barrier. Tony Howard's 'Conference Special' team for the BBC had come up with a 'jolly wheeze'. The female stars of the Party conference were plainly Amaranth and the Dance of the Seven Veils, and Hyacinth, the YC who had gone on camera beyond the point where even Sir Robin Day had dared to go. She had taken on Mrs T and lived to tell the tale. And she had danced with John Major.

They were both very pretty, major and minor, fair and dark, one of a certain age, the other very much *en fleur*. Why should they not interview each other for the delight of the political classes? It would be more fun than ten minutes with Michael Portillo.

The producer mumbled something about expense, but Howard persuaded him to offer them fifty quid each.

Just before nine o'clock, Joshua and Felicity moved into the lounge and found a place in range of a television set. Jeffrey Archer was about to tell all. The room was packed and the noise level high. At the sight of the newsreader, silence fell, and the viewer was immediately transported to Brighton.

Jeffrey Archer, sitting in his Bridal Suite upstairs, was being interviewed by John Cole. They were both drinking champagne.

'More Krug,' said a voice from the back of the lounge. It was immediately shushed.

Archer's story had little of the narrative charge that so many of his earlier books possessed. There was little Cain and no Abel. No, he had not done an Agatha Christie (how much he admired her plots), he had just had enough of rioting and gone back to his penthouse flat on the Thames, from the windows of which he could look down on the House of Lords. It had been quite outrageous how his party had been broken up by thugs, who had drunk his Krug and finished up what was left of the shepherd's pie.

His guests, among whom he numbered *la crème de la crème*, had been forced to flee for their lives, and the hotel was in a state of utter chaos. He had simply taken his motor from the garage and driven through the night to London, arriving in the small hours. He had found the midnight drive curiously relaxing. The penthouse was empty – his wife Mary had a singing engagement in a club in Swansea – and he had slept soundly until lunchtime. The telephone was switched off.

'You've no idea, John,' said Archer, refilling Cole's glass, 'how very hard we politicians work.' After a light lunch from the ice-box, Archer had returned gently to Brighton. Had he not listened to the car radio? 'No, I played my tapes. *Turandot*, actually.'

It was not until he had returned to the Grand and been passed through security by two Bengalis, that he had realised that anything was wrong. Hence his surprise at the press conference in his honour.

'It seems,' said Archer, 'that in my absence all sorts of people have claimed to have kidnapped me, and what is more, demanded large sums of money for my freedom.' Cole, sipping his champagne (one could not get stuff this good in Bangor), asked if Lord Archer had realised the fuss his absence had caused, the police time wasted, and the trouble he had made for the leaders of his Party?

Jeffrey said he was beginning to, and offered his apologies, especially to Tim Renton who, he understood, had fainted quite away at his unheralded reappearance. He would dedicate his next novel to the former Minister for the Arts.

The cameras faded, and returned to the studio. The police, it was reported, were doing their level best to discover the identity of all those who had misled them, the Animal Liberation Front, the 'Friends of Le Pen', *et al*. When their identities were discovered, charges would be preferred.

The next item was a film of the Heseltine conference speech, and Felicity excused herself. They would meet in ten minutes' time. As he waited, Joshua noticed a large black man sitting on his own in the foyer. Sneaking a closer look, he decided it must be Leroy Burns, the heavyweight boxer. He had seen him fight at the Albert Hall several years ago, and had read somewhere that he was attending the conference as a delegate from the Midlands.

'Mr Burns?'

Leroy agreed that he was.

Joshua told him that he was a steward of the British Boxing Board of Control and had seen him fight several times. 'You had a good chin.'

'Too good for my own good,' said Leroy.

'And a good left hand,' added Morris, placatingly. He looked at Burns's photo-pass and saw he was part of the Arden constituency party. 'One of Ralph Grunte's little lot.'

Burns bridled, but Morris hastened to reassure him. 'We all think the world of Grunte.' It was the whitest of white lies.

Burns then told him of Grunte's trials and tribulations. Angela Cartwright was out to get him. So, too, were the

Swans. So what if Sir Ralph drank a bit and chased the girls; who didn't? Pinched the Mayor's daughter's bum, he did, but David Swan was no bloody bishop. His wife had caught him in the act with Hy Scragg. What was more, Swan had spent the last day or two hanging around Amaranth Wilikins, the 'strip-tease artist'. She was another Burns was keeping an eye on. She was hoping to succeed Grunte as their MP.

Felicity joined them and Joshua introduced Burns to her. After a moment's small talk, they said goodbye, and left the Grand for the Metropole next door. They would witness Hyacinth's coronation as Miss Birmingham Young Conservative, return to the Grand for a drink, and take a cab back to Wenlock Manor for an early night. The Rover could stay where it was.

Since the proscription of the Young Conservatives earlier in the day, a great deal of revamping had taken place. A new slate of officers had been confirmed in office by the remnants of the old national executive committee, and were standing ready to greet their guests. Murdo Fraser, a respectable Scot whose Thatcherite views were tempered by Calvin, had been made – for the second time – the National Chairman of the YCs. The new politburo had replaced the old. In place of the tattoos and T-shirts, the Tartan Ale and the denim trousers, the new officers all had the Daks look, as if they had been kitted out in the sales at Simpsons, Piccadilly: tweedy jackets, yellow waistcoats and grey flannel trousers. Joshua saw himself as he must have looked forty years ago as an officer of the Hampstead Young Conservatives, Lord Finsberg's Own.

Hyacinth was standing on the stage talking to the 'Newsnight' team. Then the band struck up, and after the MC had called for silence, she was crowned 'Miss Birmingham Young Conservative' by Sir Norman Fowler who, besides being the Chairman of the Party, was the Member for Sutton Coldfield, the suburb where all good Brummies wish to end their days. He said something nice about Hyacinth who, in a silver and red dress and long ear-rings, looked a bit like a Spanish version of a Christmas Tree.

She made a brief and charming reply. This was the most exciting week of her life. Her bosom heaved beguilingly. She had been offered a job on the telly and crowned Queen, and on Tuesday night she had danced with John Major. She gave Fowler a deep kiss (there was much applause and some embarrassment on her victim's part) and then she jumped down from the stage. The cameras flashed and the hacks gathered round her.

At that moment, Amaranth was led up on stage by a solicitous Tony Howard. She was looking (said Felicity) rather like a prize-winning greyhound.

Television is a confrontational medium and Howard had the bright idea of putting the rivals in a late-evening contest. There can be too much straightforward politics on the box.

'It's as if Joan Crawford had been asked to interview Bette Davis,' said Joshua. 'Sparks will fly.'

It was soon evident that he was right, although Hyacinth, as the questioner, held the advantage. Perhaps she had been inspired by her coronation, to say nothing of her embrace with Norman Fowler. Thrusting the mike beneath Amaranth's chiselled nose, she asked whether she was about to take her clothes off.

'Don't be ridiculous,' said Amaranth. 'What a stupid question!'

'Some people,' Hyacinth said with Warwick gentility, 'will do anything to attract attention. Is it true you are trying to get an MP kicked out?'

'Of course not,' Amaranth replied. 'Why on earth should I do that?'

'Because you hope to get his seat yourself.'

'Are you crazy?' was all Amaranth could think of in reply, to which Hyacinth retorted, 'I'm the one who's asking the questions. Answer this one. You've been chasing several men at this conference, but when one made a pass at you, or so you say, you reported him to the police. Why?'

Amaranth looked round as if she was seeking escape. She was clearly losing her temper.

'Mind your own business,' she said.

'What are you going to do when you leave Brighton?'

'I'll tell you what I'm going to do. I'm going to write an article about this conference, about the way people behave. About what it's like to be interviewed by a tart like you, who goes about poking people's eyes out on the telly. I'm going to—'

At this, Hyacinth took a menacing step forward, only to have Howard and his female producer throw themselves between the contestants like referees at a big fight. The lights were switched off, the furry microphones lowered, and the two women were led away in opposite directions, Hyacinth shouting that she would kill the old bag. Amaranth took a sip of the BBC's water, and left the stage, taking what was left of her dignity with her. Joshua awarded the fight to Hyacinth, on points. He thought he saw a man waiting for Amaranth as she reached the door of the hall. Perhaps a congenial shoulder to cry on.

Any plans Joshua and Felicity had for an early night soon evaporated. Tony Howard invited them to join the television team for a drink, and they sat for the rest of the evening discussing the week's events.

'That interview was all on film,' said the producer. 'We weren't live. I will have to ask my boss whether we can use it. The BBC is in enough trouble with the Tory Party as it is. Bias and all that jazz.'

'Whether we show it or not,' said Howard, 'you can't keep a thing like that quiet. It will be all over tomorrow's papers. One of your new respectable YCs is probably on the blower to the Press Association at this very moment.'

In fact, the Amaranth *v.* Hyacinth contest went on the air within minutes. It was far too good to be left in the can. Their clash was witnessed by, among others, John Major, Kenneth Clarke and several members of the Cabinet. (John Gummer had been sent downstairs to the bar to fetch a plate of salt-beef sandwiches.) They watched the dust-up in silence. As Hyacinth's threat 'to kill the old bag' died away, Major groaned aloud.

' "Who will free me from this turbulent wench?" ' he asked.

'Which one?' asked Richard Ryder.

'Both of them,' Major replied.

' "Turbulent priest," ' Clarke murmured, 'Henry II, about Thomas à Becket. Whatever happened to Kenneth Baker?'

It was after midnight when Joshua and Felicity returned to the Grand. They were subjected yet again to a search and found in the foyer a group of people talking in hushed yet excited voices. They included Kenneth Baker and John Gummer with their wives. Terry Dicks, a cheerfully Philistine back bencher and thorn in the pink flesh of the Minister for the Arts, shouted on seeing Joshua, 'Here's the bloody detective. Tell him, Ken, what's happened. He could be of help.'

Baker did not seem to be willing to respond to Dicks's suggestion, so Joshua went over and asked him.

'You'll know soon enough,' said Baker, a touch ungraciously, 'so I might as well tell you. Amaranth Wilikins is dead. We found her body on the beach fifteen minutes ago; the police have been summoned and are on the strand now. As to how she was killed I have not the slightest idea. She seemed very wet.'

Baker was then joined by two senior police officers and a plain clothes man (his private detective?) and they all went swiftly upstairs. They were bracing themselves to meet the attentions of the media. After all that had happened . . . now this.

There were several moments of stunned silence. Felicity, white at the gills, sat down and Joshua hurried to bring her brandy and water. Mrs Dicks was crying. Mesdames Gummer and Baker made their excuses and left. Their shoes were covered with wet sand.

'We'd been out to dinner,' said Terry Dicks. 'We were walking back along the beach and found her sitting in a chair under the old, ruined pier. The tide was coming in and we had to wade out to see who it was.' Dicks presented his muddy shoes and socks for inspection. 'Ken's security man radioed for help, and the fuzz are down there now.'

He looked shocked, as well he might be. Joshua brought over two more brandies. Felicity, her colour restored, whispered to Joshua that it would be sensible to visit Amaranth's room, and see if it were possible to find her calendar, a list of her engagements, and whether anyone had called to see her.

Unconvinced, Joshua went over to the reception and asked for the number of Mrs Wilikins's room. The girl behind the counter intoned, 'Mon Repos, 14 Gardner Street, although she lives here most of the day.' She was dabbing on nail polish remover with a tiny brush. Perhaps, thought Joshua, it would be wiser to telephone; the police would in all likelihood have gone there already, and he did not wish to invite a snub. The girl gave him the number, and Joshua dialled.

It was answered by a youngish-sounding man with a pansy voice. There were several minutes of consternation and then consultation with someone else. Eventually the youngish voice returned, and said he had absolutely nothing to say. 'Are you the police?'

Joshua said that he was a Tory MP anxious to help in any way.

'Nosey Parker!' cried the voice, and the telephone was slammed down.

'We would not be made welcome at "Mon Repos",' Joshua reported to Felicity, 'but unless they are out-of-work actors of some standing, I don't think they had anything to do with Amaranth's death. They seemed terribly upset.'

Joshua ordered a cab for the drive back to Wenlock Manor. Outside, on the opposite side of the front, an ambulance and three police cars were drawn up, their blue, swivelling lights illuminating the small crowd that had gathered to gawp. As they climbed into the back of the cab, three men could be seen putting something on a stretcher into the back of the ambulance.

'Poor Amaranth,' said Felicity. Joshua put his arm around her.

'More trouble?' asked the driver. 'We had enough of it last night. I wish you bloody – no disrespect – politicians would stay away. You bring nothing but trouble with you.'

Joshua remained silent. He had no wish to encourage the driver.

'Do you think anyone will ask you to help this time, like John MacGregor did when Emma Kerr was killed last year?' asked Felicity.

'I doubt it very much,' said Joshua, 'but it would be fun to keep our hand in. We'll get up early and return to the Grand for breakfast.'

'You are a Nosey Parker,' laughed Felicity, 'and no one will thank you for it.'

Friday

By lunchtime on Thursday the morale of the Party's 7,000 'representatives' (no one is delegated at Tory Party conferences) is at its highest. Routine has taken over; oratory carries with it its own addiction. And there is a certain comfort to be won from the presence of so many of the like-minded. Lubricated by alcohol and warmed by good-fellowship, at Thursday lunchtime Tories are at their best, prepared to show charity, if not to the Smiths and Goulds of this world, then at least to the Attlees, Wilsons and Callaghans. Some even have a good word to say for Tony Benn.

Friday lunch, on the other hand, has an air of departure, of finality, about it; of the need to rally one's strength to meet the challenge of the Leader's speech, due to be delivered at two-thirty in the afternoon, a performance that is the climax of four days of sustained enthusiasm, and which can be as draining as an orgasm.

Lady Thatcher with her remorseless uplift and brassy self-confidence was to the taste only of the most committed (many of whom were bussed in from the neighbouring countryside). In her day there used to be what came to be called 'the flight of the MPs'; the hurried departure of the more faint-hearted of the Tribunes who, breaking through the police cordon thrown around the arena, ostensibly for its protection, made for home before the first blast of the trumpet.

John Major was more downbeat and altogether less demanding. Sleep, which had been impossible in Queen Margaret's Golden Days, came more easily under the new dispensation.

Norman Fowler was awake long before the arrival at seven o'clock of the day's newspapers. The heavies all carried large photos of Jeffrey Archer, whose 'death' and subsequent resurrection were the subject not only of the lead stories but of much irreverent comment from the 'funnies' within. Craig Brown, Miles Kington and Andrew Rawnsley had all spread themselves having fun at Archer's and the Conservative Party's expense. Auberon Waugh had suggested a lying-in state in Westminster Hall, the four corners of the coffin guarded by the managers of the largest branches of W.H. Smith's.

The obituary pages, which had obviously been cleared to carry long appreciations of the author, written by his enemies, were full of the obits of Peruvian poets, Dutch tulip-bulb-growers, and retired Belgian station-masters. It had not been an easy day.

The tabloids, which go to bed much later than their more respectable cousins, led with photos of Amaranth when alive, and of her shrouded body arriving at the Brighton General Hospital. The *Sun* shouted 'Outrage at Brighton', and the *True Brit*, which carried Amaranth's life story 'written by her own fair hand', carried only one nude photograph, but the coarse screen had done nobody justice. It was, the tabloids agreed, a clear case of murder most foul.

The Brighton Constabulary were making their inquiries, and were concerned that the end of the Party conference, scheduled for three-thirty on Friday afternoon, would disperse so many potential witnesses across the country. Anyone who could help the police to account for Amaranth's movements that evening should quickly get in touch with them. The fact that the body had been discovered by a former Home Secretary was commented upon unfavourably by the *Mirror*.

As he read the papers, Fowler was cast into gloom. The Tory Party conference, for so long the model of how these esoteric functions ought to be conducted, had turned into a 'soap' in which the bit players had stolen the limelight while the 'stars' of the show, accustomed as they were to respectful admiration, had been regularly upstaged. There was not even a photograph of Michael Heseltine and the reports of his conference speech were, at best, perfunctory.

Fowler, with the help of Michael Portillo, had been up half the night writing John Major's end of conference speech. Once the whole bloody circus was over, Norman would retire to his cottage in Northampton post-haste. Never again would he seek solace at a seaside resort out of season.

Joshua and Felicity, too, had slept badly. They drove silently by cab into Brighton, having arranged with the L'Hermittes to stay over Friday night, and to dine in. They had to wait half an hour to be served breakfast at the Grand, where the news of Amaranth's death had caused a decently modulated consternation.

'A damned bad show,' was the view of a retired Grenadier. Nora de Crespigny was very upset. There was a move by her, and many others, to demand an emergency motion at the morning conference (which is in normal times given over to a series of mini-debates, the subjects of which are actually chosen by the rank and file) in favour of the return of capital punishment for murder. Others, of a like mind, wished to amend the motion to include the return of the rod. There was much to-ing and fro-ing between tables, and signatures penned on pieces of paper.

Joshua ordered a kipper and instantly regretted it. Felicity read her *Times* and toyed with an expatriate croissant. 'The police,' said Morris, 'will have the hell of a job. They will have to go back over all Amaranth's movements since Monday night, and try to trace with whom she had been seen, wining, dancing and dining. I doubt if she was ever alone, day or night. It says here [pointing to the *Telegraph*] that she had apparently been drowned, and her body placed on the deck chair later. It could have been an accident, or even suicide; it does not have to have been murder.'

'It might have been manslaughter,' said Felicity. 'She hadn't gone swimming – she was wearing a dress. An accident is most unlikely. And why on earth should she kill herself? In three days she had made herself the Belle of the Ball, or the Toast of the Town.'

'Adverse publicity?' said Joshua. 'I wonder what the tabloids make of her this morning.' He went out into the hall and brought back the *Sun*, *Star*, *Mirror* and *True Brit*, which carried her life story. Joshua began to read.

'It teeters on the verge of libel,' he said. 'Not the sort of thing she would have enjoyed reading about herself.

Especially if she were daft enough to have written it. I wonder whether she did?'

'The only people who might tell us anything are those two out-of-work actors at "Mon Repos",' said Felicity. 'I know they called you a Nosey Parker but let's chance our arm. If we can establish our good intentions, they may help us.'

They agreed that was a good idea and on the way out of the hotel, Joshua asked Tom Arnold if he had seen anything of Amaranth during the week.

'Only in the line of duty,' was the response, 'but she did have lunch with old Grunte on Tuesday at Langan's Bistro. But he couldn't hurt a fly unless it were stationary.'

The *prominenti* in the Grand Hotel were gathering their strength and papers, and setting out for the conference hall. The mood was sombre, and a winter's wind and a cold sea accompanied them in their struggle along the front. What had previously been a stroll in the sunshine, had become a chilly dash from door to door. The more brazen stole lifts in ministerial cars, while the faint-hearted remained behind in the warmth to watch the proceedings on the hotel's many television sets.

Joshua and Felicity decided to wait some moments in the hotel until the crush was over. They could then take a cab to Gardner Street.

They sat in the corner of the lounge. Felicity asked Joshua if he had still got Amaranth's note, and they re-examined it.

' "Sneeped"?' said Joshua.

'Nobody would use that expression unless they were from the Midlands,' said Felicity.

'Very large, the Midlands.'

'More specifically,' said Felicity, 'the Potteries. Very small, the Potteries. I wonder whom she had been seeing since Monday night. She had so much publicity of one sort or another it should not be too difficult to make a list of her suitors.'

Joshua, spotting a cab for hire, led Felicity into the gale.

The door of 'Mon Repos', a pretty, if small, Regency house on three floors, was opened by a middle-aged man wearing a designer-butcher's apron. His visitors asked politely if they could enter and were shown into the drawing room. They introduced themselves as friends of Amaranth's. The apron seemed to recognise Joshua Morris's name and shouted for Lancelot to join them.

'My partner,' he explained. 'We've run "Mon Repos" for the past ten years ever since Lance ruptured himself at the Old Vic.' Lancelot was the younger of the two; he had a feather duster in one hand and a copy of the *Independent* in the other.

'What a terrible shame,' he cried. 'We were fond of Amaranth, weren't we? A lovely lady. Who could have thought of doing her in?'

The elder, whose name was Stephen, muttered something about an unpaid bill, but the point was not taken up. They offered coffee, and did their best to be helpful. 'Sorry about the Nosey Parker bit when you rang last night,' said Lance. 'I thought you were from the *True Brit*.'

It appeared that Ron Barton had been the bane of Amaranth's life. He was the one who had written what purported to be Amaranth's life story in today's edition of the rag. Joshua and Felicity said they had read it.

'She didn't write it, of course,' said Lance. 'That swine

Barton did, even though she begged him not to. Did you know he assaulted her? He had also dug up some naughty pictures of Amaranth in the buff, taken from a skin-mag of some sort or other.' Lance gestured towards a coffee table on which there lay copies of *Field*, *The Stage* and the *Sussex Magazine*. 'Not our sort of publication.'

Felicity asked whether Ron or anyone else had rung for Amaranth or had been round to 'Mon Repos' in pursuit of her.

'Ron was often on the phone,' Lance replied. 'He offered her a lot of money at one stage to go exclusive, but I don't know what the outcome of that was. And there was a tall, good-looking man of about thirty-five brought her back here late on Tuesday night after that kerfuffle in the Grand, but I don't know his name. Fair-haired. Looked a bit like the young Jack Watling. Do you remember Jack? Used to play Spitfire pilots and younger sons in red MGs. Now appears as Nestor in bloody "Bergerac". Time's winged chariot and all that.'

Felicity said she recalled seeing him in black and white on BBC2. 'Who else?' she asked.

'Another bloke came round yesterday afternoon with a note for her, but I said she was not to be disturbed,' said Stephen. 'Lance put her to bed with a hotty at lunchtime, she was so upset, but I must admit that after two hours' kip and a cup of Earl Grey, and a bath, she seemed as right as rain. Put on her glad rags and made off. Probably back to the Grand Hotel.'

Joshua asked them for a description of the second visitor.

'Common-looking,' said Stephen, 'the sort you get coming to Conservative conferences nowadays. Dark, middle-aged, quite trim, name of Swan.'

They were shown over Amaranth's room – the police had rung to say nothing was to be touched – and given a conducted tour of the 'public rooms'. Joshua and Felicity agreed that 'Mon Repos' was both pretty and very comfortable.

'We do dinner, too,' said Lance. 'B&B from £20 single, £35 double; dinner sixteen quid.' A card was pressed into Felicity's hand and they were shown off the premises with cries of goodwill.

'I would be quite happy to stay there,' said Felicity, as they struggled against a rising east wind. 'Back to the Grand.'

Angela Cartwright woke on the Friday morning with feelings of guilt and indecision. The guilt was not so much due to the encouragement she had given Sir Ralph (it was difficult for her to think of Grunte just as 'Ralph') – she was, after all, on holiday, and it had been a very long time indeed since anyone had made her anything remotely resembling a proposition. The guilt was due to her ill temper when Grunte had admitted to her that he had 'disposed of her blasted hat'.

She was perhaps too touchy about her hat. Her sister had said last Christmas that it didn't suit her complexion. The local YCs had stuck it on a pole in the course of her visit to their dance in Arden that summer and paraded around the floor with it, until the Member had stepped in and handed it back to her. Perhaps her bad temper was due to 'having drink taken', for Angela drank little, save for an occasional sweet sherry and nothing whatsoever at lunch.

Her indecision sprang from her growing doubts about

what to do about Grunte's de-selection. She began to
regret that she had summoned a meeting in her room at
the Queen's Hotel for ten o'clock that morning. When it
came to Grunte's future, better the devil you know . . .

At ten o'clock the conspirators assembled in her
room, squatting on the side of her narrow bed, and
sitting uncomfortably on hard chairs. The hotel
resounded to the sound of vacuum cleaners.

Paul Franklin thought Grunte should go. Leroy Burns
said that Grunte's enemies would have to reckon with
him. Hyacinth Scragg ('I can only drop in for a moment,
I'm "on air" at ten-thirty') said something about sleeping
dogs.

The Swans seemed surprisingly undecided. David,
who certainly looked the worse for wear, his face
covered with wisps of cotton wool where he had cut
himself shaving, said that if it came to a Special General
Meeting he might well vote against Grunte, but that he
would not be one of the fifty signatories. 'A row of this
kind would do the Party in Arden no good at all.' At
this, Paul Franklin read out aloud the letter that Swan
had written in last week's *Recorder* calling for the MP's
de-selection. The meeting listened in silence.

'Has he given you a job, too?' Franklin asked Swan
offensively. 'Hit by the slump in property? And what
about Grace's bum? It's become public property as it is.'

There was a general intake of breath. Carole Swan
hissed at her husband to control himself, and, with an
obvious and even alarming effort, David Swan managed
to do so.

Only Leroy laughed. 'Poor Grace. I'm the only one of
you what's entitled to be both black and blue.' At this
sally the Malcolms looked embarrassed.

Hyacinth laughed merrily and left the room. 'I'm for Grunte,' was her parting shot. 'Take care.'

Conscious of her duties as chairman of the meeting, Angela Cartwright turned to Janet Malcolm, who was rummaging in her shoulder bag for a sweetie. What did she think? 'Kev and I have been giving it a lot of thought.' She was still full of cold. 'We think we should give Sir Ralph another chance, but that you, Mrs Cartwright, should write him a stiff letter as to his future conduct. We want him to spend more time in the constituency, and indeed more time in the House of Commons. He must drink less, lose some weight and stop' – here she looked coyly at Kev – 'chasing the girls. And at his age! Don't you think so, Angela? Shouldn't a letter like that come from you?'

Leroy was looking out of the window, David Swan was examining his finger nails, Kev Malcolm was admiring his wife, and Carole Swan was staring at Angela Cartwright. Couldn't get it up, could he, she thought grimly.

Mrs Cartwright said she thought that it would be an extremely good idea, and that it was plain that there was not a majority among the officers for any attempt at getting rid of Grunte. 'I'm not sorry,' she said. 'Lord Wakeham told me yesterday that he didn't know what the Party would be like without Sir Ralph.'

Firmly, she closed the meeting.

The long queue of conference-goers waited impatiently before the necessary fumble for security. A large man of battered appearance complained bitterly that terrorists had been permitted to bring everything to a grinding halt. 'We are too soft,' he asserted. 'We should string 'em up.'

Two frail elderly ladies with blue hair moved up and down the lines of the waiting Tories selling raffle tickets for the East Grinstead Conservatives' Christmas Bring and Buy. The first prize was dinner at No. 10 with Norma and John Major. Dutifully, everyone paid up. Some studied their conference agendas, booklets plump with advertisements from industrialists in search of knighthoods and with a raft of 'motions for debate' submitted by constituency parties up and down the country that had not been starred by Central Office for discussion. The Tories of Reigate had demanded that 'this Conference would like to see the teaching of the National Anthem compulsory at all schools and for it to be sung on special occasions'. The occasions were not specified. There were several in a similar vein.

Many others read their *Telegraph*s, sharing Charles Moore's dismay and Oliver Pritchett's whimsy. Having at last passed underneath the metal detector they picked up pace, only to be checked by Virginia and Peter Bottomley who had stationed themselves at the door leading directly into the conference ante-room. They were handing out small packets of contraceptives as part of the campaign against Aids. Peter had a cheery, and Virginia a kind, word for everyone.

The unmarked packets were not immediately recognised for what they were. Some, believing them to be sweets, were suitably grateful; others, who supposed them to be a promotional material on behalf of a privatised industry such as BT, put them away soundlessly in bag or pocket. A Sapper General in his seventies gave his packet back to the Bottomleys, wondering loudly what on earth the world was coming to? Such largesse was too much of a good thing. Whenever he had wanted any of the damn things he had had his hair cut. He had reached the time of life when, if he were obliged to travel, he did so only with toothbrush and paste.

John Major would not be there until the afternoon. He had made a request that, this morning, he should on no account be disturbed. He was doing his exercises. With his eyes closed, he breathed deliberately and relaxed the muscles of his legs. The Brixton Method had much to be said for it.

After his exercises he ordered breakfast in bed (Norma was spending the morning in Peacehaven, talking to its senior citizens), but Kenneth Baker felt it necessary to report to him the news of the discovery of Amaranth Wilikins's body. John Major went into spasms. Recovering, he told Gummer to take care of the details: make statements of regret to the press, inform the next of kin, etc. And Gummer would represent him at the funeral. Useful chap, Gummer. Every Cabinet should have one.

He then read Fowler's draft of the speech that he was due to make at the conference rally at two-thirty that afternoon. It read really very well. There was a bit about classlessness and even more about the Citizen's Charter. There was even a hint that in future he would be less free with the twice-yearly honours list which his predecessors had used, sometimes outrageously, to reward placemen, sycophants and the time-expired. Portillo, who was a clever fellow, had included a telling quote from Robert Peel: 'The honour of the unadorned name.'

Major would, of course, make use of the 'magic mirrors', the American device introduced into this country by a man who had once worked for Billy Graham, enabling the speaker to read, unseen by his audience, the text of his speech. It took a bit of getting used to, and the text had been known to stick. It was like riding a bike with no hands, exhilarating once you had mastered it.

Changes had been made in the afternoon's proceedings since Margaret's day. John Major had stood down the six trumpeters of the Blues and Royals who had blown Lady Thatcher a regal welcome. Vera Lynn had not been invited to entertain the meeting before the Leader's arrival singing 'The White Cliffs of Dover', and there was to be no barrage of a thousand blue balloons, each one bearing the leader's name which, in Margaret's time, had been released from nets suspended from the ceiling. The Young Conservatives had applied their fag-ends to many of them, and the proceedings had, on one occasion, ground to a halt to the accompaniment of a volley of 'shots'. It had been likened by unsympathetic journalists to the overthrow of a banana republic.

The compulsory standing ovation was proving more difficult to do away with. In Margaret's time it had lasted more than ten minutes, and had been timed to the second by hacks standing with stop-watches, a measurement used to compare one year's performance with another.

'We want the meeting', John Major told the officers of the National Union of Conservative and Union Associations in July, 'to be more like Norwood than Nuremburg.'

Major's bedside telephone gave a modest buzz and a red light started to flash. It was Lady Thatcher.

'John?' Her voice had that gritty quality which suggested that she was in no mood to stand for any nonsense. 'Is that you?'

Major admitted that it was indeed he. 'I am doing my exercises.'

'I've had Dame Vera Lynn on the phone. She is most upset. I gather you have cancelled her engagement this afternoon. It is most reprehensible. What is more she is threatening to take her account away from Dickins and Jones. I shall not put up with it. And will there be balloons?'

Major sighed. 'Margaret,' he said, 'you have left Downing Street. I am Her Majesty's First Minister. I do not want Vera Lynn and her bloody blue birds. And I hate balloons.' There was a silence from the other end of the line. Major hastened to fill it.

'Margaret,' he said, 'have you thought any more about my offer of the Governorship of the Falkland Islands? The climate, I am told, is rather like the North-east of Scotland, but the natives are friendly.' There was the noise of a receiver being replaced.

Major returned to his exercises only to be interrupted ten minutes later. It was his Principal Private Secretary. 'Lady Thatcher is determined to take the chair for your meeting this afternoon. She says she has a message for the nation. What am I to tell her?' Major, abandoning any further attempt to relax, leapt from his bed.

'Find John Wakeham, and ask him to go and have a word with her. She won't listen to anyone else.'

Back at the Grand, Joshua and Felicity ordered coffee, serving themselves from a scaldingly hot metal pot. Several uniformed policemen were standing about the foyer of the hotel, which was unusually full of Tories for the time of day, the weather having discouraged them from attempting the 200-yard dash to the conference centre so they sat gloomily watching on TV a parade of speakers mount the rostrum, their soundless gestures conducting an invisible orchestra.

'I bet Inspector Morse would have solved the crime by now,' said Felicity. 'Let's go over what we know.' It did not amount to much. Amaranth had in three days lunched with Grunte, dined with Harvey, been persecuted by Ron Barton, and pursued by David Swan. Any one of them might have been responsible for her death, whether deliberately or not.

'What was the motive?' wondered Joshua. 'She was beautiful but not inviolable. If I were to be unkind I might say that she gave every appearance of treating the Party conference as if it were a casting-couch. She had no money; I gather she was broke. I was told she did some part-time modelling, and dabbled for a time in Public Relations in that firm run by John Gummer's brother. I suppose she might have been killed out of jealousy, by someone whose favours she had refused, or she might have been blackmailing someone.'

'She could have had something other people wanted very badly, besides her body,' said Felicity, 'although I have no idea what that could be. Look! There's Grunte. Ask him to join us for a cup of coffee. He did take her out to lunch.'

Joshua was at best only a nodding acquaintance of Sir Ralph's, but he grinned broadly in Grunte's direction and invited him to take coffee. Grunte came over and, bowing low over Felicity, kissed her hand with all the aplomb of a stage Italian. He was wearing a red tie with horses' heads on it and seemed to be in a very good mood indeed.

'No conference this morning?' asked Joshua.

'I have had my fill of speechifying,' said Grunte magisterially. 'Too much cant.'

Felicity said how awful it was about poor Amaranth, such a pretty woman. They remained silent, waiting for Grunte to tell them about his lunch. But all he said was, 'A very bad business.' He blew his nose loudly, and peered into his handkerchief. He then looked directly at Joshua.

'You drive an old Rover don't you, Morris? A "D" registration 825?'

Joshua said he did. The Japanese engine had made all the difference to Rover cars.

'Trade it in, dear boy,' said Grunte. 'I'll give you a fair deal. Great mistake to drive a motor in our line of country with more than fifty thousand miles on the clock. Let you down some dark night on the motorway. All right if you're a woman on your own, they'll come and fetch you pronto. They won't do it for us blokes. You can sit on the hard shoulder ringing up for hours.'

'Did Amaranth drive a Rover?' asked Felicity winningly.

'A Fiat,' said Grunte dismissively.

'Any idea how she met her end?' asked Joshua, desperately.

'You don't have to drive the car to Arden, you know,' said Grunte. 'I've got a London depot. Fix the whole thing up over the telephone and deliver a new car straight to your door. Sold one to Anthony Beaumont Dark only the other week.' Joshua thanked Grunte for the suggestion and said he would consider it seriously.

'Just had some good news,' said Grunte, confidingly. 'You may have heard I've had some trouble with my lot in Arden? Always whingeing about something. All over and done with. We've kissed and made up. Took a stern line with 'em.'

Sir Ralph looked at his watch. 'I'm expecting my niece any moment, a sweet child. We are going to look at the Pavilion – a bit of culture you know – and then we're going out to a slap-up lunch.' As he spoke, a girl of about sixteen in school uniform, pretty with ginger hair, a grin and freckles, came into the lounge. 'Here's Amanda,' said Grunte. 'We must be off. Lovely to have made your acquaintance,' he said to Felicity. 'Don't forget about the motor.'

He placed an avuncular arm around the girl's waist, and they moved in stately fashion towards the door. Amanda gave them a wave.

'Bloody old Grunt,' said Joshua. 'He took us to the cleaners. We ought to go round to the Hospitality Inn and see if Amaranth did, in fact, turn up at eight last night. And if she did, with whom? I think we can safely leave the Party conference to the delegates.'

The lounges of the Grand were full of weather-shy Tories, some sleeping gently, others watching the debates on television. Joshua opened a glass door leading to the main lounge and sound immediately reinforced the picture on television. 'Far too many of our policemen are being shot,' proclaimed Geoffrey Dickens MP, a colleague who had once gone nine rounds with Don Cockell, the old heavyweight champion.

'How many does he think would be about right?' asked Joshua. 'I would have thought that one would be one too many.' The Friday morning conference free-for-all provided a sort of political dustbin in which the dotty and distressed were permitted to have their say.

Joshua and Felicity took a cab to the Hospitality Inn.

As they passed through security, they noticed Charles Harvey in the hallway talking to a tiny man in grey shoes, wearing a dirty mac. It was Ron Barton. They seemed to be having some sort of row.

The Hospitality Inn is a hideously modern edifice built round a central sky-lighted well, with swimming pools, solariums and all the latest American vulgarities. It reminded Joshua either of an airport or of the Princess Margaret Private Hospital in Windsor where he had once been taken for a scan: four stars in Beverly Hills. It had a reputation for comfort (was not Lady Thatcher a guest?), but at £250 a night for a suite one could expect no less. He had been told that its restaurant, La Noblesse, was good; good enough indeed for Ralph Grunte to have entertained his delegation there for dinner.

They had no luck with their inquiries. The Manager was 'on leave' and his deputy had not been on duty the previous evening. The girls behind the desk were svelte but unhelpful; they, too, went off at six p.m., and the second shift would not be available until later that afternoon.

The Head Porter in a brown uniform coat, top hat and yellow spats reminded Joshua Morris of his colleague Nicholas Fairbairn, whose curious habit it was to design his own clothes. He did remember seeing a smart blonde woman who might well have been Amaranth Wilikins ('the one what took off her clothes?') but he could not remember whom she was with. He had not spotted her leaving the hotel. Joshua and Felicity tried the Brasserie, but it was too early to get much sense out of the few waiters who were busily laying tables. None of them spoke French, let alone English, while the doors of La

Noblesse, tucked away in the bowels of the building, were still locked and barred. Frustrated, they returned to the lounge and ordered yet more coffee.

'Joshua Morris?' A tallish man, with an Ian Botham moustache, and wearing a greenish suit, presented himself.

'I'm Paul Franklin. You don't know me, but I know all about you. "The Shropshire Sleuth" and all that. You were mixed up with the Emma Kerr business in the House of Commons, weren't you? Are you taking an interest in what happened to Amaranth?'

Joshua admitted cautiously that he might be.

'What line are you taking?' asked Franklin.

'I suppose the most important thing is to find out with whom she spent her time.'

'Well, there's that bugger Swan for starters, I can tell you all about him,' said Franklin. A third cup of coffee was ordered, and Franklin, having dropped four lumps of sugar into his cup, unburdened himself. 'I'm from Arden, one of Ralph Grunte's little lot, although I have no time for him.'

Joshua closed ranks. MPs do tend to stick together in public whatever their private views about each other might be.

'I work for Jaguars in Coventry. I have known Swan, on and off for years, mainly "off", but I do know something about his background. Are you interested?'

Joshua admitted that they would both be very interested indeed. 'Fire away,' commanded Felicity. Franklin added a fifth lump of sugar.

'Dave Swan – the David came later – was from Burslem originally. Very ordinary background, council house, father worked for the council as a gardener. As a

young man, eighteen or nineteen, he laid his hands on a
JCB, an earth-mover. Some people said he pinched it.
Anyway, he set up in business on his own. Prospered
too, I gather. After five years or so, his company
demolished a listed building, a seventeenth-century
black and white manor house, near Eccleshall, I think,
one Sunday morning. Much local outrage and newspaper
publicity. Got away with it, and he must have made a
couple of hundred thousand on the deal.

'Anyway, he moved his business to Birmingham, and
got married to Carole – big busty woman, one of our
Arden crowd. He leads her quite a dance. He was made
Mayor of Arden a few years ago. Carole's been back
there twice this week already in a huff. First Swan
frightened her to death by jumping out at her from
behind the bedroom door, you probably heard of the
false alarm in the Grand on Tuesday night?'

Joshua said that they had indeed heard all about it.

'Well,' continued Franklin (Felicity was staring at his
bright yellow socks), 'Dave was all over Amaranth
Wilikins, took her out to lunch at some Indian place on
Wednesday, but whether he scored or not I'm not sure.
Perhaps not, as Carole found him in bed with Hyacinth
Scragg on Wednesday night. You know Hyacinth
Scragg? Another one of our delegation. A right goer.'

Felicity said they both knew of her. A very striking
girl. The Arden Tories seemed to be a very lively lot.

'Is Swan still in business in a big way?' asked Joshua.

'He was,' said Franklin. 'He's just the sort who did
well under Mrs T, ruthless, go-getting and greedy. But
the recession has hit him like it has everyone else. You
know what's been happening at Jaguars?'

Morris said he did.

'Swan built a housing estate in the early 1980s, but, as you know, we've put a stop to council house building. He buys up bits of land, builds bungalows that he sells to the old who have small amounts of capital and can pay cash. No need for mortgages and inconvenient gaps between his prices and the mortgage companies' valuations. Did business with Grunte once, but they fell out over something or another. Two of a kind.'

Morris let it pass. He was still smarting a little from his brush with Grunte earlier that morning in the Grand.

'Since when,' Franklin continued, 'he has been trying his best to get rid of Ralph Grunte, writing offensive letters to the local press and making a fuss about Grunte pinching his daughter's backside in the House of Commons. She was lucky that was all that happened to her. But, for some reason, Swan has changed his mind. We had a group meeting earlier this morning at the Queen's Hotel. Grunte is in the clear.'

Felicity murmured something about the news accounting for Grunte's euphoria. 'He's taking his niece out to lunch,' she said.

'His niece?' said Franklin. 'Grunte is a world-class luncher.'

'You don't know whether Swan saw Amaranth Wilikins here in this hotel, early last night?'

Franklin said he didn't, thanked his hosts for the coffee, and made to leave. 'Keep my name out of this,' was his parting shot.

The wind had let up a bit, and racks of cloud hurried over Sussex from the Pas de Calais. Four miserable donkeys passed by in line astern led by an Asian wearing a duffel coat and a fez.

'Make a nice photograph,' said Felicity. 'Arty,

symbolising the end of another wretched season. Just the thing for the *Observer* Review Section.' They changed their minds about walking along the front and took a cab.

'We've got the Labour lot coming here next year,' said the cabbie. 'What on earth will they be getting up to? You're a hard act to follow.'

Joshua was still wearing his photo-pass. 'You'll find the Labour Party to be much more respectable. They still want to build the New Jerusalem; we are much keener on turning it into an Enterprise Zone.'

Back in the womb of the Grand Hotel, they sat for a time in front of one of the many tellies. The Home Secretary was having a hard time. A line of Tories from the floor, each carrying a hangman's noose, were on their feet, waving their ropes and their fists in the direction of the platform. It was an experience that in the past had been sat through by other senior Conservatives, such as Rab Butler, Reggie Maudling and Willie Whitelaw. Hanging was widely believed to be the answer to violent crime, although the evidence for the assertion was clearly lacking.

'If we spent as much time trying to catch criminals, by improving the police force, to say nothing of the legal system, as we do on sadistic visions of public punishment, we'd be a lot better off,' said Joshua pompously. It was not a point of view that went down well with his constituents. Capital punishment was a subject avoided whenever possible by the more sensible Tory MPs.

'Never mind the general, back to the particular,' said Felicity. 'Let's go over what we know and what we don't. Question one: what did Swan want from Amaranth besides her long, white body? Question two: was Swan the last person to see her? Was he the one she left with after her row with Hyacinth? Question three: what part did Charles Harvey play in the affair? Was he just out for a good time? Question four: did Ron Barton want anything more than just digging the dirt?'

'And five,' put in Joshua, 'what about the note?'

John MacGregor, the Minister for Transport, came up to them and said, 'Good morning.' He was wearing a kilt of the Macdonald tartan. Had he ambitions to become Secretary of State for Scotland? God knows there were few enough Scots Tories.

'Have you solved the mystery yet?' he asked. 'The police are thinking of asking everyone to stay on an extra night to help with their inquiries, but the hotels are full. I understand there is a Thames Water sales conference booked in here, plus wives. Or should I say spouses. It's just not on. The fuzz will have to do without us. And I'm due to weekend in Balmoral.'

Joshua and Felicity decided to go their separate ways; Joshua to the conference hall in search of Charles Harvey; Felicity to talk to Ron Barton, whose diminutive figure could be seen in the adjacent lounge, talking into his mobile telephone. They would meet again in the Grand for a light lunch.

By the time Morris had been admitted through the Croatian lines, the debate on capital punishment had come to its bitter end. The motion had been passed by an overwhelming majority, despite the pleas of the platform not to tie their hands, an unhappy phrase which was met with counter-cries of 'tie the knot'. A harassed Kenneth Clarke was being interviewed by Sir Robin Day. Television was making a meal of the remains of poor Amaranth. For the umpteenth time it showed her now famous strip-tease and replayed interviews with her.

Hyacinth Scragg, with hairy Angus and camera crew, fell upon Joshua with happy cries. 'Will you be interviewed, Mr Morris? You are, after all, the President of the Sherlock Holmes Society.' Joshua declined the invitation. His reluctance served only to fuel their enthusiasm, and Hyacinth went on air alone to say that Joshua Morris himself was hot on the track of Amaranth's killer. Joshua watched the 'interview' with growing irritation. The media, who were threshing around in search of some sort of lead – the Brighton Constabulary was proving to be most unhelpful – were desperate for information. The news that he was 'on the scent' would make him the target of every hack in Brighton.

He spotted Charles Harvey in the bookshop talking to the two Fionas. They were hanging on his every word. He went and stood next to Harvey, holding a copy of *Room at the Top?*, John Gummer's autobiography. Harvey, turning his back on the girls, greeted him without pleasure.

'I've no doubt you want to ask me about Amaranth, too,' he said, 'but there's nowt to tell. I bought her dinner, chatted her up at *The Times*' cocktail party, helped write her speech. For your ears only, I rogered her on Wednesday night, but by Thursday I had decided she was too hot to handle. When it comes to the girls I'm a bit of a shit. But then you probably knew that anyway.'

Morris put his face into neutral. 'I don't know how you bloody Ministers find the time. I would have thought you would have no scope for dalliance what with road, rail and Channel tunnel. But then you are still a comparatively young man.'

Harvey looked peeved. His good looks, he had been

told, were of the kind that would last indefinitely.

'You didn't tell her anything that would be of interest to a third party?' Joshua asked.

'What do you take me for, a bloody fool?' was Harvey's reply.

Meanwhile, Felicity, having failed to find another copy of the *True Brit*, was obliged to borrow one from the girl at the reception desk. The front page carried a coloured photograph of Amaranth beneath the headline, 'All Washed Up'. There were two other photos: one of the pier, the other of an ambulance, with its doors open. The centre-spread carried Amaranth's so-called 'life story', with another range of pictures. The bogus account was introduced under the heading, 'World Exclusive from Beyond the Grave'.

Felicity shuddered. What sort of person could buy this poisonous rubbish, let alone make it up? Ron Barton was still visible through the glass doors of the lounge. He was sitting on a bar stool, gazing into space, his little legs a foot from the parquet floor.

Felicity read Amaranth's story.

'I came to Brighton determined to make my mark. My friend Charles Harvey, who is a junior Minister for Transport in charge of Britain's roads programme, gave me a helping hand with my conference speech.

'Charles, as I now call him, is a very handsome man who has set more hearts than mine aflutter. He has become a dear friend. [There was a cross heading in bold type: 'Minister befriends Conference beauty', which could not have pleased the Harveys.]

'Among the busy Tories I have met during the week are Sir Tom Arnold, MP, who was very kind to me,

Norman Fowler, the chairman of the Party, who has asked me to dine with him when the House resumes next week, and Sir Ralph Grunte, the playboy Midlands MP, who played footsie-footsie with me in a smart restaurant and has promised to give me a Rover.

'Who said we Tories are a stuffy lot? Lots of fun and games. I was told that Edwina Currie's feathers were ruffled by my success, but who cares any longer about Eggwina? She's well past her sell-by date . . . '

Edwina won't like that, thought Felicity, not that it now much mattered. She heard a sound, looked up and found Ron Barton standing next to her chair.

'How nice to find someone who actually reads "the comic",' he said. 'Aren't you Joshua Morris's friend?'

'Good friend, actually,' said Felicity. 'Do sit down, I'd love a word with you.'

'Ditto,' said Ron, drawing up a chair. 'Your turn first.'

It soon became obvious that each wanted more from the other than either was prepared to give away. Felicity wanted to discover Amaranth's last movements; Ron Barton wanted to know whether Joshua had been asked to investigate and, if so, by whom, and what progress had been made.

'You're a lot prettier than Dr Watson,' he told her.

'I hope so,' retorted Felicity, 'but I see myself not so much as Dr Watson to Sherlock Holmes, more Tinker to Sexton Blake.'

Barton looked nonplussed. Wasn't Blake a Russian spy?

Felicity told him that Morris had not been asked to investigate – her curiosity was a perfectly natural one. Barton said that if he could get the editor to agree, would Joshua and Felicity be prepared to conduct the investigation on the paper's behalf? There would be money in it for them. Several grand. Felicity said she was sure the answer would be 'no'. Pointing to her copy of the *True Brit*, she asked Barton whether Amaranth had really written her life story. 'We have been told she knew that you were going to write it, and without her permission. She was very distressed.'

Barton shrugged. 'She should have played ball with us. In the end I was left having to write it. Her death has killed it, though. Readers want to know how she came by her end and who did her in.' Barton got to his feet and stood, scratching his backside idly with a Biro.

'Take care,' he said. 'I'm off to find Charles Harvey. He's quite a lad, that one.'

'Which leaves us with David Swan,' Felicity said on Joshua's return from his meeting with Charles Harvey. 'If he's not in the Grand, he could be anywhere in Brighton. His wife's a delegate, of course. She has probably been voting in favour of the rod and the rope. How was Harvey?'

Joshua recounted briefly what had happened. Harvey had said he was a shit where women were concerned, but that he had not been indiscreet.

'In what sense?' asked Felicity. 'Did he mean that he had not flaunted his affair too publicly, or that he had not told her anything which he shouldn't?'

'There was some talk,' said Joshua, 'that Harvey had passed on some information or other about a new motorway. And the press were all given the impression that Harvey had had more than a share in Amaranth's success. He had forced his way into the press room after her strip-tease on Wednesday afternoon in order to

225

rescue her from the *True Brit*.'

'What could he have told her that could have embarrassed him later on? A declaration of love?' said Felicity. 'The actual line of the new motorway?'

'Do lovers talk about lines of new motorways? Not in our day,' said Joshua.

Felicity asked for a glass of white wine from the bar and said that they should think laterally. Joshua said that they had been discouraged from so doing in the Tory Party as the exercise almost always led to a leadership election.

Felicity produced a scrap of paper. 'Look,' she said, 'I have sketched out Amaranth's calendar. Tuesday she lunched with Old Grunte, lucky girl. In the evening she dined with Charles Harvey. Could she have told him something about Grunte that might have been of interest?'

'She was more likely to be seeking information herself,' said Joshua. 'As you know, she was very much in the market for Grunte's seat. And the *True Brit* says Grunte offered her a car, another bloody Rover, no doubt, but he could also have talked business of some kind. Grunte has quite a pay-roll. He is supposed to employ two girls as his Commons researchers, neither of whom can read or write.'

'Has Grunte any other local problems, besides de-selection and all that? Supposing he had an interest in the motorway also? Or that someone wanted to pull down the Stratford Theatre and rebuild it next to the Birmingham Conference Centre.'

'Harvey would know about the roads programme,' said Joshua, 'but planning on the scale you suggest would be a matter for the Department of the Environment, and its left hand never knows what its right hand . . . '

'Darling,' said Felicity, 'go and ring up the press office of the Department of Transport. Ask them what plans they have for the Warwickshire/Arden area. And when such plans are due to be made public.'

Joshua returned with the news, wreathed in smiles. 'You're right. There's a motorway spur designed to connect with the M40. The route has been fixed, the announcement is not due to be made until later this month. The bloke said he would put a map in the post, but not until after the fifteenth of October. Harvey would have known about it. And the route cuts across Grunte's patch all right.'

Felicity consulted Amaranth's calendar.

'Look,' she said, 'Amaranth lunched with Grunte, dined with Harvey, and lunched with David Swan at the Black Chapati on the Wednesday, before her speech. I know that because Ron Barton told me. So, how's this for lateral thinking? Grunte tells Amaranth about his motorway problems – who knows, it might cut his tennis court in two – she tells Harvey who, in turn, and in order to impress her, lets slip the outline of the new route. She then lunches with David Swan who is a local property developer – if Franklin is to be believed – and tells him what Harvey has told her. The question is, does all this give anyone a motive for killing her?'

To which Joshua replied, 'Let's have a sandwich in the bar, and listen to the news on the wireless. We shall dine well tonight at Wenlock Manor. The police are bound to have found out more than we have been able to do.'

The weather forecast is one of the longest five minutes in broadcasting, although more palatable on radio than it can be on television. Lord Reith would certainly not have approved of its mateyness, but then there was little in current broadcasting of which Lord Reith would have approved. He might have sanctioned James Naughtie (provided he appeared before the microphone wearing a dinner jacket) on the grounds that they were both North Britons, but even he would have been thought far too familiar and disrespectful.

The news came directly from Brighton, from the Grand Hotel, itself. 'It has not been a good conference for the Tories,' asserted Naughtie, who then proceeded to interview Tory Party chairmen, past and present.

Fowler said that it *had* been 'on the whole' a good conference. The platform and the Party saw eye to eye on most things. The morning's vote on the restoration of capital punishment was understandable, given the deplorable circumstances of Amaranth Wilikins's death. It would be for Parliament to decide. There had been, it was true, 'little local difficulties'. Jeffrey Archer's vanishing act had not been an altogether welcome diversion. The standing down of Wullie Robertson's Young Conservatives was bound to have happened sooner or later. The party was in good heart, its leaders in good shape, and its policies tailor-made for the British people.

'What a nerve!' remarked Felicity.

Norman Tebbit, a former Party chairman, was then interviewed. His conclusions were roughly the same as Fowler's although they disagreed on everything else. The YCs had been guilty of 'youthful high spirits', Jeffrey Archer's disappearance had 'contributed to the gaiety of nations' and he, for one, welcomed the return of the rope. 'And we have a good Tory, name of Peter

Bruinvels, who has, once again, volunteered to become the public hangman.'

'But he is only four feet, six inches tall,' said Naughtie.

'He can stand on a chair,' was Tebbit's splendid response.

There was, of course, an item about Amaranth's death. The body was believed to be undergoing a pathological examination. Death, the BBC had been reliably informed, was caused by drowning, and there was bruising around the face and head. Until the post-mortem had been made available, the Brighton Constabulary would make no statement, save to say they were concerned to discover Ms Wilikins's whereabouts after she had been seen leaving the foyer of the Metropole Hotel at around 10.15 on Thursday evening. A telephone number was given for those wishing to divulge any information.

Mr Gerald Kaufman, who had been in Brighton covering the Tory conference for the BBC, said that the week, which had begun as a farce, had now ended in tragedy.

'Which is the exact opposite of what has happened to Kaufman,' was the view of a man in a green corduroy jacket standing at the bar. He must have been a journalist.

The last item was frankly speculative. Lady Thatcher had every intention of taking the chair at the meeting this afternoon when John Major, the Party's Leader, was due to give his closing address. The chairman of the conference, Sir Charles Webb-Bowen, whose task it was to preside over the meeting, had announced his willingness to give way to the former Prime Minister, but it was, once again, reliably reported that John Wakeham, acting on a request from John Major, had spent the morning trying to argue Lady T out of her intention.

Whatever the result of the morning's disagreements, it was clear that Margaret Thatcher was no 'back number' to be relegated to the accessories counter of Dickins and Jones and permitted only the occasional foray into political life in order to raise funds for her Foundation.

She was still 'larger than life'. The Conservative Party conference had proved to be one of the most controversial in living memory, dogged by bad luck, claimed Naughtie. 'Are its proceedings now to end with a bang or a whimper?' he concluded.

By two o'clock the conference hall was besieged by eager Tories, many of whom had been bussed in from the hinterland, ready to sit at the feet of the Leader of the Party. Some of the faint-hearted, it was true, had slipped through the police cordon and made for home, feeling that three whole days of politicking were more than enough. It would always be possible to catch John Major's drift as the highlights of his speech were bound to be repeated on every television bulletin that night. An early departure meant a seat on an empty train, or a trouble-free drive back to Gatwick, the M25 and London.

For the more robust who were prepared to stay, the atmosphere within the hall was devotional, tinged with excitement. John Major was no orator, but Tories distrust oratory, preferring the silver spoon to the golden tongue. Let the Michael Heseltines of this world raise the roof; what the Party looked forward to was the truth simply told, as Major had so ably done at the election.

But would Margaret make an appearance? Would she speak, and, if so, what would be her message? Would she rock the boat? The noise level of the hall rose steadily as 7,000 pilgrims waited for the platform party to arrive.

At Brighton the platform is filled from behind as the party's leaders make an entrance from a door on the left of the stage, and pass one by one, to varying degrees of applause, to their places along the platform. John Major would sit in the middle of the dais, flanked by Norman Fowler and the chairman of the conference, or whoever would be taking the chair with the task of introducing the Prime Minister and proposing a vote of thanks. John Gummer would be drawing the raffle, a ceremony which, with its quasi-religious overtones, had long been an essential part of any Conservative Party gathering, large or small. The first prize was an Audi.

One by one the gladiators entered. Some of the *prominenti* went quite unrecognised, such as Ian Lang, Richard Ryder and Peter Lilley. Cranley Onslow, the former chairman of the back bench 1922 Committee, was greeted by a small cheer raised by his relatives. Lord Archer was welcomed, rather rudely in the view of Mrs Nora de Crespigny, by hoots and whistles, a reception to which he responded with a cheery wave of the hand. Sales, he had just been told, were quite definitely up.

It was the opinion of General Sir Brian Wyldebore-Smith, the party's fund-raiser for more than twenty years, that whatever one's view of Archer, the 'feller bobs up like a cork'. The General was sitting in uniform in the gallery. He was later to lead the mass singing of 'Land of Hope and Glory'. Mrs Virginia Bottomley was warmly received, while Michael Howard entered unnoticed. Kenneth Clarke was smoking a cheap cigar.

Once the less important had taken their places, there

was a pause before Michael Heseltine and Douglas Hurd, two members of the triumvirate which controls the destinies of the Party, made their entrance, *main à la main*. Silence fell. As David Dimbleby put it on BBC2, 'You could have heard a pin drop.'

The silence was broken by an unmistakable voice that came from behind the entrance door. 'Let them know I'm coming.'

A hand came round the door, and then slowly, magnificently, as it was later reported, appeared the figure of Margaret Thatcher. She was dressed in flowing white robes and a red cloak and she carried a trident in her right hand. On her head was a brass helmet of the sort once worn by provincial fire brigades.

'A party,' she had told John Cole, 'deprived of Dame Vera Lynn, must not be denied its Britannia.'

'Thank God it's all over.' Such were the prayers said by leading Tories as they sank into the back of black Rovers, the careful hands of their lady-drivers tucking tartan rugs around their bony knees. The convoy, with its escort of police cars, marked and unmarked, made its way through Brighton on to the London Road.

'All that noise and, my dear, the people,' said John Gummer, aping the famous comment of a Guards officer who had been evacuated from Dunkirk.

Norman Fowler said that Margaret's performance had been the last straw. He had been obliged to give a brief press conference once the former Prime Minister had been led away from the platform by men in white coats. She had gone quite easily.

'Overwork' had been the first explanation. There had been stocktaking at Dickins and Jones, and the pressures of a nine to five job, when coupled with international fund-raising, were known to be very great. Off the record, strictly off the record, Fowler had suggested that Lady Thatcher might be 'one Taco short of a combination platter', an Americanism which quite defeated John Cole. In fact, Margaret had been taken to a retreat near Basingstoke where she would be spending time in 'Rest and Recreation'.

On top of everything, the magic mirrors, the bloody speech-machine, had stuck, and there were parts of John Major's oration that had been extempore. As happened under Margaret, policy had perforce been made once again 'on the hoof'. As the convoy of weary fugitives breasted the Downs, John and Norma relaxed in the style of Brixton. 'Start with your big toe, dear,' said Norma, 'and work steadily upwards. And don't worry. I'm sure it won't matter much that you have committed the Party to the privatisation of the Monarchy. Rupert Murdoch, or "Tiny" Rowland are bound to put in a bid. And there is always Hanson. We are lucky it can't be Robert Maxwell.'

'Buried beneath a mound of olives,' Major murmured.

Joshua and Felicity returned to Wenlock Manor in the early afternoon. They watched the beginning of John Major's speech, and Margaret's demonstration. 'Poor woman,' said Felicity, 'she did so much for us.' They fell asleep, made love, and fell asleep again.

Over Madame L'Hermitte's farewell dinner (scallops in pasta, salad, and *îles flottantes* with a bottle of Gewürz, Cuvée Anne, Schlumberger '89), they were joined by a Detective Inspector. He was in plain clothes and, for a policeman, quite humble. He did not have the rustic simplicity of Wexford, or the public school gloss of Dalgleish. Had Mr Morris and his companion any ideas about what might have happened to Ms Amaranth Wilikins? He understood that they had a small reputation for being good in his line of work. Felicity beamed with pleasure. The policeman accepted a glass of wine.

Joshua and Felicity ran quickly through the events of the past three days, and listed those who, in their view, had some grounds, however slight, for desiring Amaranth's disappearance from the scene. Of course, her threat to write articles for the *Daily Mirror* about her adventures in Brighton had been a danger to Grunte, Barton, Swan, Harvey, and anyone else with whom she had been in contact.

Joshua advised the Inspector to make inquiries about the route of the new motorway and about David Swan's development plans in Arden. He asked whether the pathologist's report had been prepared yet.

'Not yet,' said the inspector, 'we only have a preliminary report. And we're in trouble there. It seems certain that she either fell or was pushed from the pier into the sea. There is an unaccounted for bruise on her forehead. It could have been the result of a blow, or she could have struck her head on a strut of the pier as she fell.

'There was no water in the lungs, but that does not necessarily mean that she was not alive when she hit the water. The sudden shock of unexpectedly hitting cold water has stopped many hearts, and in these cases death can be instantaneous. She was wearing an evening dress, and nothing else.'

'What about the contents of the stomach?' asked Joshua.

'She had eaten clams,' was the response. 'There's a lot of shell fish sold in Brighton, and we've yet to establish where she ate them.'

'Good God,' said Joshua, 'just like Bob Maxwell.'

The Inspector looked grave. 'We want to know who she was with last night and, whether or not he had a motive to kill her. On the other hand she could have fallen into the sea. Or she could have committed suicide. And who was it who fished her body out of the sea and plonked it down on the deck chair. The killer, or a tidy-minded passer-by?'

Joshua refilled the Inspector's glass and asked Felicity to show the policeman the message that Joshua had rescued on Thursday night from behind the wastepaper basket in the lounge of the Grand Hotel. The Inspector examined the piece of paper. 'Sneeped?' he said. 'What on earth does that word mean?'

'Miffed,' said Felicity, 'but that is the whole point. The word is very significant indeed. It is in common usage in and around the Potteries in North Staffordshire. But nowhere else. Look, we've been doing some research. We have spent the earlier part of the afternoon checking with the reference room at the House of Commons. Grunte was born in Bridgwater, Somerset – only later did he move to Brum; Harvey, in Chelsea Reach; Barton, as far as we can tell, in Catford, in South London. None of them ever came from Staffordshire, and certainly not from the Potteries.

'But Amaranth went to the Obadiah Sherratt High School for Girls in Burslem, headmistress a Mrs P. Halfpenny, and David Swan was born and bred in Burslem, the rough end of the Potteries. When Swan wrote "sneeped" Amaranth and he, and only those two, knew what they were talking about. It was as good as code.'

The Inspector thanked them, took Amaranth's salvaged message from Felicity and placed it carefully in his wallet, made his apologies and left. Felicity and Joshua returned to their bedroom and switched on the telly to listen to the ten o'clock news on ITN. It was much as they had expected. John Major had put the record straight about the Monarchy. There was no question of the Sovereign being put in the private sector. John Cole, misquoting Fowler, had gone on about Margaret being one sandwich short of a picnic. Joshua switched it off and climbed into bed.

'Where is the conference taking place next year, darling?' asked Felicity.

'Blackpool,' said Joshua. 'Wild horses wouldn't drag me there.'

The Diaspora continued throughout what had become a mild October night. A yellow, Prince Regent's moon hung over the sea, a tribute to the town of illicit love. For four days, more than 7,000 Tories had congregated at Brighton, ostensibly to put the world to rights, in reality to have a jolly good time. By the early evening most would have returned home either by car or train, weary wives to cook an eggy supper, chastened husbands to open a sheaf of assorted and neglected bills. Northern Tories, of hardier stock, swung away from moorland motorways and spoke kindly of past conferences when Lord Woolton had been the chairman of the Party, Lord Hailsham had rung his bell and the Good Lord himself had smiled upon their doings.

'Fings,' said a Teesside alderman in bad cockney, 'ain't what they used to be.'

'You can say that again,' replied his tight-lipped wife.

Sir Ralph Redvers Grunte let himself into an empty 'Copper Beeches' and opened a tin of Campbell's soup and a bottle of Tesco champagne. (Marjorie was with her lover at a Jilly Cooper Evening organised by the Chipping Camden Young Farmers.) As far as he was concerned, the conference had been a remarkable success. He had smitten his enemies, and the threat of de-selection was lifted. And it appeared, from what he had heard on the news, that David Swan was in deep trouble. Something about 'helping the police with their inquiries' in the search for Amaranth's killer. There would be no more letters from him in the *Arden Recorder*. Grunte wondered whether he might not write one himself, calling for the restoration of capital punishment.

The outlook was not altogether rosy – that would be too much to ask. He had been obliged to invite Angela Cartwright to lunch with him at the Commons next week. On the other hand, Amanda had shown great interest in becoming his research assistant. Unlike the two whom he employed already, she could at least add up, even if she could not spell. And he had sold Nigel West a Rover.

He switched on his electric mock coal/log fire, put his feet on the fender and, having undone the buttons of his waistcoat, fell into an easy slumber.

Peter Worthington Evans sat in his flat in Dolphin Square sifting through a pile of photo-passes worn by the House of Commons' secretaries, marking on the back those whom he thought to be uncommonly attractive.

Some of them, at least, would have to be found alternative employment, if scandal were to be avoided.

Would compensation be payable for loss of office? He would ask the Attorney General.

Hyacinth Scragg was entertaining her friends to a breathless account of her successes. After her contretemps with the unlucky Amaranth had been shown on 'Newsnight', she had been obliged to answer questions by the Brighton police. 'They were charm, itself,' she told them. She was, she admitted to her friends, 'really quite famous'. She had been informed by Angus that a contract from TVS was in the post, and a career in telly beckoned.

'I will give in my notice at "Back and Sides",' she told her admirers, 'and, who knows, I might even stand for Parliament.'

'In place of Grunte?' asked someone. Amid laughter, they drank to it in Bulgarian chardonnay.

Jeffrey Archer had gone to bed early, exhausted by his adventures. But sleep evaded him, and in desperation he counted Tory back benchers leaping over stiles in a vain attempt to achieve unconsciousness. He gave up when he got to Sir Donald Thompson. Later, he tried to compose the speech he would deliver at the Guildhall, having won the Booker Prize. That did not work either, so he calculated his royalties instead. In five minutes he was fast asleep.

Sir Brian Wyldebore-Smith and Sir Charles Webb-Bowen dined together at the Carlton Club, sitting under the portrait of Arthur Balfour. 'Damn bad show,' said Sir Brian, who had discarded his uniform. 'Don't know what the party's comin' to.' Webb-Bowen muttered something about a different class of person. The lamb was overdone and the vegetables overcooked but they did not seem to mind. And there was no redcurrant jelly. But the service was properly deferential and they were drinking a Chateau Talbot, '70, the year Ted Heath won the election. 'Thought you did frightfully well with the singin',' said Webb-Bowen. 'Saved the day.' Sir Brian said he had done what he could. He had been taught to cope. 'And what about that bare-arsed lot of Scots?' he asked.

'Took me back to my days at m'Tutor's,' was the reply. 'They should all have been at Eton.'

Angela Cartwright told her husband, Bert, that she had changed her mind about Grunte.

'We don't want to wash our dirty linen in public. Grunte's not a bad old stick, and he's offered you a job.' Bert said he would believe it when he saw it. There had been a parcel waiting for Angela on her return home, a parcel from a Munich-based mail-order firm, which had supplied her hat. It contained a dirndl, as gay and flowery as a Bavarian meadow. Would she dare to wear it for her lunch with Ralph next week at the House of Commons?

Ron Barton clambered into that curious mobile room which at Dulles Airport, Washington DC, serves as a transporter from aircraft to arrival lounge. He had flown Virgin, first class, and had disregarded all the good advice given by the well-meaning never to touch alcohol above ten thousand feet. He was drunk on cheap champagne.

The charge of sexual assault which Amaranth had made against him had, of course, been dropped, as she was the only witness. But there were several reasons why he should quit the United Kingdom, not least his notice which had been served over the telephone by the editor of the *True Brit*.

'You made a proper balls of the Tory Party conference,' he had been told, 'and Kelvin Mackenzie says you are a disgrace to the profession.' A severance cheque of a year's salary was 'in the post'. Barton bought a ticket to Miami, Florida, a city with a certain sort of vice. It was a good base, he thought, for a freelance reporter with his particular gifts.

In the Brighton nick, the genial policeman in plain clothes who had drunk wine with Joshua and Felicity at Wenlock Manor, unlocked the door of the cell where David Swan had spent the last twenty-four hours. The one-time Mayor of Arden was not looking his best.

'It's all right, Mr Swan,' said the detective, 'you're free to leave now.'

'So I should think. What right had you to detain me?'

'It was that word "sneeped" that made us suspicious.'

'But I told you I didn't know what it means.'

'Even if you did,' said the policeman with a sigh, 'it wouldn't really have stood up as evidence against you in a court of law. We are not making any charges. At present.'

Epilogue

From: Det. Inspector
Tomkins

To: Det. Chief
Supt. Arbuckle.

Re the late MS AMARANTH WILIKINS
Further to my previous reports re the above, three weeks
have now elapsed since her death, and I have to report
that the investigation into the circumstances surrounding
it is no further forward. It seems unlikely that any
further progress will be made.

As you know, the pathologist's post mortem report
confirms the preliminary medical findings, so we are no
further forward as to the cause of death. Yesterday the
Coroner recorded an open verdict.

Ms Wilikins's death could have been the result of:

(a) Accident. She could have had a heart attack, and
hit her head when she fell over the pier.

(b) Suicide. Possible motives include (i) disappointment at not being selected for the safe Conservative seat
of Arden; (ii) fear of exposure by publication of the nude

photos in *Penthouse* magazine (attached); (iii) her complicated financial situation which she mentioned to Mr Charles Harvey, MP (Accountant's report attached).

(c) Murder. The following suspects have been interrogated (Reports attached): (i) Sir Ralph Grunte, MP (ii) Mr Charles Harvey, MP (iii) Mr David Swan, former Mayor of Arden (iv) Ms Hyacinth Scragg (v) Mr Leroy Burns. If his evidence is believed, it also provides an alibi for Sir Ralph Grunte, who, according to Mr Burns, was drunk and incapable at the time of Ms Wilikins's death (vi) Mr Ron Barton, formerly reporter on the *True Brit*, now believed to be living in Miami.

As will be seen, all the above had a motive of one sort or another and any one of them could have been involved in the death of Ms Wilikins, but as there is no conclusive evidence that she was murdered no charges have been brought.

It should be added that it was brought to my notice that, after the altercation on television between Ms Wilikins and Ms Scragg, the Prime Minister made a comment in front of several members of the Government to the effect that he wished one of them would dispose of 'a turbulent priest'. Could he have meant Ms Wilikins? While not believing that any Minister would have taken this literally, I ventured to apply for an interview which was granted. I interviewed Mr Major at 10 Downing Street and asked what he had intended this comment to convey. He replied (a) he had been misquoted and (b) he had been referring to the Bishop of Durham.

No further action is contemplated.

*More paperback entertainment
by Julian Critchley
from Headline*

HUNG PARLIAMENT

(an extract)

An observant motorist driving northwards over Westminster Bridge at night might wonder why a small lantern burns in the tower of Big Ben higher up than the illuminated clock face itself. He could not fail to notice the great bulk of the Palace of Westminster on his left, its lights ablaze like those of an ocean liner, and the people standing or sitting on the terrace. The light tells London that the House of Commons is still sitting: the Palace itself, with its thousand rooms and thousand politicians, to say nothing of as many cooks, clerks and bottlewashers, has all the confidence of a *Titanic* bound for New York on a far from maiden voyage. So it seemed on the evening of Monday 7 June 199–.

In the early hours of the following morning, Tuesday 8 June, a prominent woman Conservative MP, whose face had been long carried into every home in the land, was to be found dead in what the Sergeant at Arms said gravely were 'unusual circumstances'. However unusual they may have been, the fact remained that the news of her death was not made official until noon on Tuesday, several hours after the murder had been committed. For much of that morning, while rumour spread as to the victim, who was thought by many to be Mrs Edwina Currie, the authorities published no statement of any kind. However, at midday the Leader of the House, John MacGregor, made a statement to the journalists of the parliamentary lobby. He was speaking in the Bernard Ingham Room. 'It is true,' said MacGregor, looking like a solemn Scottish fifth former, 'that an Honourable Member has been found dead. It was not, as we all now know, Mrs Edwina

Currie.' He paused at this point. 'It was a case of mistaken identity. I am very sorry to say that the victim was Mrs Emma Kerr, the Member for Corve Dale.' At this the ears of the lobby pricked up. Had not the lovely Emma been described by Mr Robin Oakley of *The Times* only yesterday as the 'Tory Party's sweetheart'?

ISBN 0 7472 3836 7   Price £4.50

Available from all good bookshops or newsagents, or can be ordered direct from the publisher. Please fill in the form below. Price and availability subject to change without notice.

Headline Book Publishing PLC, Cash Sales Department, Bookpoint, 39 Milton Park, Abingdon, OXON, OX14 4TD, UK. If you have a credit card you may order by telephone – 0235 831700.

Please enclose a cheque or postal order made payable to Bookpoint Ltd to the value of the cover price and allow the following for postage and packing: UK & BFPO: £1.00 for the first book, 50p for the second book and 30p for each additional book ordered up to a maximum charge of £3.00. OVERSEAS & EIRE: £2.00 for the first book, £1.00 for the second book and 50p for each additional book.

Name ....

Address ....

....

....

If you would prefer to pay by credit card, please complete: Please debit my Visa/Access/Diner's Card/American Express (delete as applicable) card no.

Signature ....Expiry Date ....